RED BLOOD

JACK FORBES

THEYTUS BOOKS LTD.
PENTICTON, BC

First Edition

Theytus Books Ltd.
257 Brunswick Street
Penticton, B.C.   V2A 5P9

Book Design & Typesetting: Marlena Dolan & Regina Gabriel
Cover Design: Marlena Dolan & Greg Young-Ing

Special Thanks: Kateri Akiwenzie-Damm, Lil Scheps
& Hartmut Lutz

Printed and bound in Canada

Canadian Cataloguing in Publication Data

Forbes, Jack D., 1934-
  Red Blood

ISBN 0-919441- 65-3

  I. Title.
PS3556.0667R42 1997   813'.54   C97-910418-1

The Publisher acknowledges the support of the Canada Council,
Department of Canadian Heritage and Cultural Services Branch of the
Province of British Columbia in the publication of this book.

TABLE OF CONTENTS

*Dedicated to grandmother Estella and
great-grandmother Cary Ann*

Red Blood

Chapter One: Rainwater

Everyone thought that Rainwater was an Indian name. Well, it was and it wasn't. Jesse let it be, he let people think what they wanted to. But really it was a name brought over from England, probably, carried by some Colored or White people who later inter-married with mixed-Indians in Louisiana. And so now it was, truly, an Indian name, a good earth-type name anyway.

Jesse, as a boy, was always intrigued by the fact that he had been born in Oklahoma instead of California. He never grew tired of asking his mother Elisa: "Why was I born back there? Weren't you and daddy already living out here?"

Elisa would say something like: "Well, it's a custom among us Delawares to have our babies at home, and home for us is where the old people are – your grandparents and my grandparents. So I always have tried to go back to Oklahoma for each baby, including you.

You see, Jesse, it's a lot easier for me that way. Out here I'm all alone, except for Cousin Claire. But back there I've got a lot of womenfolk to help me with the baby. So it's better that way."

She kind of laughed. "And Jesse, I always enjoy going back there to see all the family and my old school friends, so having a baby is a good excuse for a nice trip that's a lot of fun for me!"

Jesse's older brothers and sisters, Andy, Dewey, Cary, and Ladell, had also been born in Oklahoma, some of them before the family had left to move to Kansas and then to California. Jesse, born in 1945, was the last.

Many times, especially on a weekend when it was raining, they asked questions about Oklahoma and about the Delawares. Growing up on a one-acre alkali flat between Long Beach and

Paramount, California, and going to school mostly with children of Mexican or poor White background, they were all a little puzzled by what "being Delaware" was all about.

Teach us some Lenápe words tonight," Cary might say. "Yes, please Mama, we want to have our own talk. The Mexican kids can all talk Spanish. We need our own way of talking," would chime in Ladell.

But Elisa would only give them a few words. "Yúkwe ki-íshk-wik, that's the way to say today."

"Yoo-kway-ki-ish-kwik," they would all repeat.

"How do you say dog?"

"Mo-é-kan-ih."

"What does Dálamoos mean? Dálamoos, our dog, what does her name mean?"

"Dálamoos means my pet."

"And turtle, how do you say that?"

"Tulápe, turtle, tulápin, little turtle."

Elisa spoke fluent Lenápe but she seldom used it in California. She had gone to a Bureau of Indian Affairs boarding school and had been punished for speaking Indian. After that experience she spoke only to the older people in Lenápe, speaking to her younger relations in English.

Eisa had decided not to teach Lenápe to the children. As she said to Andrew, her husband, "I don't want them to have to go through what I went through, with those White teachers looking at you like you are a savage or stupid, just because you speak a different language or have a different way of pronouncing. Oh, it was so hard on me. I used to be so embarrassed and ashamed!"

Andrew understood some Delaware, but he was mostly of mixed Houma Indian background from Louisiana and never felt completely comfortable with Lenápe. The children tried to find out also about Louisiana but Andrew never said much.

"Sometimes it's best if you don't know too much. Some kinds of knowledge can just get you into trouble. I haven't seen any of my relations for years. They might all be horse thieves, so it's better not to talk about it."

Andrew had grown up with the fear of one who was from a state where even a little bit of African ancestry might prevent you from being regarded as an Indian. Also, in Oklahoma, it was illegal for an Indian who was part-African to marry an Indian who wasn't part-African, even if they were members of the same tribe. It was also against the law for an Indian who was part-Black to go to the

White schools, whereas any other kind of Indian could attend.

Andrew never spoke much about his brothers and sisters. From the Oklahoma perspective, many of them had married "wrong." They had picked mates who had visible African ancestry, people of the Creek, Cherokee, or Seminole nations who were caught in between the Indian and Colored worlds. Of course, many Indians were married to Red-Black people but it always created problems because of the way the Oklahoma caste system worked.

Andrew rejected that caste system but he wouldn't talk about it when Jesse was young. "I left Oklahoma to get away from all of that and I don't want my children to suffer from it," he would tell Elisa. And that was that.

But the kids were always asking, "Why did we leave Oklahoma? Why can't we live back there with Grandmother and Grandfather? Then we could learn to talk Delaware good!"

Andrew would respond: "Well, the Indians lost a lot of land. And then the Depression came on and I just couldn't get any regular work. We couldn't make enough for all of us to live on from the land that was left. So when the war started I moved up to Wichita to get a defense job. Then we came out here so I could work in the airplane factory. There's a lot more work out here, even now. So that's why we stay – and here we have our ducks, chickens, and other animals, so I can feed all of you big eaters!" Then they would laugh and forget about the many things left unsaid.

Soon after Jesse had learned to walk and say a few words he was taken back to Oklahoma to visit his grandparents and other relations. They made quite a fuss, not a new experience for him, being the youngest child in a close-knit family. He had inquisitive, deep brown eyes, set in a somewhat chubby, good-natured medium-brown face and long black hair that his mother hated to cut. His nose was somewhat prominent, but his childish fatty cheeks obscured the high cheek bones which would later become more noticeable. Jesse was an easy baby to raise.

He managed to imitate a few Delaware words on that visit but, most important of all, he learned to like the Old Ones who, in turn, liked him. Grandparents, either adopted or natural, were to be very important to Jesse. He was drawn to them and loved to listen to them talk. He could just sit, even as a toddler, and listen to the musical sounds of their voices as they bathed him in the rhythmic cadence of Delaware. Many times the Old Ones were hardly even aware of his presence but he was there watching the expressions on the wrinkled faces, listening to words he couldn't understand but which sounded like lullabies.

Jesse's family included lots of animals. Animals had always been important to the Delaware people – they used to keep pet bears in the old days and even had a ceremony to help the bear adjust to going back to the forest when it grew too big to remain 'at home' anymore.

So the old Delawares helped animals to grow up and oftentimes plants and animals helped humans in return. And it was true, really, while Jesse was growing up. Jesse wasn't turned out into the woods at puberty to get a vision, in the old Lenápe way, but he was helped all the same.

Even Elisa used to say, "Jesse, I believe that Dálamoos took you on as her child, kind of like a loving little auntie, or like your teacher. She surely has watched out for you."

As soon as Jesse came home, still in his crib, Mother Fox Terrier adopted him as her own. She stood up on her hind legs to see that he was all right and slept beside him at night. Nobody asked her to do that, but she was part of the family and she knew her job. She felt that Jesse's personality really depended upon her, his future quality as a person.

When Jesse got a little older she played with him, kissing him on the face, making him feel loved. Of course, Jesse's human relatives did that too but Dálamoos knew that she had to provide a different kind of love. Did you ever notice how dogs love without asking anything in return, how they love you no matter if you've been good or bad, how they're always right there to support you? That's the way we humans learned to be human, thousands of years ago, from the old wise dogs who 'domesticated' us. That's where, even now, we learn how to love one another.

Some people don't learn that, of course. They are the ones who are not raised by animals or whose brutish or selfish parents teach them to hate animals or to just think of animals as 'things.' Poor souls, they're the ones who grow up to be patients of psychiatrists – psychiatrists who weren't raised by animals either and who can't help them.

As a toddler Jesse always had Dálamoos close by. If he fell down and cried she was there to lick his face. And when he was old enough to sleep in a bed, she woke him up every morning, jumping into bed and kissing him until he got up.

It's funny how dogs understand humans so well. They see that little children need to develop their coordination, their strength, their agility. So they are always coming up with a stick in their mouth, challenging the child to pull on it. That way they teach the child to use his little fists and arms to coordinate his eyes and hands. Some dogs also are ball players. Maybe Babe Ruth was trained by such a dog. They let people throw balls for them and they bring them back so they can be thrown again. Jesse learned how to throw a ball that way. The dogs were happy when his arms got stronger and he could throw it a long way.

Dogs like to teach people how to run too. They run around and the young children chase them, trying to keep up. They can't, of course, but the dog always circles back to encourage them, to reassure them. Jesse learned to run that way.

Dogs take children on walks too. They show them how to find trails and how to smell the air and how to stop and look around. Some dogs raise up a leg to point to something worth looking at, others just stare hard hoping the child will see too.

Dálamoos felt that her responsibilities were primarily around the house. Jesse's best friend outside was Laddie, a big mixed shepherd that lived with an old lady not too far away. Laddie took Jesse on when they first met and he taught him a lot about sticks, ball games, and hiking.

Later, Laddie taught Jesse a lot about love, old age, and death. As Laddie got older, he couldn't move so well and Jesse just sat with him, stroking his hair, and resting against him. Later, as Laddie grew weaker, Jesse lay down with him, keeping him company. Once in a while Laddie would get stronger and act young again but Jesse knew not to play ball too long or throw too many sticks. Finally, Laddie went off to die and Jesse found him. He said prayers for Laddie, tears in his eyes, thanking him for all of his love and thanking Kishelemókong for the joy of knowing him. Then he and his father and brothers helped bury Laddie in a special place, a cool shady place where he had always liked to rest.

"All things come from the Mother Earth, and all things must return to the Mother Earth. That is the way it has always been. We will miss our friend but someday we will all join him. His 'That-which-Separates' is happy now, because it is free. His old body was getting tired. That's the way it is. We are sad now. Something good has gone from among us. But our hearts will heal again. We are thankful that his memory will always be with us, giving us joy. Wanishi!"

Later in life Jesse read that dogs had been living with humans for tens of thousands of years. He also read about how Indians in the old days had lots of pets around all the time: bears, coyotes, possums, turkeys, parrots, and even mice, and how the South American Indian children are literally surrounded by pet birds and animals of all kinds. He also read the stories of how Indians got their knowledge of medicine from the otter, the bear, or other healing animals. One story, in *Pawnee Hero Stories and Folk Tales*, told how a young Pawnee man was devoted to unselfishly curing people who were sick but he himself was made ill by a jealous doctor. The animals helped him though, and a Bear-doctor brought him back to consciousness.

The Bear said, "Now, Nahurac (animal doctors), this is what I can do. I do not care how dangerously wounded I may be, I know how to cure myself. If they leave any breath at all in me, I know how to cure myself."

The head of all the animal doctors, a Beaver, told the boy about medicine. He said, You must imitate us. Do as we do. You must depend on us, but still, if anything comes up that is very difficult, you must depend on Tirawa (the Creator). Ask help from the ruler. He made everything."

The boy went home and became a great doctor, teaching all the other Pawnee doctors how to cure.

There were many other good stories in that book. One was about a man who was kind to a baby bear and, in turn, the bears brought the man's son back to life after he had been killed in battle.

After the son was well, a big male bear said, "None of all the beings and animals that roam over the country are as great and as wise as the bears. I'm going to make you a great man, but you must not deceive yourself. You must not think that I am great, or can do great things of myself. You must always look up above for the giver of all power."

So Jesse learned about animals and about humility as well. The animals worship the Creator and they are not so arrogant as to believe that they are all self-sufficient as some humans do. "The gifts that come to us come from the Great Mystery," said Jesse to himself, "my drawing, my writing, whatever I can do. It is a gift to me. I must not be conceited. Whatever I can do I must do well but the start of it is with Moxúmsa, Kishelemókong, grandfather, Great Mystery."

But when he was younger the animals themselves taught Jesse many things. The goats taught him, not only love, but also how to play and kick up one's heels (like sheep do also). The cats taught him how to be loving without being possessive, how to just rub against another without trying to cage the other up.

The ducks taught him a lot too. He learned to understand their language, and it was a good one (so he never could believe those White teachers who said that only humans had invented language!). He watched the ducks play, how the females would sometimes imitate a male, crawling on each other's backs and then they would start a yelling which was like laughter or elation, an expression of joy. Some of them would then run around in circles, darting very fast, and they would have a good time.

The geese were Jesse's good friends. They were so brave and dignified, yet so soft and gentle if you were their friend. He loved the way they held their heads up high, and looked at you, as grand as any emperor. And how they would announce the arrival of any strangers. Jesse knew also how they would fight to protect their babies. Once he found a female who had been attacked by stray dogs. She had fought them off, resting with her back against a bank of dirt so she could use her beak, wings, and feet. She was still alive but badly wounded. Jesse picked her up, very gently, her eyes looked at him with gratitude but said, "I am going to die. There is no hope." Jesse took her home, put medicine on her wounds, gave her water, and watched over her. But she was right, her wounds were too great. Jesse tried to help many hurt animals – pheasants, birds of all kinds, snakes, lizards, dogs, cats. Some lived. Many died. He learned that it was always worth the effort.

Of course, Jesse had to kill also. We must kill to eat and he was raised in the country where chickens and other animals helped to keep the family alive. So Jesse learned to do that but he learned to do it with sadness and with a prayer. "It is good to suffer with those that we are going to eat. Never harden yourself against other creatures' pain. If you do, you will lose something. You will become less than a man," said Antonio Chavis many years later.

Jesse spent a lot of time watching insects and wild animals. He let the bees crawl on him and he watched the wasps. He never got stung except once or twice when guard-wasps thought he was too close to their nests. Jesse dreamed about wasps and bees as a young boy. In his dream he could talk with them and they helped him. They were his friends. So he always picked up hurt bees and put them where people wouldn't step on them, and he helped wasps when they were attacked by ants.

He wondered later if that was some kind of a vision-dream, like one of Black Elk's early visions. Anyway, he never bothered wasps, or mud-daubers, or bees and they didn't bother him, except for yellow-jackets. Sometimes he had to shoo the yellow-jackets away from food but even then they didn't sting him.

In later years, when he was living in the city, Jesse often went to the zoo. He liked to go when few other people were there, mostly because the people were often noisy and pushy. They made you watch them because they were the strangest creatures to be seen anywhere.

Jesse liked to visit the caged animals quietly, standing for a long time, silently, to set up some kind of communication. Usually the animals wouldn't look you in the eye, they always tried to gaze past their audience, looking at something beyond. But once in a while Jesse had the thrill of meeting an animal face on. Once a jaguar not only looked him full in the eyes but began talking to him in low growls. Jesse knew that the jaguar was doing something special, telling him, "You are different. I can see you are a Native of this land just as I am. I can see you are a spiritual being. The White people are crazy. Frenzied, they run around in a big cage which they make for themselves. You and I, though, we can be free because we are creatures of a different order. We live in the spirit as well as the flesh."

"I might hurt you or even eat you, but you would understand. The Whites would only hate me, and never forgive. They kill and eat more than any other creatures. They are voracious, like weasels and skunks. But they have no balance, no understanding. They hate in others that which they do so unremittingly. You and I are different. We are of this land."

Jesse's feelings toward animals and plants were confirmed by reading Indian books, especially, *Black Elk Speaks*.

"Is not the sky a father and the earth a mother, and are not all living things with feet or wings or roots their children?...the earth, from whence we came and at whose breast we suck as babies all our lives, along with all the animals and birds and trees and grasses."

Black Elk was able to make understandable many of Jesse's feelings. The way he felt about rocks, about the ocean, about clouds in the sky, about oak trees, about waterfalls, about the earth itself. All of these things evoked the deepest feelings, mysterious yearnings and a sense of joyous peace, and yet he could not put any of it into words. And nowhere in the White churches or in school did he learn anything that helped him. Were most White people devoid of such feelings? Were they truly empty? Or did their culture force them to suppress the mystical in order to be single-mindedly ruthless in the material world?

Gradually Jesse learned that his feelings were legitimate. It was all right to cry for Mother Earth. It was good to have tears in one's eyes when freeways caused the destruction of thousands of trees, plants, and snakes, and created huge scars on the hillsides. In the 1960s and 1970s Indians began talking in public about their love for Mother Earth. Jesse was fortunate. For a century Indians had talked only quietly to themselves about such things. And many felt guilty about being 'superstitious' and 'primitive.' Jesse would have a chance to grow up with a generation of Indians who could try to leap back in time to make contact with Black Elk and Chitto Hadjo, with Handsome Lake and Smohalla. A century of harsh oppression, of brutal colonization, of intensive brainwashing had failed. The link had been weakened but it survived. From the underworld of imperialism, Indians could crawl forth, born again as in the beginning, from the earth's own womb.

That the Native People are earth-colored is no accident.

Jesse learned, little by little, that an Indian never need be alone. When one has trees and plants and rocks for relations, one has a world of kinfolk always close by, always at hand. White psychology was a mystery to Jesse, all hung up on relations between humans, spending millions to talk to someone about relations with other people. Sure that is important, but incomplete. Of little use because it is so terribly incomplete.

Jesse learned to sit on a ridge or a hilltop with a big pine tree or an oak close by. Can you believe that that tree 'looked' at Jesse, that it took pity on him if his mind was sad, that it soothed him, caressed him, 'spoke' to him?

The mystery of 'place' was another thing that Jesse discovered. We all have special places in this world but most people never find them because they don't even look. Some Indians still look for them.

When Jesse first visited the high country east of the Sierra Nevadas, he knew he was in such a place. To the west were snow-covered peaks, bare of trees, looking like the mysterious mountains of Tibet or the Andes. In the foreground were hills and valleys covered with blue-grayish sagebrush and, here and there, slopes strewn with junipers and piñons. Along the streams were cottonwoods or, more often aspens, vibrating in the breeze. In some of these places, Jesse felt that summer was transient, that winter was the real ruler. Even in July or August it seemed as if it were fall. These feelings filled Jesse with a kind of deep yearning, a melancholy longing, or often, with a sense of something impending, a promise of a coming. But a coming of what?

He also felt something similar along the coast, in the sand

dunes, especially if it was a little foggy. He found a place where the dunes had created little basins, some filled with miniature lakes, all lonely and desolate. Jesse loved to sit nearby in the utter quiet with even the roar of the ocean reduced to only a distant hum. It seemed as if he were on a planet all by himself, or that he was the last man on earth.

But the effect of each place was different. The high country promised something in the future, always coming. The dunes and the fog told of something in the past, something he should know.

Such places made him queasy in the stomach sometimes, made his hair and scalp tingle, made him extra alert so that he noted every detail, made him 'high' without drinking, made him lose track of time.

It was not that he wanted to stay in the high country forever, or that he could sit there in the dunes without ever leaving. He knew the power of the place, he knew he could go there whenever he wanted to, he knew he should return to fast and pray, to learn more. But it was too powerful to just stay there.

It seemed to Jesse that he had been there before. This was true of many places in the desert too. Why did it often seem so familiar? What was it that lay there in the back of his mind just beyond recall? Some part of his memory wanted to come out but couldn't. He had been there but when, how? It seemed to Jesse that in former lives these places must have meant something to him.

There is an old Indian belief, among some tribes, that when a person dies his spirit must visit every spot where the person had spit or maybe peed. Only after that can the spirit go on to the land of the spirits.

Maybe when we come to a place where we feel powerful longings and feelings of inexplicable recognition, those places are ones where our former bodies went in previous lives.

In any case, Jesse learned about such places and they became a part of his life-map. They became relatives, kinfolk. If a tree can be a relative, why not a place?

It makes us vulnerable to have places or trees for relatives. A place can be destroyed. A tree can be bulldozed down. Jesse knew that pain. He found canyons in the hills, later destroyed for dams or highways. He made friends with trees, later killed for subdivisions. Tears came into his eyes for those relatives. He cried for them as he would cry one day for his grandparents and other human relations. Why not?

It made Jesse vulnerable to have places and trees for relations.

But it also taught him something about suffering, about caring, about love, about being a grown up person. A grown up person has learned to give and to share, to give little bright, shiny, glittering gifts of love, like snow flakes scattering all around, and to share the love and the pain and suffering of others.

Some people are too busy worrying about themselves to even notice places or trees or animals – too bad. Can such people truly 'notice' another human being?

So Jesse became vulnerable. He grew up in such a way that he could be hurt. Oh, he had an exterior like other boys and men of this time and age – tough, cool, indifferent, but he was fortunate this exterior didn't go below the surface into his gut.

Like the old Indian warriors with battle-scars, who love to play with babies and could pray to the Great Mystery with tears running down their cheeks, Jesse learned, little by little, that the warrior's true strength is derived from caring. To suffer for others is the mark of the warrior-spirit.

As Jesse grew older, he was able, more and more, to distinguish between the 'toughs,' who are only self-centered, conceited children grown big in body, and the truly strong. He gradually learned to turn away from those who didn't care about anything but themselves, who didn't have the sensitivity to discover kinship in places, trees, animals, insects, and humans.

Buffeted about, Jesse ran into places, met trees, caressed animals, helped plants. He found beauty. Caring, he was cared for. Caressing, he was caressed. Loving, he was loved. Suffering, he was suffered for.

Red Blood

Chapter Two
Isn't It Amazing That Any Survive At All?

"Blessed Jesus, Blessed Jesus! My skin is still dark but my soul is White, because I have accepted the Lord, oh, thank you Lord, Blessed Jesus.

You know what we were like when the White people came to us? Do you know?

Pagans! Heathens! Idol worshippers! Superstitious savages, lost people who were worshipping the Devil. Not only were our skins dark but our souls were dark.

We were lost in the darkness, the eternal night of damnation. Deluded by the Devil, and damned to eternal Hell-fire and punishment.

Yes. We were lost! Lost in the lust of lewd and obscene dancing. Lost in the lust of fornication. Lost in the lust of black magic and witchcraft. Lost in the lust of wildness and anarchy.

Many of our brothers and sisters are still on the road to damnation. They still have not accepted Christ Jesus as their personal savior. They still have not submitted themselves to the Lord.

But my soul is White, clean, pure, saved! I have been born again in Jesus. Hallelujah!

You can be saved too. Your soul can be cleansed of its darkness. Your skin may still be brown but your soul can be White!

And what rewards that will bring! The reward of eternal life in heaven at the side of our Lord Jesus. The reward of prosperity right here on this earth. No longer cursed as an Indian you can live as White people do. You can have what they have! Do you want a new car? A nice house? A good job? Fine clothes?

They're all yours if you accept Christianity.

Why do the White people have these things?

Why do they own everything as far as the eye can see?
It's because of God's favor! They are in God's good grace!
You can receive the gifts of God too. Hallelujah!
Repent! And ye shall be saved.
We are all sinners but we can be saved.
Holy Jesus!...
Now, let us pray."

The Rev. Maxwell Sims was a Creek minister, pastor of the American Indian Mission. An ex Baptist, he had joined some kind of holy-roller church and moved to L.A. where he could operate on his own. He had quite a following because there weren't many places where Indians felt welcome on Sunday.

A lot of the Native People didn't really pay much attention to what Pastor Sims said. They thought he was a little crazy. They came because they liked to be with other Indians and had been mostly Christians in Oklahoma or other states. Anyway, the Christian ones had already heard most of what Sims had to say.

It was a pretty regular thing that when an Indian joined a Christian church he had to stop going to the traditional ceremonies of his tribe. The preachers said they were bad, sinful, devilish. The Christians also usually had to stop seeing their pagan kinsmen. Of course, they couldn't avoid all contact, but intimate social relations were discouraged. Thus the Christian Indians came to be a breed apart, quite separate from the traditional people.

The Rainwaters didn't like Pastor Sims but they occasionally visited the church because one of Mrs. Rainwater's cousins sang in the choir. The cousin, a lady, kept after them, worrying about their souls. Jesse went to stay with her for awhile once during the summer. She was a nice enough woman except that she hated everything Indian. Cousin Claire used White powder to lighten her complexion and she wore her hair in curlers around the house so she could have flounced-up, wavy hair at church. Her house was decorated with pictures of Jesus and knick-knacks, and a few family photographs. Nothing Indian was visible.

Jesse didn't mind visiting Cousin Claire when he was still young. He liked playing with his cousins. What he didn't like, after the first experience or two, was going to evangelistic revivals in big tents or to White fundamentalist churches. The Redneck preachers screaming "Gee-sahs, Gee-sahs" spoke about things he didn't like and couldn't relate to. He didn't feel like a sinner. His mother and father were not sinners. His grandparents were not sinners. Even Cousin Claire didn't seem like a sinner (but maybe she had done something awful he didn't know about. What could she have done that was so bad as to make her grovel so before these pasty White people? Was it that she felt so sinful just because she was an Indian?).

Jesse hated it when White ladies near him started talking in tongues and spitting. He was afraid they would spit on him, or pull him out and make him cry and scream and 'testify.' He hated it too because Cousin Claire seemed to be held up as an example of a 'good Indian,' a saved soul. The implication was always there, that Jesse was one of the damned ones, especially since he never came up to the front even though they would practically call him by name.

Cousin Claire's children all went up front and testified. They had to, but Billy (who was Jesse's age) told him in secret that he had just faked it and that he just did it to stop them from bothering him all the time. Clary, Billy's older sister, liked to sneak off with Jesse, behind the bushes in the backyard, where they would kiss. She claimed she was truly saved and said she was worried about Jesse's soul. Jesse didn't understand her evangelism and he was even more confused by her offer to show him what was between her legs if he would show her his parts. Being born-again didn't grip him but her body did, so he looked and she looked and they both felt very sinful but neither was sorry.

Before moving to Los Angeles, Jesse had always imagined Kishelemokong, the Creator, to be a very, very good, loving person or power. He had seen his grandparents, other elders, and his own mother and father praying. They all seemed happy and pleased when they were doing that. It was kind of deep and restful, a reassuring experience.

Going to the Christian churches confused them though. The 'God' they were talking about was a very frightening, vengeful, angry Big Man who sent people to Hell-fire for what seemed like unimportant things. They also talked about a Holy Ghost who was somewhere around and about Jesus. Jesse couldn't figure out who Jesus was in relation to God. He gradually got the idea that God could change himself into Jesus or into the Holy Ghost at will and that he had crawled inside a woman and came out as a baby but that the woman was still a virgin, whatever that was.

And then there was the Devil. This creature was very powerful and it seemed like the Christians felt the Devil around them a lot more than they felt God. Once Jesse said in a Sunday School class, "Maybe the Devil is really God. If God can become this Holy Ghost you talk about and can be Jesus too, then he could also be the Devil since he can change himself all the time." Everybody was so shocked that they just sat there, even the teacher. Jesse went on, "God wants to punish sinners. The Devil does the punishing. So the Devil works for God, not against him. Also, God needs sinners or he wouldn't have any use for Hell. So the Devil works to help people sin...See, the devil is really just as important to God as Jesus is, or the Holy Ghost-Spirit. So why can't God be four people, or things? Maybe he's even more than that too and we just don't know about it."

The teacher tried to explain that Satan was Lucifer, a bad angel who had rebelled against God. Patiently he told the whole story but Jesse wanted to know if there was a Hell before Lucifer rebelled, and if God made Lucifer, and if there were sinners before the rebellion. The poor teacher tried to show that Satan tempted Adam and Eve in the Garden of Eden and that was when sin appeared. He then talked about how this 'original' sin was passed on to all babies born to mankind from then on.

"Who decided that?" asked Jesse. "Who decided what?" said the teacher.

"Who decided that every baby has to be born with that sin of eating the apple, and why did God put that tree there anyway, if he didn't want them to eat its fruit?"

The teacher, now sweating and exasperated, tried to change the subject but Jesse wouldn't stop. "So Satan sinned when he rebelled, and he sinned when he fooled Eve, so that means that Adam and Eve were not the first sinners, unless God asked Satan to do all of that so he could pass sin on, just like I said before."

Jesse came to the conclusion, at a rather young age, that he didn't like churches all that much and that the Whiteman's God only reflected the way some White people acted. That is, God was kind of like a picture with two sides (or even a mirror). The White people looked at one side and saw themselves reflected there and what they saw was frightening. The Indians looked at the other side and saw beauty and kindness there.

Jesse's foray into theology was influenced by an increasing awareness of the way in which the White people treated non-Whites in the Los Angeles area. Jesse's family had moved from the country into an area that was shifting from White to non-White. His elementary school had a White majority still because it was toward the northern part of that section of the city. His junior high was about half non-White, including Chinese kids from Chinatown, Filipinos, Mexicans, Indians, and a few Blacks. The high school for Jesse's area was mostly non-White, with additional Black students, Asians, and lots of Mexicans. Most of the White kids went to a different, better high school to the north. The School District kept trying to redraw attendance lines so that the races would be kept as separate as possible.

So Jesse learned what happened when Colored people, Mexicans, or even Indians tried to buy a home. He brought it up in Sunday School once when Jesus' love for all mankind was being discussed. That's how he learned never again to believe what Sunday School teachers said.

Out in the country, Jesse had found a place where he liked to pray and to think about spiritual things, a private place near a clump of eucalyptus trees. So Jesse was not against religion. It was just that he was like so many Indians in that he couldn't separate 'religion' from 'living.' Jesse honestly expected people to live what they professed and it was a shock for him to realize that lots of Christians – the ones he saw at least – had two religions, a church religion and their main religion. The main religion was what they did when they weren't in church.

At his new elementary school in the city Jesse overheard the principal telling a White parent how good it was that the school had no Black students and bragging that most of the children were White. "We have a few Mexicans, Asians, and Indians but thank goodness most of them are refined. We have very few of the real dark Mexicans so we haven't had any problems yet. Ours are mostly of the Castillian Spanish type." At school Jesse had teachers whose minds never became cluttered with notions of cultural pluralism or multi-cultural education. They stuck with Christopher Columbus, Daniel Boone, and Davy Crockett, proven winners for sure.

When Jesse got to Harding High, the non-White students had become a large majority. The Civil Rights Movement had started, the Mexican-American community was beginning to organize, and even one teacher of Mexican background was 'putting ideas' into some students' heads.

Intellectually, though, Jesse had to lead a dual life. His history and social studies classes, not to mention literature, art, and music, were all 'lily-white' and Anglo-Saxon to boot. The textbooks that were thrown at him were full of racist attacks on Native People or terribly stereotypical distortions. Jesse read about the 'savage and brutish men, which range up and down, little different from the wild beasts.' Supposedly, these were Jesse's relatives who had befriended the Pilgrims at Plymouth Rock. All the texts made it very clear that

Indians, Blacks, and other non-Whites were not 'Americans.' Instead, they were the 'American's' enemies, slaves, or problems.

Pupils resist racist schools as best they can. Jesse tried the usual ones – ditching classes, breaking rules, smoking, drinking, wearing defiant styles of clothing, and so on. But he was lucky compared with most of the rebels since he had some high cards to play, cards that the school couldn't take away, cards the school didn't even know about.

On several occasions, Jesse went back to Oklahoma to spend part of the summer with his grandparents. Once he got to go back by himself, taking a Greyhound bus to Oklahoma City and then changing to get to Tulsa and Bartlesville. His parents were reluctant for him to go alone but he had demonstrated his independence many times, so what could they say? Jesse had ridden buses and streetcars all over L.A. and hitchhiked as far as Santa Barbara. And with members of his family he had been to Oklahoma several times. Riding a bus for a couple of days is not much fun for most people. But Jesse loved to watch the details of the countryside and he was also a people-watcher. Things that were going on around him were important somehow. Maybe it was his artistic sense, everything being a potential drawing or painting. Or maybe his inquisitive mind was simply trying to comprehend the nature of life.

Part of the way, Jesse sat next to a Tejano, a Mexican from Texas, who was on his way back home. This man, a farm worker basically, was returning to his wife and children near Lubbock after working for awhile in the L.A. area. He spoke English but Jesse wanted to practice Spanish so they talked a lot in that language. They shared a lot of information about the plants that could be seen in the desert, about the common racial heritage of Indians and Mexicans, and about the way the Red-Brown Race was treated in Tejas. The Tejano told many stories of how he had been beaten up by Texas Rangers, of how he couldn't go into many restaurants in Lubbock, or Amarillo, or Midland, and how the farmers and police prevented them from unionizing. "Here it is, 1961, y la mayor parte de nosotros are still living like perros, in shacks that won't   keep out the rain or the cold. I voted for Kennedy but the government doesn't do a thing for us. And I had a hell of a time even being able to vote. It was the first time I ever voted in this country and I'm thirty-nine years old. But now, I've saved up some money and I'm going back to bring my family to Califas. There's no future in

Lubbock. The best we can hope for there is to get a job in a shoe store where Mexicanos trade, or get a job picking up garbage, or something like that. No, Tejas is bad, Lubbock especialmente."

Together they rode across the Mojave Desert at night. The moonlight cast an eerie light across the flat basins and the rolling grades and Jesse watched as long as he could stay awake. They talked about desiertos since el Tejano had hitchhiked across it several times and had also worked in the Phoenix area and the Imperial Valley. His family originated in Chihuahua and Zacatecas so his heritage was that of the arid world. El Tejano knew about lots of desert plants and trees – ocotillos, chollas, nopales, magueyes, mesquites, and many others. He even knew a little about peyote since his mother was a Tepeguana and used peyote as a medicine, even then. She was a kind of curandera and used many yerbas as a part of her folk medicine.

The desierto seemed to call to Jesse and he knew he would have to get out there one day. He had felt that way on train trips and now he felt it even more through the bus window. It was hot when they stopped in Barstow and in Needles, too, but Jesse found the warmth of the night somewhat pleasurable, especially as he was half-asleep. It's funny how the world is seen differently when you walk out of a bus, half-asleep, into a strange town, at three or four o'clock in the morning. The senses seem dulled but the feelings, for some people, reach out like antennae and take it all in.

Jesse saw occasional Indians, in Barstow a few Navajo laborers, in Needles a big Mojave guy standing around, some Walpais in Peach Springs, and lots of Navajos and Pueblos from Flagstaff on. He and el Tejano talked with a few of them, saying nothing of consequence but just making contact like Brown people do in a White world. Sometimes it's just with the eyes, no words being spoken.

Past Needles the desert changed. Ocotillos and saguaros, and then Piñon and juniper later. Finally, pine forests for a stretch around Williams, and then the high desert of Navajo land. Jesse watched Indian families walking along the highway, the women with bandanas around their hair and bright-colored dresses. He knew some Navajos in L.A., at the Indian Center, and he thought of some of the girls. Their dark-brown skin, high-cheekbones, long black hair, and intriguing eyes flashed into his mind. He remembered dancing with some, and one in particular. He began to get a hard-on sitting there in his seat, and he tried to shift his mind to the scenery outside.

Jesse had brought some things along to read but the bus gave him a headache. Anyway, el Tejano was there to talk to and the new things to see kept him pretty busy. He also kept his eyes on a light-brown Colored girl who had gotten on the bus in L.A. too. She was somewhat skinny with long, thin legs like some Black girls have, and she was flat-breasted, but she had a cute button-nose face and, since she was alone, Jesse kind of watched out for her. After traveling all night together, he felt they were old friends who just hadn't been introduced yet. He smiled at her several times when they got to piss-stops and at Flagstaff, when they had breakfast, he talked with her a little.

Ella, for that was her name, was on her way to Oklahoma City. She had a nice smile but one that she revealed only cautiously since she was somewhat nervous among so many strangers. But Jesse was able to open up a conversation by talking about what high school he was from, and so on. She ate with an older Black lady who sat next to her on the bus. "Is that your mother?"

"No, I just met her at the depot in L.A. She's going to Chicago."

So Jesse knew that Ella would be all alone after Albuquerque and since el Tejano would also be leaving, going on a separate bus... "Well, maybe.. Anyway, somebody else might get on the bus. I'll just wait and see what happens."

It wasn't that Jesse was under any illusions. He just liked people, especially girls, and he enjoyed starting little friendships even if they never had any chance of being more than brief encounters. When he got older he realized that it was wonderful to be able to give a little love (for isn't friendship such a thing?) to another person, even if it was only a two-minute contact with a cute Chicana waitress in a Mexican cafe, or doing some little favor for an old person.

In Gallup, the bus stopped several times at traffic lights and Jesse saw lots of Navajos standing around, seemingly waiting for something. The men looked like Indians who had suddenly been transformed into cowboys with black cowboy hats, cowboy-style shirts, levis, and boots, but without their dark red-brown angular Indian features being modified at all. They all seemed to have big metallic belt-buckles and a bowlegged horsemen's way of sauntering.

Jesse got out at the tiny bus station to stretch his legs and look around but he couldn't see much more than rows of motels and stores. Trucks went by with old Navajo ladies and children sitting in the back and there were a lot of cars from Illinois, and Iowa, and even California with tourists in them. One or two Indians were waiting at the depot but none got on the bus.

The ride to Albuquerque was interesting. Jesse saw hogans and little corrals off in worn-out hilly land south of the highway. He saw lava flows and pueblo houses around Laguna and Acoma. The big, round earthen ovens were just like on post-cards and he even spotted a little girl helping her mother put something in to bake. He also saw 'trading post' after 'trading post' with fake tipis or false-front adobe walls and huge, repetitive signs to trap the tourists. Like spiders, the operators had set out webs to snare the unwary. But the cement or plywood tipis and garish signs were irritating. They reminded Jesse of old mildew-smelling fun-houses at the beach where stuffed two-headed calves were exhibited. Only here it was Redskins as the come-on.

The difference between the White and Indian societies was never so clear as along the U.S. highway from Gallup to Albuquerque. Jesse learned in later years that here you could jump from the plastic world of fake tomahawks and high mark-up jewelry to the real world of the Native People in a matter of minutes. Dramatically, the hustling sucker-traps symbolized White society very effectively while the plain brown hogans or sturdy adobe houses symbolized that of the Native Americans.

But the tourists didn't know that. "Can you imagine New Yorkers standing in front of a cement tipi that a wino slept in the night before, getting their picture taken?" commented el Tejano.

White towns like Grants depressed Jesse but whenever they came near an Indian community or a majestic peak or a formation of cliffs and juniper-covered mesas, he peered fixedly out the window as if to try to absorb something, as if to try to understand questions that had not even appeared yet in his conscious mind. El Tejano sensed his absorption and let him look without interference but after Laguna, and especially from the Rio Puerco to the mesa above Albuquerque, they talked a lot about los Apaches and los Comanches, about old stories that el Tejano had heard from his antepasados. Somebody had said that his father was part-Comanche and he liked to believe that since the Comanches had fought so well against the Texas Rangers.

Whether el Tejano was really part-Comanche or not didn't matter that much. We should make our own road-maps for life and it is good to make a map that gives one courage, pride, and meaning, thought Jesse. Of course, it can't be fake; but if we live like a part-Comanche doesn't that make it real?

The Albuquerque depot was a big one and it was there that

el Tejano and Jesse had to go separate ways. Each had an hour or so to wait, however, and not wanting to eat Greyhound food they decided to go to a nearby Mexican cafe. Jesse spotted Ella and her friend, a Mrs. Brown, and on the spur of the moment asked them if they wanted to come along. Mrs. Brown, although a tiny bit reluctant to go somewhere with strange men, was fed up with bus station dining as much as they. Besides she was a Chicago school teacher taking her biggest trip in years and her adventuresome spirit decided the matter.

They went about a block to a little Mexican cafe. El Tejano helped everybody pick out good dishes and the meal was a welcome success. Mrs. Brown was especially pleased and said that it was the best food she had had on her trip. Jesse kind of liked the school teacher. She was very dark, a little on the stout side, and with a rather vivacious personality in spite of her fifty or sixty years. Jesse found it hard to believe that she was a teacher, especially a high school literature teacher. She was somehow alive and vital, not dried up like a prune, not squinchy and taut.

The ad hoc group of friends stayed as long as possible, sharing bits of their lives, enriching each other, giving and not taking. Jesse had a knack for setting up such encounters, without thinking much about it. Mrs. Brown had read a lot about the Southwest and Mexico but on her entire trip she hadn't ever really met an Indian or a Mexican, thus she was an enthusiastic listener as el Tejano talked. Someday, she said, she planned to visit Mexico, and she promised to learn Spanish too.

El Tejano's bus left first. They said goodbye, he and Jesse shaking hands warmly. His real name was...oh what does it matter! Just another Tex-Mex trying to make a decent life for his mujer y ninos. Jesse never saw him again but he long remembered Horacio Sotomayor, tejano, campesino, unionista, tepeguano y Comanche.

Mrs. Brown stayed a little while longer, listening to Jesse tell about his disappointments with high school. She wrote out a list of novels for him to read, books by Richard Wright and others and told him not to give up, that someday maybe he could be a teacher and do things differently. She said, "Go to the public library, search through the stacks, look and read. Don't stop until you've read what they don't want you to know. Find out what it is. And try to find a Colored bookstore or a place where all kind of books are sold. Keep your eyes open, now hear, and don't stop your learning just because of poor teachers. This applies to both of you."

Jesse knew that she was right. He told her about the museum

library that he had seen and about the L.A. Public Library. He promised he wouldn't give up. Ella also said that she would look for the kind of books her school didn't use even though it was an almost totally Black high school. Then it was Jesse and Ella's turn to gather up their stuff and board the bus for Oklahoma City, so they said goodbye to Mrs. Brown. "Visit me if you ever come to Chicago, either one of you. You have a place to stay, hear!"

As Jesse had hoped, he and Ella were now friends. He asked her if she wanted to sit by the window. She was cute, with yellow-brown skin and kinky, short brownish hair. Being somewhat reserved, she had not talked much at dinner but her smiles and laughter had made her a full participant.They now had a long trip before them, across the rest of New Mexico and on into the Texas Panhandle and western Oklahoma. Ella was a little nervous now, since she had never been down South and even going through part of Texas was upsetting to her. Luckily, she thought, she wouldn't have to get out of the bus to eat until morning. Would they still have White-only restrooms in Amarillo and Elk City? She was glad that she had met Jesse. Even though he was not of her race he was surprisingly nice and seemed to be someone who would help you if he could, although only a teenager like herself.

Jesse and Ella talked for a long time, clear past Tucumcari and the Pecos River, and almost to the Texas line. They talked about music, movies, school, sports and the usual getting-acquainted subjects, and then they talked about boy friends and girl friends and drinking and adventures and other more confidential matters.

"You know you're a cute girl, and pretty light-skinned too. Does that make any difference in the way people treat you?"

"Thanks, Jesse, for saying I'm cute. But my light color? I don't know really. Most White people just take one look and they know I'm Black and that's that. Maybe they'd rather have me around than a real dark person but I'm not sure. I do know this: I've been called names, chased, and beat up by very dark girls because of my color."

"Why is that? I would think you all would stick together."

"That happened when I was younger. Maybe people favored me because I was light skinned, maybe the teachers. Anyway, some of the dark girls just kind of hated me, for no reason that I could see. I tried to be nice but I was scared. Anyhow, it got better later on."

"I could understand that if you had real straight hair and looked more White, but you have African hair and all. I still can't see why they got after you."

"Oh, the girls that are real light and look White, in their facial features I mean, with wavy long hair, they are the elite. Everybody worships the ground they walk on, especially if they have a good figure. Everybody will practically fight to get to see who carries their tray at lunchtime. But me, I'm skinny and not that pretty really, or, as we say, my nose and features aren't 'fine' enough and my hair is 'bad.' So maybe they take out their feelings on me."

"You know what? Somehow I've read this too, that White racism has made a lot of Black people hate their blackness so they are filled with hate. Maybe they hate White people too, for doing that to them but they can't get it out. So, anyway, they take it out on each other and you just got in the way of that...Oh yeah, and I want to say this: You're a little on the thin side, Ella, but you have a nice figure. And I think you're cute. You're a nice person, so don't ever feel bad about yourself. Can I touch your hair?"

Ella was pleased at his words but worried about his touching. Jesse just went ahead anyway. Her hair felt soft and wooly like a nice fur coat or the lining on some jackets. It was good to touch and he liked it. In a way it had more texture, more of a feel than did straight hair.

"It feels good. I like your hair. I never touched a Black girl's hair before so I hope you'll forgive me. I just wanted to see for myself. I mean, it looked nice so I wanted to see if there was anything so 'bad' about it. You shouldn't ever call it 'bad' hair. It's good hair."

"I like you Jesse. You're very unusual. I never met anybody so... so honest as you, about your thoughts and feelings I mean."

"Forgive me if I was fresh in touching your hair. I get carried away sometimes. I could make a fool out of myself easily. In fact I have already, several times."

"No, it's all right," she said, putting her hand briefly on Jesse's arm. "Talking with you has been good for me. Are all Indians like you?"

"No, I've been raised in the city and I'm probably a little more of a talker than most. Oh, I can be the silent, stoic redman when I want to be all right, but I usually am pretty open, at least around non-Whites. I have a lot of friends of different races, Filipino, Mexican, and Colored from my school...But one thing I think is true, no, two things, Indians are very honest when they choose to speak, from what I've seen, and they are very accepting. They have to be, you know. We have so many different tribes and all shades of color and all the rest."

"Well we have all kinds of colors, shapes and sizes in the Black community but I don't know if we're really all that accepting. I guess we have to be. I guess we are when you get down to it, but there still is a lot of tension sometimes like if a Black man marries a White woman. The Black women do not like it at all. They won't accept her at first. After a while they might, if she sticks around and doesn't act all high and mighty...I don't know though, there are so many of us. Maybe every neighborhood is different."

"Well, there are differences among Indians too. Some dark full-bloods are ashamed of their race while others are prouder than hell. Some mixed-bloods get kidded a lot in L.A. but I guess that in Oklahoma the mixed-bloods rule the roost. I'm sure there's a lot of hate among Indians too. I've heard a preacher try to convince us that we should all be White!"

She touched his arm. "Thank God you ain't White, Jesse, or we wouldn't be here talkin' together. Don't ever want to be White, Jesse, you are finer than any White person I could ever dream of!...I wonder if I'll get to meet any other Indians while I'm staying with my aunt?"

"Not too likely. You might, of course, but from what I've heard the Indians in Oklahoma are mostly too scared to be friendly with Blacks. They're scared that the Whites will get down on them. They even made it illegal for Indians to marry Colored people there."

Ella was silent for a time.

"But don't feel bad" said Jesse. "I hear there's a lot of Red-Black people, mixed Indian and Black, so there must be something goin' on. Maybe some of them go to Colored churches in Oklahoma City. Maybe some Indians even go there, for all I know. You see, I don't know anything much, just what I've heard and seen when I was younger."

"What are you going to do, Jesse, when you get older?"

"I don't know for sure. I like to draw things. I'm always drawing. But I like to read too, and I write some poetry and things. I could be an artist, I guess, but I don't know anythin' about it, I mean, I don't know if you can make a living doing that."

"It sounds wonderful though. You should try hard. Do you have any pictures with you?"

He turned on the little overhead light and showed her a couple of drawings. She thought they were good, so he gave them to her, writing on them "To Ella from Jesse."

"What do you want to be?" said Jesse.

"I might want to be a teacher like Mrs. Brown, or maybe a doctor. But I'll probably get pregnant and have babies and that will be the end of going to college."

24

"Why should you have babies if you don't want to?"

"Jesse! How can you ask that? The boys are always trying to get us to...to go all the way. They say we're stuck-up and mean and call us bad names if we don't. I mean, they just expect us to do it with them."

"Well, I can understand that but you don't have to, you know. I mean, I've never...uh, I've never slept with a girl and I sure as hell would never put a lot of pressure on one. You know, I wouldn't want it that way. And anyway, I would have to go to work to take care of the baby."

"You're different, Jesse. But you're right too. There are boys who don't do that, and I've never slept with anyone. But still it's hard after a while to always keep saying no when you would like to find out what it's like too."

"Ella, you have to run your own life. If you want to be a teacher or a doctor you're going to have to just fight them off. They'll respect you more, even if they don't like it. Or...I'm kind of embarrassed. I never talked about this before!" They both laughed.

"What I mean is, you can make them use prophylactics or whatever. I don't know, but they say they keep you from getting pregnant. Ella, you seem like a smart girl. There's a lot you can do for your people. You should concentrate on that, and you know, you've made me think about that too. There's no denying that I've wanted to have sex. It's kinda hard to figure out what to do, but I think I'll be careful. Good jobs are too hard to get for somebody that hasn't got any training in anything."

And so they talked, and the next day they said goodbye. Jesse and Ella never saw each other again, but, on the other hand, they never parted either. True friendships, no matter how brief, have no ending. They're always there.

RED BLOOD

CHAPTER THREE: LENÁPE ENDALAUSIT

"My relations.
I give thanks, this day, that
we are thinking how the blessings come
when our Father the Great Spirit remembers us.
That's why we are gladly rejoicing
when we see all things how they are growing
and our grandfathers the
trees they are putting on fruits.
Now all the whole world looks fine.
All vegetation and also grains and
what we pick, all is growing
And also we feel the heat of our
elder brother Sun
He sympathizes with us.
And besides these our grandfathers the
Thunder-Ones do the same when they give us enough
water.
Everything is that which is made by our Father
the Creator
It is said, even that every spirit prays
because sometimes we hear our grandfathers
the trees that they pray earnestly as when
the wind there goes by.
That is enough to cause anyone to think
and to bring happiness
when one sees our Father's wonderful works."

Prayers, prayers, always prayers. Did any people ever pray so much, with such deep feeling and humility? Around little towns such as Copan and Dewey prayers rose up from the old Delawares like mist rising when the sun comes up after a rain. You could almost see the worshipful thoughts spiraling upward with corn-husk-tobacco smoke, curling upward in a sacred manner, rising to form an uninterrupted continuous umbilical cord, wispy but solid nonetheless, between humans and their Creator.

For such was the life of the older generations of Lenápeyok, a life revolving around thoughts of the spiritual world because the evidence for that world, to the Lenápe, was everywhere, to be seen all around everywhere in Elemahákamik – the entire universe.

"Yukwe gatati wemi awen wichemanen moxúmsena. Now do your utmost, all creatures, to help our grandfather."

"Ketemaksíhena. We are pitiful. Wicheminen koxwísuk. Help us, your grandchildren."

Prayers, prayers, coming from a people who believed for ages that they were older brothers or grandfathers to the other Indian tribes. Prayers, also, coming from a people still worshipful in spite of the visible decline in their national strength.

"Long ago, back in the east country, when the Lenape lived there, we had many kinds of ceremonies. Here now we are pitiful because we are very lacking in strength. But we were warned long ago by our ancestors that the Lenápe will be unable to do things."

Still, even in adversity, one must recognize the gifts and the power of the Creator.

"Wanishi Grandfather Thunder and you also Wind Spirit. I beg of you that you pass somewhere else. Have pity on us your children. Do not run over our land. You see us. We are pitiful, Grandfather. We sacrifice him our Grandfather Tobacco. Help us. Listen to the pleading of your children. That is all I can do. Pity me. Again, I say, wanishi."

Jesse heard many prayers that summer and by then he was old enough to learn and understand a little more. He learned not only from the words, but better still , he learned from watching those old Delawares, how they really did live humble, spiritual lives, how they really believed what they were doing. Their gentleness, their kindness, their deep concern was evident everywhere. Most of them were poor but they were not concerned with material things.

Many of the old Delawares were cheated; cheated by the government, cheated in land sales, cheated by lawyers. But they did not allow themselves to become sly, defensive, deceitful, or even shrewd. They did not build a barrier around their honesty. Honesty and dignity and straightforward dealing was the very fiber of their being.

But all of that was changing. The rough waters of avarice were continuously breaking against the rocks of Lenápe spiritual life. And gradually the rocks were worn down, chipped off, ground away to be absorbed into the shifting sands of dishonest tribal "politicians" scheming with White bankers, oilmen, and speculators.

Jesse learned from the grandfathers how it all started:

"We had a hard time when we came down here from Kansas but for a few years we were pretty well left alone. We lived together in little settlements and helped each other. We all worked together, and everybody helped to put on the ceremonies. We had a lot of them then, the Bear Ceremony for pet wild animals was one. Then we had the Mask Dance, the Mesingk Ceremony, that was a big one put on by a mask owner and other people who helped him.

We also had the Rain-making Ceremony, Enda Sokalanheng, the Spring Prayer, the Corn-Harvest Ceremony, the Scratching Ceremony to get ready for something important or dangerous, and many others.

It is pitiful, grandson, but we have now lost all of these. We are poor, miserable today, for we have lost all of them, now for almost thirty years they have been gone."

"Can't they be brought back?" asked Jesse. "Why did they stop doing them?"

"A long time ago, in the 1880's I think, we started having a lot of trouble. The White people were trying to get our lands and they were always around bothering us. The government broke the treaties and took over our tribes. They did what they wanted to do. We couldn't fight back.

Finally, in the early part of this century they took all of our lands, the lands we had bought ourselves. They just took them and gave us each a small farm. The rest they took and they brought in White people to live on that.

We faced starvation. We had to abandon our villages, our settlements, and go to live on little separate farms. Many of them were poor, hard to work.

We had hard times, clear up to the big war, the last big war. The Whites poured in, for oil and land. They killed the animals and then said we couldn't hunt or fish for what was left. They hired game wardens to keep us from hunting on what was truly our own lands.

We became very poor, most of us, especially the older people. It was hard times, very hard.

No longer living together, being very poor, the people could not afford to put on the old ceremonies. How could you feed all of the people? How could you take off from working to do all of the things that were needed? How could you even hold the ceremonies when the White people were getting the land?

But the Elders tried hard, the old ones, they cried to themselves and tried hard. They sacrificed to keep them up, clear into the Depression. But that was the end of it.

The Depression ended it. Lots of people had to leave. The younger ones went off to the BIA schools or when they came back they were ignorant and couldn't help, or wouldn't.

Our older ones, with all of the knowledge, they were dying. Most are all gone now. And the young ones didn't learn.

It takes a long time to learn Indian ways, the prayers, the dances, the right way to do things. Now the younger ones they feel ignorant or sometimes they don't believe any more because of the Indian schools.

The Elders didn't give up. But they were too poor, so they turned to Father Peyote, so that is our Indian religion now."

"I don't understand why it cost so much money to keep up the ceremonies," said Jesse.

"Well, it cost a lot because all of the food had to be bought, or most of it. You had to feed a lot of people and you had to buy a steer because you couldn't hunt deer anymore. People just didn't have even an extra dollar to spare, in those days. They could hardly feed their families.

But even more it was a matter of time. It took a lot of time to study and get ready for ceremonies. And the men had to be off working for White people to feed their families."

"Did the government try to outlaw the Lenápe ceremonies like they did in other places?"

"Not directly, but the Indian Bureau schools and officials were always after the younger ones, always telling them to keep away from the ceremonies, to forget their Indian talk, to stay away from peyote. They punished them all the time in the schools and took away any peyote or Indian things."

"So, in a way, the Bureau took away the young people and cut it off that way," said another elder. "They didn't have to stop the ceremonies with police. They just took our people away from us. Broke us up, divided us. What is it that they do to people's minds?"

"You mean 'brainwashing'?"

"Yes indeed, that's what they did to our people. They washed their brains out, washed everything out until they were empty.

Then they filled them up with White ideas."

The old ones kind of smiled and chuckled to themselves, thinking about the BIA teachers washing people's brains out. It wasn't really that funny but it gave them a laugh because they were convinced that many of their children and grandchildren were, indeed, rather empty and ignorant, very much looking like fools as they imitated White ways as much as possible.

Jesse asked, "How did the peyote ceremonies get started?"

All looked towards an old grandfather who was a devout spiritual leader. He thought for a while and then told a story about how, many years before, an old Indian woman and a young boy were left in the desert down towards Mexico. The boy became frightened and left to find his people while the old woman, although very weak, thought nothing of herself but set out to save the little boy.

"Then, when she was in a pitiful state, a strange Indian-looking being appeared before her. It spoke her tongue and told her that the child was safe.

The Spirit, which was Peyote, went on talking to her. It said: 'When I have left, take up the peyote and eat as much as you can.' Then he taught her the ritual and the original songs which are still sung today by the Comanche, Kiowa, and other tribes, and even up here among us Delawares."

"What tribe got it first?" asked Jesse.

"Well, they used to say that the Comanches learned about peyote first. But lately I heard that the Lipan Apaches used to go down into Mexico to visit their friends, some Mexican Indians called the Carrizos or Hulimes. These Hulimes taught the Apaches and maybe the Apaches taught the Comanches.

But I don't really know, Taktani. Maybe the Comanches and those other Indians that went down that way each got peyote directly from the Peyote Spirit. It could even be that some Delawares were among the first. Some of our people – the Absentee Band – used to live in Texas with the Kickapoos, Caddo, Tonkawa, and a branch of the Cherokees. But that was long ago."

"How did peyote meetings get started up here then, from Comanches coming around?"

"No, two Delawares brought it over this way in the 1880's. Jim Wilson brought the Big Moon ceremony and Elk Hair brought the Little Moon. The Little Moon is just like the Kiowa and Comanche way. The Big Moon is different but not in the main things. Father Peyote is the main thing."

The old ones sat silently then, quietly examining their hearts.

Perhaps their minds wandered to other times and places. Perhaps they thought of the other world. Jesse lay back on the grass, closed his eyes, and listened to the flies buzzing in the shade of the big trees under which they were sitting. Some of the old men half-dozed and Jesse too felt sleepy. All of the dogs were quiet, stretched out to place their bodies on the coolness of the earth.

Summer is good. Can one soak up enough heat to carry one through the winter? Can one learn enough from the Old-Ones to carry a person through the disappointments of life?

Red Blood

Chapter Four: Coyote Road

He saw a coyote cross the highway just ahead. It did not hurry. It did not move like a coyote. Instead, it walked methodically, something like a horse on parade, leisurely, carefully, looking straight ahead. Jesse slowed down the car but the coyote-person paid no attention. It headed directly to the south, disappearing into the creosote brush.

Jesse knew it was a spirit-coyote. No ordinary animal moved that way. It wasn't until much later, though, that he learned from an old Navajo woman that it could have been an evil power. "Witches lots of times turn into coyotes and travel that way," she said, "But since it didn't look at you it's all right. It was going after someone else, I think."

Jesse, not knowing any better, felt good about seeing the coyote-person in broad daylight. He felt it was a special gift to him and he day-dreamed that perhaps he would have some good thing happen soon, or that the experience could help him understand things better.

Driving in the desert, even in the hot summer, was pleasing to Jesse. With the windows down he didn't mind the heat, except in the canyons where the wind didn't blow strong enough. But climbing up the steep grades in his old car was hard on both of them since the car's heat gauge kept moving higher and higher and Jesse had to strain to help the car find the strength to make it to the top.

The sweat poured from his forehead and his body was wet by the time the first big summit was ascended. He felt like he could just squeeze himself and fill up the steaming radiator but instead he coasted downhill for a few miles letting the air cool both the car and his body.

Sometimes he could make it up the second big grade without stopping but on this day he felt that the gauge was still too high. "Kshilánte. Gishte amalsi, it's hot, I am sun-hot," he said to himself. So he stopped where a row of atholl trees, brought over from North Africa, shaded the side of the road. The car cooled down some with its hood propped up by a stick that Jesse carried. Some added water in the radiator helped it to get ready for the next climb.

Jesse liked the desert. He especially liked a certain kind of desert. He didn't care so much for the broad basins covered with creosote brush but the bare-ribbed, wind-polished, sun-glazed skeletons of mountains and the deep canyons and the piles of rock-bones left behind by long disappeared peaks or hills and the hidden oasis with their tell-tale native palm trees, these parts of the desert created a sense of mystery, of wonder, and expectation in him.

The desert was like radio in contrast to television. With radio you could use your imagination, creating your own private pictures in your head. Television took that away. In the same way the green coastal mountains filled your mind with their images while in the desert you could use your mind freely. The desert only gave you a skeleton, bare and suggestive. You could fill in the rest, especially at night. At night, in the desert, you could be surrounded by huge trees, and all kinds of imaginary things, beyond the veil of the dark shadowline. Yet in the daylight all disappeared except in the deepest canyons where every turn offered the chance of something inexplicable, unpredictable and impossible.

Hours later Jesse reached the place where he wanted to camp. It wasn't far from the house of Antonio Chavis, his old friend from Los Angeles. Jesse had often visited him in the city and he continued to do so after Antonio moved to the desert. Jesse liked to sleep out in the spaces between the creosote brush, where he could be away from anything human, but he always spent a lot of time during the hottest part of the day sitting under Antonio's ramada or in the evenings on his porch on the north side of the little cabin.

Antonio had several dogs, old friends of Jesse. But his official greeter was a huge male turkey who came out front whenever a car drove up. The turkey, known as Don Pascual, was somewhat treacherous like a lot of roosters. That is, he would attack a stranger when they were least expecting it, when their back was turned. Jesse was always careful at first because Don Pascual had a short memory for faces (or smell, or whatever). After awhile he got used to you, or realized that his sentinel-duty, although willingly and conscientiously performed, was no longer needed, then he could go back to just being a turkey again.

Antonio had a lot of animals, none of which he ever killed, except for an excess rooster now and then. He did, however, rely on the eggs the hens produced and supplemented this with beans, corn, chilies, tomatoes, sunflower seeds, squash, and chayotes raised in a little garden. His place was also surrounded by prickly-pear orchard fences from which he harvested the tunas and nopalitos regularly.

Jesse noticed that many tunas growing from the prickly pear pads were deep red and plump with their juicy, sweet pulp. He made a mental note that he would later brush off the small spines and have a tuna fruit feast. There were very few young, immature pads on the nopales so he figured that Antonio was mixing chilies in with his scrambled eggs now instead of nopalitos.

The gobbling of old Don Pasqual and the commotion raised by three dogs, a dozen hens, several roosters, and a pair of geese had, in the meantime, aroused Antonio from his afternoon siesta in the shade of the ramada which stood a short ways from the east side of the house. The ramada was Antonio's favourite place since it provided cool shade, open pretty much on all four sides to whatever breeze was passing through. A hammock, acquired in southern Mexico, was suspended from a center post to one of the corner timbers. It was from this hammock made of matting that Antonio arose to greet Jesse.

Antonio Chavis was a stocky, powerfully built man. He was the color of dark mahogany with a reddish-brown luster that seemed to penetrate through the darker overlay. His features resembled those of the West African but his hair, although heavy and somewhat coarse, was long, cascading down his back in waves. A blue kerchief, folded into the shape of a narrow band, kept his thick head of hair, now with greyish streaks or tones in its dominant blackness, from swinging into his eyes (eyes that reminded one of an Egyptian mural or perhaps a Maya carving).

Antonio's face was still relatively free of wrinkles but it had a parchment quality due, perhaps, to the dryness of the desert and exposure to much sun. It was a face that showed great strength but also much kindness and, still more, good humor. For Antonio was a man who, in spite of much experience with pain and even violence, had long ago arrived at an age in which quiet laughter, gentleness, and good stories were his trademark. He was a complete mixture. Antonio's father had been a North Carolina Black-Indian man of the widespread Chavis race, a man who had wandered into south Texas, discovered Mexican women, liked what he had found, and then wandered still deeper into Mexico where he had married several ladies. He had brought his last wife, a woman of Yaqui-Mexican ancestry and Antonio's mother, to Arizona and then to Los Angeles along with seven children. That was in 1912 when Antonio was a teenager.

Jesse had learned all of these things and many more while sitting beside Antonio listening to stories which, taken together, had formed a major part of his education about the world. With his own grandparents living far off in Oklahoma, Jesse had found, in effect, a substitute abuelo in Antonio Chavis.

"Jesse, I knew you would be coming. I could feel it," said Antonio as he put his arms around the young man. A very self-sufficient person, content to live by himself, Antonio nonetheless deeply enjoyed Jesse's company, especially since his own grandsons were uncomfortable around him. His way of living, to them, was too indio, too primitive, too reminiscent of a poverty that many Mexican-Americans wanted to bury forever.

"Como estas viejo. I am sorry to have interrupted your siesta but old Don Pascual thought you ought to know that somebody had come."

"Did you have any trouble con su coche? The radiator seems to be hissing a little at us like an angry snake. Did your tires do okay? I thought you might not come til after dark."

"I just poked along and took it easy. No choice, anyway. I didn't want to wait for dark, you know I was too much in a hurry to get out of the smog. You're looking younger, has a lady been visiting you?"

Antonio laughed from way down and winked slyly, "Well, there is that old White lady who keeps coming by wanting me to be born again, but I think she is the one who wants something. But, I'm afraid of her. She is a little too, how shall I say, voracious, that's the word, too voracious for me. She's young you know, hombrecito, only fifty or so, and very hungry to be reborn. So, what have you been doing? How is your father and mother, y sus hermanos?"

"Everybody is fine. I haven't been doing too much. Working, saving a little money, trying to save enough to go back to Oklahoma in the fall. And, well, I go down to the Indian Center on Beverly Boulevard once in a while. That reminds me, I met a Yaqui girl who works in a laundry near my job, but well, she smiles at me at least, but I haven't been able to take her out. She always has to take care of her baby, or help her mother, or something. Maybe she has a man, although she says not. I have to talk to her in Castellano so I don't always understand her...I said hello to her in Yaqui the other day and she really got a kick out of that, but then she rattled on in su idioma and I couldn't understand anything she said after that."

"Well, Jesse, you're too much of a gringo, you know, even though your skin is brown...maybe she is waiting for a Yaqui man, comprendes? They're pretty tight. My father had to really woo my mother and even then he only got her because she was starving on account of the porfiristas. But once they fall in love and you give them a baby or two they make tremendous wives, like my mother, she was a santa, in every way."

The two friends, one in his sixties and the other seventeen, talked as they walked together to the shade of the ramada, sitting there on old chairs whose backs had disappeared years before. The dogs, who had preceded them, lay luxuriously on the cool, packed earth. The hens, on the other hand, grew bored and wandered off to search for bugs in the shade of the nopales or beneath a mesquite tree. The geese and Don Pascual had withdrawn out of sight, probably to a water trough that Antonio kept near the well.

It was still too warm for serious conversation, so Antonio and Jesse chewed on mesquite pulp or sunflower seeds and smoked a cigarette, occasionally sharing thoughts or jokes but saving important matters for the cool of the evening. Jesse drank water from an olla hanging from the roof and relaxed, letting his eyes glide along with the shimmering of the desert until he too was only a silent mirage. Antonio slept once again in his hammock. With a blanket for a pillow, Jesse lay back upon the earth and also slept.

After the sun had lowered itself behind the distant hills the dogs and other animals began to stir. Antonio got up from his hamaka and, with Jesse's help, began feeding his big family. Don Pascual and all the others were talking loudly letting the humans know that it was dinner-time. Once the food was scattered they all went to work on it, but occasionally a goose would look up and make a few satisfied sounds as if to give thanks.

Antonio liked to cook outside in the summer. With a minimum of effort he whipped together a meal of corn tortillas, beans, fried squash and chilies, and small ears of green corn. They also had some dried meat strips, charqui, that Antonio had made himself.

Strong coffee followed the meal and with its stimulation the two friends settled back for an evening of conversation. Jesse always encouraged Antonio to tell stories about life in Mexico and the Southwest and Antonio was more than willing to oblige.

"You told me once that there were still some Apaches living in the mountains down in Mexico. Can you tell me anything more about that? I just finished reading Geronimo's story of his own life," said Jesse.

"One of my uncles used to go up into the Sierra between Chihuahua and Sonora," responded Antonio. "He used to trade with those Apaches. The ones that the U.S. Army never was able to capture. They live in a very remote section of the montaña, back in some little valleys. I went with him once and I got to see them. He knew them and since he was a Yaqui they got along very well. They still spoke their language then and probably still do now.

There are also very deep canyons back in that country and down in the bottoms are caves and cliff-houses just like in New Mexico and Arizona. People are still living down there in those caves, people who don't even know that there is a Mexico. There are probably a lot of small Indian tribes still living back in there. Lots of Yaquis hid out in those areas during the time when the Mexican government was trying to enslave them. That's when my father befriended them and married my mother."

"Were the Apaches still fighting with the Mexicans when you went down there?"

"No, they just wanted to be left alone. They had guns, though, and they were very tough. No strangers went in there without their permission."

"There's one thing I don't understand, Antonio, and that is why the Mexicans, who have so much Indian blood, seem to always be trying to kill Indians or to take their land. I would think that they would feel a kind of kinship with each other."

"Oh, no! Now you've asked me about something! It will take a long time to explain that but then we have all night, so why not?

You've been to those Mexican cafes around Chinatown and Olvera Street? Remember those colored pictures on the walls of Mexican women in colorful costumes, or the pictures of Popocatépetl and the woman Ixtacihuatl? Do you recall what color their skins were? Did they look like Indians? Did they have Indian-looking eyes or high cheek bones?"

"No, they did not! They were creamy-skinned Spaniards!"

"There you have it in a nutshell. Even the pictures of Indians look like Spaniards before they are considered 'fit' to go up on a restaurant wall."

"Do you mean that Mexicans are ashamed of having Indian ancestry like a lot of people up here try to hide any Indian or Negro blood? Now I understand why my high school principal wouldn't let me write about the ancestry of the first settlers in Los Angeles. They were all Indians or Blacks or of mixed race!"

"Eso es. There are a lot of powerful people around Los Angeles who pretend to be Spanish-Californios. They don't want anyone to know that their ancestors really came from Mexico and that they had Indian and African blood. So they try to cover-over everything. After all, one of them was a big official and lots of them have Anglo names and are intermarried with White people."

"I've noticed that a lot of Mexican kids just look at me kind of funny when I say that I'm Indio, even though they may be darker than I am. Sometimes they'll call some other Mexican 'el Indio' but it's like a nickname and it's strange because why should one be `el Indio' and the others, just as brown, be something else?'"

"Well, let me go on with my story," said Antonio. "Then it will be clearer perhaps.

Mexico is a very complex country. Each area is different but, nonetheless, certain things are true in most places. Por ejemplo, the rich Mexicanos are very proud of the pyramids and monuments built by the Aztecs, Toltecs, and so on. They are also proud of being descended from those ancient, old-time Indians. But, and this is a big one, they are also very glad to be descended from the Spanish invaders. They call themselves Mestizos today but a few years ago they were all blancos, no matter how brown.

Oh, they will tell you that Cortés was bad, that Malinche was a traitor, and that Moctezuma and Cuautémoc were heroes. They will pretend to be on the side of the old Indios, but at night, in their prayers, they will thank God that they have enough Spanish blood so that they can pretend to be White. And if they don't have enough Spanish blood, they will use powders and creams to hide their brown-ness. In the old days the women, especially, would stay indoors to keep from getting a tan.

The saddest thing is, though, that when a dark-skinned Indio rises to the top, he will usually call himself a Mestizo and invent some Spanish blood. He will try to go against the Indios as much as possible to prove that he is not one of them, that he is truly a persona de razón.

An Indian, by definition, is backward, stupid, foolish, or just a plain country hick in Mexico. So to be considered as a civilized person, a rational being, one has to stop being an Indio. That is the general rule, proven even by Benito Juárez since he was a bad president so far as Indians were concerned. He dealt his own race a death blow although it took Porfirio Díaz to fully carry it out."

"You know, Antonio, that sounds like the U.S.A. An Indian up here has to get a 'certificate of competency' from the BIA before he can handle his own property and those certificates say that 'so and so is now a competent person and is no longer an Indian.' I've seen one. So it's the same everywhere."

"Well, in Mexico, everything runs against the Indian. A lot of people are ashamed that they talk an Indian language so they try to pretend that they speak only Spanish. I'm glad to say that the Yaquis are different and I've heard that the Mayas way down south are the same. But in general it is the Indians who are always being cheated and taken advantage of, so when they leave their village to go to the city or come north they usually pretend that they are Mestizo."

"Is there any real difference between Mestizos and Indios?" asked Jesse.

"Yes and no. On the one hand, there is no absolute racial difference. I have seen Indios, many times, who had lots of European blood, or African, but they spoke Indian so they were Indian. I have also seen many Mestizos, in fact whole villages of them, who were very Indian-looking. But they spoke Spanish and therefore were not considered to be Indios. Comprendes? It is very complicated!

You see, there has been so much intermarriage in Mexico, especially in the eastern, central, and northern parts, that almost everybody has some Spanish, or Moorish, or African blood even if it is only a little. But, likewise, everybody has some Indian blood and, for most people, it outweighs all of the rest combined.

Of course, there are tribes like the Yaquis and Mayas and Seris and many in the far south who are still almost purely of native race, but the bulk of the rest of the people, even those who talk Indian, are mixed to some degree."

"You started to say 'on the one hand.' What is on the other?" asked Jesse.

"Hombre, it is complex because humans are complex creatures. The big difference is that many of the Spanish-speaking Mexicans, whether of Indian blood or mixed, act and think differently from los Indios and even from the Mestizos who live in smaller Mestizo villages. Anyway, these last are really Indios, you understand. They just lost their idioma, maybe a long time ago.

So anyhow, who are these different ones? They are the ones who want to be White, who want to be light-skinned, who want to be 'successful.' They are the pushy ones, the scheming ones, the ones who open up small stores or who loan money to people. They are the ones who become army officers, who run the government and the labor unions.

When they get rich they, of course, get an education or at least educate their children. Then they pretend that they are very 'cultured' and 'refined.' But when they first start out they are often what we call 'coyotes' which, in Mexico, means a Whiteman or a Mestizo but especially one who tricks people. These are the crooked labor contractors who cheat the braceros but in the days of the porfiristas the coyotes were kidnappers who stole Indians to work as slaves in the plantations or in the mahogany-cutting camps."

"They sound almost like some of our tribal leaders up here, who do whatever the Whites want," said Jesse.

"Maybe so. But the coyotes were, and are, often vicious. They may be of pure Indian blood but they have put on a pair of pants and try to look like a Whiteman. They get a gun, if they can, and in the old days they would get a horse. Indians usually had no guns or horses."

Anyway, the coyote often will sell his own mother to get a little money. He is especially vicious with Indios because he wants desperately to prove that he is macho and mestizo.

So it's very sad. The poor Indian race is enshrined in the museum and raped on the streets. And I guess you could say the same is true in este país also."

"Do you think the Indians can ever win? Can they ever establish their own nations or build their pride up again?" asked Jesse.

Antonio was silent for a long time. The last faint light of the sun was slowly disappearing and a few stars could be seen. A wisp of wind briefly stirred the leaves of a cottonwood tree near the well, and then it meandered around the ramada, caressing the men's faces and moving their hair slightly. The cooling night wind felt good on their bodies. Jesse shut his eyes briefly, in order to better to give his full attention to the woman-like air caressing his arms, shoulders, neck, and head.

Antonio poured some more coffee and said, "I don't believe that I know the answer to your question. Times change. The Black people are waking up in this country. They are saying 'Black is beautiful' and 'Black power.' Well, no one is saying 'Brown is beautiful' in Mexico yet, or 'Indio power,' but who is to say it might not happen.

Perhaps in Peru or Bolivia or Paraguay or in the south of Mexico it might be possible. The Indian race is still an overwhelming majority in those places. Who knows?

But Jesse, you must keep this in mind. For centuries the Whites in the southern part of this country had a way of life called 'watching the niggers.' You know what that means? That they concentrated a good part of their energies on keeping a close eye on the Blacks so that the Colored race could never, ever get out from under them. They wanted to be on top. So they watched the Blacks very closely and they figured out every possible way to keep them divided, scared, ignorant and helpless.

Now it's just the same in Mexico and South America, except there the sport is 'watching the Indios.' The object is the same, to keep the Indians divided, ashamed, frightened, ignorant, sub-servient, and on top of that, malnourished, physically weak, and incapable of political activity. And it's worse now. They've still got armies, guns, and all the rest to kill the poor Indios but on top of that they have the schools, which seek to systematically destroy the Native languages, and radio and television. Do you think they allow Mexicano, Otomí, Yaqui, Maya, Quechua, or Zapoteca on radio or television? Not on your life!

No, everything is well calculated to destroy what is left. What has survived all of these five centuries is now going to be destroyed by TV, radio, Sears Roebuck, and Walt Disney.

Am I wrong? I hope so. But you know what happened in Guatemala. When it looked like the Indians were getting guns and a real revolution was going to occur our famous president, Ike Eisenhower, ordered in the CIA. The CIA organized all the rich White riff-raff, trained them in Honduras, and re-established an old-fashioned White military dictatorship! The same thing will happen in Bolivia where the Indian tin miners are armed. No, if the local Whites can't keep the Indios down the U.S. will!"

"You know, it's interesting that Eisenhower and his people also implemented the termination program against U.S. Indians. Do you suppose that the invasion of Guatemala and termination are connected?" asked Jesse.

"Absolutely," said Antonio. "I don't mean that the same man ordered both of them for exactly the same reason. But they are con-nected because the U.S.A. is still a Whiteman's country and the government cannot tolerate the idea of Indians ruling any territo-ry. Don't you see? They could never allow Indians to have even a lit-tle bit of land under their own control in the old days. Why should they change? That's how they make their money, by stealing other people's land or making them pick bananas for nothing."

Jesse was quiet. He was not really very pleased with the con-versation. He knew that Antonio was probably right but in his heart he still hoped that somewhere, someway an Indian people could pull off a successful struggle for freedom.

"Antonio, why is it that Indians, of all peoples, have such a hard time organizing and developing a revolution or a war for independence? I'm thinking of the Czechs, and the Albanians, and the Irish, how they have all rebelled at one time or another."

"Jesse, you know that los Indígenas have many strikes against them. First, you yourself know how localistic Indians are. Up here there are all different tribes and reservations, many of whom are jealous of each other. The government is always able to use one against the other. In Mexico each little pueblo is separate from the rest. Each has its own customs, and so on. There is no national consciousness except perhaps among the Maya of Quintana Roo or among the Yaqui. Each little pueblito goes its own way. The only time they work together is in a big general uprising and then all they want to do is to get some land back. As soon as they kill their own local Mestizo landlords they stop fighting, not realizing that by staying local they have left the state and national governments in the hands of their enemies.

So they get a new, maybe even more oppressive set of landlords as soon as they lay down their arms.

Indians are also very democratic and individualistic, or I should say 'family-istic.' There really are only Indian families, extended families, no tribes, no nations, no pueblos even, just interlocked families. They are often jealous of each other and distrustful of any authority outside of the family.

This was a wonderful society, before the Whites came, very free, very democratic. But the Whites are too clever. They can always use one Indian, which is to say his family, against another."

"Yes, that's true," said Jesse. "The BIA always picks out certain Indians and gives them favors, usually the Christian ones. Then they and most of their relatives support the BIA against everyone else. We had a group like that among the Delawares, the Journeycake faction. The government made Journeycake chief even though he was a Mixed-blood and no chief at all. But he was a Christian so they used him. He and his relatives lived completely separate from the rest of the tribe."

"Except among the Yaqui and a few other groups there are no united Indian pueblos or nations," commented Antonio. "There are only related Indian families struggling to survive. But on top of that you must remember the tremendous ability of the Whites to exploit every Indian weakness, every facet of Indian character.

The Whites, and not just anthropologists, are Indian-watchers. They study where the pressure-points are, where the cracks exist, where there is a weak, ambitious man with greedy eyes. They locate such persons and such points and they use them deftly. After all, they have been rulers for four hundred years. They would be stupid if they hadn't learned anything. Compañero, we must remember again that the Whites have been very clever in taking away the Indian's very own heritage, his own history. In Mexico and in Peru, por ejemplo the Whites and Mestizos have the gall to claim descent from the Aztecs, Toltecs, Mayas, and Incas. They claim that the old Indian aristocracy intermarried with the Spaniards and that they, the Mestizos, are their true descendants. The Indios of today are nothing but the descendants of the former peasants, or landless masses, ignorant, dumb people who created nothing then or now.

By means of such lies the Mestizos, who cannot prove their ancestry in any respect, seek to take away the pre-columbian greatness and give it to themselves.

The Indios, of course, are kept generally as ignorant as possible about the greatness of their past and when they are told about it, as in the rural elementary schools, it is not their past but a heritage belonging to someone else.

How can a Mexicano-speaking Indian of central Mexico, living today, possibly relate to the Mexicano-speaking people who created the greatness of the Toltec civilization? He is told nothing but lies and, since he is treated like a dog, he becomes ashamed or at least confused. If the Mestizos exalt the Aztecas and he is an Azteca how can he be so low? Obviously the Mestizos must be the Aztecas and he must be what? He does not know what. He is just an Indio which means poor and backward.

He doesn't even know that his Mexicano language, which is the same language as that spoken by the Virgin of Guadalupe and by Cuautémoc and by Moctezuma and by Quetzalcóatl, that his language is one of the great languages of the world. To him it is just what he is born with and more often than not it is a curse since the government cheats him in Castellano."

Jesse thought for a long time. "Antonio, I can see that education is a must. I would have been badly screwed-up if it wasn't for books and what older people have been able to teach me. The schools tried to destroy me with lies too! So what I mean is that we must use true education, the truth, to reach Indian people."

"Maybe through more books, or by means of art, and maybe music, or whatever we can use, we can develop our own way of getting across the truth.

It's very discouraging, but Indians have managed to survive. You have survived racism, Jesse. Other people have. So that is a great thing. We have survived!

Now we can go on and do more than just survive."

They sat for a long time after that, mostly just listening to night birds, to the wind in the brush, or to coyotes barking in the mountains. Finally Jesse took his bedroll and went off to the clear space in the desert where he liked to sleep.

His mind worked hard for a time but finally he relaxed and went to sleep. Antonio's words had stimulated his mind, though, and sometime during the night he had a dream. In the dream two White Europeans were talking to each other, arguing about what they should do with the Native People they found in the Americas. One of them said: "We are intruders on this land. We must respect the Native People." But the other one, a man with aluminum eyes, said: "This is our land. The Indians are only a myth. We don't really believe they ever existed. They are a creation of our museums.

This is our land. We have a right to take whatever we want. We have a right to use the Indians as draft animals or to kill them off as we please. It is completely up to us whether we shall be merciful and let them live on as slaves or be cruel and wipe them out forthwith.

By forcing the Indians into smaller and smaller places, and by taking away their land, water, and food-supply we can slowly starve them to death. Those who choose to work for us as laborers will starve more slowly.

If we deprive the Indians of good food and restrict their knowledge solely to what they need to know to work for us, then we can create a new sub-human, a draft animal whose only source of pleasure will be derived from pleasing his White master.

What shall we do with the people already living in the Americas? That is very simple. We shall make them work for us. Those who do not want to submit we will kill."

"What if so many are killed that no one is left to work for us?" asked the other Whiteman. "Then we shall go about the world looking for others who can be brought to this land and made to work upon it."

"How will we be able to take free men and make them work for us? Won't they rebel?"

"That is also simple. People can be broken like horses. Haven't we broken our own peasants and serfs? Remember, in breaking a horse one uses the whip (terror) and kindness (food). The horse soon learns to obey, since he must avoid the whip at all costs. At the same time by the use of food and other kindnesses the horse can even be made to love his master. Our object, then, is to use terror to break the spirit of the people. But terror alone is not enough. One must then use food and the Christian Church to teach them to accept, and then to faithfully love their oppressors.

We shall oppress them. That is our necessity and our destiny. It is their destiny to serve but not merely to serve resentfully. They must serve willingly and lovingly."

RED BLOOD

CHAPTER FIVE: AN EAGLE, A JAGUAR

A Chuckawalla lay resting on a rock. He was watching Jesse out of one eye. He knew full well that Indians used to eat Chuckawallas so he was prepared. If Jesse came too close Old Chuckawalla would scurry into a crack and swell up his belly so that he couldn't be dislodged.

But Jesse had no desire to eat that Chuckawalla. In fact he had no hunger at all. His mouth was dry from hiking in the desert sun and he was now absolutely still in the coolish canyon shade, with a small pebble in his mouth to bring out the saliva. Jesse could feel his body heat. He felt like a radiator, still giving forth heat into the air, heat from the sun and heat from his own inner fires. So he was letting the shade cool him down. And he was absolutely quiet, not moving an eyelash.

Chuckawalla was not fooled. He knew that Jesse was not just a hot rock. So he kept an eye on him but he was hungry, so he watched for flies or bugs that he could catch with his tongue.

When one is absolutely still, in a state of near-meditation, one can see and feel a great deal. Jesse saw several lizards chasing each other. One, a blackish lizard, went up on a rock and did a dozen or so push ups. Jesse wondered what push ups meant to lizards. Bees flew by and Jesse conjectured that there might be water ahead, somewhere up the canyon. Most of all, Jesse felt the canyon. It was still except for the hum of insects but he knew it was alive. He could feel the canyon, the smooth rocks against his back, the sand underneath his feet and behind.

After a time Jesse's eyes became accustomed to the intricacies of the canyon walls, the crevices, outcroppings, clumps of plants, setbacks, and shelves. Then he was able to notice markings on a smooth surface, an intricate design pecked onto the rock, a design which looked so natural that one would easily pass it by. This discovery led him to look for others and soon he found many.

Some of the writings were high up on the cliffs. How did anyone get up there? Others were on big boulders jarred loose ages ago. Their shapes were various but most commonly appearing were barbell like patterns and geometric designs sometimes resembling a Japanese sun-ray flag. One looked like a man carrying a dead rabbit.

It was clear that the old Indians had frequented this canyon and spent many hours pecking out designs. Perhaps many others, of even more ancient origin, had been long ago covered by desert patina or washed away by water or wind.

Indians had prayed in that canyon, Jesse was sure of that. He felt good to be there, but it also made him sad to think that less than one hundred years before, Native People had lived as free men and women in that desert and that now, if any descendants were left, they perhaps knew nothing of that canyon. The White people called it "Coyote Hole."

Jesse knew from his reading that as late as the 1860s and perhaps even into the 1880s the only people living out in the desert were Indians. A few White miners and cattlemen had wandered in after that, seizing or fighting over most of the sources of water. Some murders had occurred near a place that Jesse liked to visit, not too many years before, but that was a case of Whitemen killing Whitemen. Somehow the Indians had disappeared as if into thin air. Maybe, thought Jesse, the White cattlemen or sheepmen had driven them away in an unrecorded attack or perhaps the government had forced them to go to a reservation somewhere.

A large national monument had been set aside near where Jesse was hiking, and he was glad of that because he loved the Tree Yuccas and other plants and wanted to see them protected. Nonetheless, it revealed the White people's avarice and racism because it was designed for their recreation and edification. No such area had been set aside for the desert Indians, just an acre or two at a nearby oasis which was too small for them to use.

As Jesse sat in the canyon he thought too of the language of the desert people and how not a trace of it remained. He could not think of a single place where the Indian name was recorded except at the oasis of Maru and in the name Morongo Valley. Why didn't the National Park Service (which Jesse still respected in a typical layman's way) ever seek out older Indians to record the ancient place-names and the rich history of the area? Jesse dreamed how nice it would be to know the real names on the earth and all the details of the past. Who had camped in the canyon? What bands? What had they done here? Was there more water then, more animals like wild sheep?

For a time Jesse felt helpless and sad. What could he do to overcome the blindness of the White race? Weren't they also being cheated by their own racist approach to history? Then, for a time, Jesse let his mind wander into soothing fantasy, a fantasy in which he helped the desert Indians to defend themselves so that the High Desert could be preserved for them and for all the animals.

After a while, in a more composed frame of mind, Jesse began exploring the canyon once again, noting additional writings and many other things – mysterious little side canyons, rock-shelter caves, and beds of cholla or other plants on steep fans sloping into the gorge. Finally, he came to a bend in the cañada and there he saw a waterfall.

No, it wasn't a real waterfall with water flowing. It was what a waterfall would look like if you took the stream away, leaving only a tiny trickle of liquid, just enough to form a small pool down below. But it was enough water for the bees, and wasps, and birds, and all the other creatures for miles around. It was the only natural water for perhaps ten miles in any direction, or maybe twenty.

So here it was. A beautiful little tiny pool in the sand, marked around by many footprints, not too appetizing perhaps to a city-dweller, but wondrously beautiful to desert creatures. A jewel indeed. Something precious, to be preserved.

Jesse squeezed the side of his hand against the thin wet ribbon on the rock surface of the former waterfall and let the liquid accumulate in his palm. Then he drank, a little at a time, thanking the water, the canyon, and the Creator for this gift of life.

After drinking, Jesse moved a little away and sat back to think about that place so sacred. He knew it would be a dangerous place if a sudden rainstorm came because there was no place to get away to. But the sky was clear and, in any case, summer storms were uncommon in that area.

Jesse had read that many thousands of years before, at least 3,000, that desert had been wetter, with many running streams and lakes. Before that, another dry-spell and then the Ice Age, more than 10,000 years ago. "So," Jesse thought, "that waterfall was carved many thousands of years before and for the last two or three thousand years it has been just as I'm seeing it now, except during storms."

He imagined that he could see the water pouring over the falls and filling the canyon. The water got quite deep even then, he could tell, because the rocks were smooth and light up to a certain point. Then they darkened with desert patina above that. The sand in the water kept rubbing away at them, making them smooth, so smooth it was a pleasure to touch the rocks near the bottom, smooth and cool in the almost-continuous shade of the narrow gorge.

Later, Jesse climbed up above the waterfall and lo and behold- no more canyon, just an ordinary looking desert wash. When he returned to the canyon he studied the rocks around the waterfall. The water must have been eating, bit by bit, at those rocks, and the waterfall simply marked the present terminus of the water's bite. Someday, if the weather ever changes again, he thought, the waterfall will be ground up into sand and a new one will exist in its place, farther back still.

"All that sand out there in the desert, all that sand spread out like a fan, all that is ground up rock form the canyon and above, spread out over thousands of years," mused Jesse. "One can really understand eternity here. How short my life is compared to just this waterfall! I am in a place that has not changed for two or three thousand or more years. Hardly any people, except Indians, have ever been here. I could just sit here and look at the past, the past is right now, here, in this place."

There, in that canyon, Jesse felt a sense of peace, a kind of mental state that taught him something non-verbal. It was as if he could suck in knowledge or feelings through every pore, and yet it all remained wordless. He and the canyon were communicating. Canyons don't talk, in the ordinary sense, but they do communicate. They know when someone is in them. Maybe they can feel it, like we feel a fly or a butterfly. We might flick the fly off, irritated, but the butterfly we might cherish, letting it stay as long as it cares to. So it is with canyons in the desert. Some people are flies to be chased away with ominous silence but others, like Jesse, are butterflies to be caressed and soothed.

It was dark before Jesse left the canyon and then, in the twilight still, he climbed up tiers of rocks to the top of a high bare-ribbed hill. He saw a coyote, a small one, scurrying off and he stopped to watch.

In the distance he could see the lights of a growing White suburb in the desert. The lights were pretty enough but they made him reflective. The White people were pouring into the desert, not just the old self-styled desert-rats who could stand the heat and who truly loved the place. No, a new breed now, ones with air-conditioning and lawns and big houses and television and central heating for the cold winters.

"Air conditioning is the curse of the desert," he thought. "Electricity and air-conditioning. They get a plot, kill the native plants, build shopping centers, and destroy the desert. What are they looking for?

Technology is bad beyond a certain point. Wow! I used to believe in inventions, but now I can see what they're doing. They're trying to conquer the whole world, the deserts, the cold country, everywhere. They're pumping the water up and wasting it, not to grow food but just to swim in and water a lawn.

We should pass a law outlawing air-conditioning in the desert. Only wood-heating in the cold places. That's the way! Then they won't come. They'll stay in their cities!"

Jesse had already seen Palm Springs. It hadn't impressed him. Tahquitz Canyon he had liked, Mt. San Jacinto also, but Palm Springs? It was just another Wilshire Boulevard to Jesse.

Perverse Indian Jesse! The enemy of everything the White society dreams of! If he could have wiped away air-conditioning with a stroke of his hand he would have. And what about cars, and TV, and electricity? Jesse pondered all of these things, deciding that TV could go but electricity for reading and cars for travel were okay, although if he had to he could do without cars since one could use horses or, if they were left, trains and buses.

Jesse decided that he didn't object to all inventions. "Maybe everyone had all that they needed by the 1920s," he thought. "But the inventors don't know when to stop inventing. They just never consider anything except making money. Maybe after the real desert is all gone they can figure out a way to invent a fantasy desert."

Then a frightening thought occurred to him. "Maybe someday all we'll have left are little parks and monuments, little caged up pieces of deserts and mountains and forests. Oh God, those horrible beaches with miles of asphalt parking lots and trash cans and fire-rings and bodies crowded together like sardines trying to avoid the smog blowing overhead from the cities left behind. The world is going to become a zoo!" Jesse shivered to himself. "Everything wild or natural is going to be fenced off in cages. That's why they have national parks! That's why Indians have been penned up on reservations! What chance do we have?"

Jesse saw himself in the coyote. Like a coyote he would have to learn to hide, to scurry, to eat the cast-off garbage of the spreading cities, to be shot on sight, to be driven into a corner, to be cunning, to be poisoned by bait, to be trapped in big bear-claw traps, to be captured and put on display, to be strafed from the air, to be hunted by helicopters or motorcycles, to be forced to adapt, to become small and scrawny, to be infected by diseases, to howl at night, not out of joy but out of terrible sadness, crying for a lost world.

He saw, as in a vision, the identity of the coyote and the Indian. Their destinies were the same, after all. When the White people invaded an area with their cows or their sheep or their suburban houses, it didn't matter with what, or when, when they invaded an area the native coyotes became pariahs, interlopers, vermin, a menace, a scourge to be eradicated – and so, too, it was with the Indians.

Jesse remembered back to what the White historians had written. Now he understood fully! What they believed in was not even White people. They believed in machines! Machines, and buildings, and dams, and highways, and power plants, and factories, and canals, and yes, bombs, and guns, and tanks, and battlships, and more machines. Whoever had material things, whoever wanted more material things so badly that they were willing to kill, rape, lie, cheat, make their own lives empty, exploit, invade, conquer...those were the people who deserved to win! Whoever made the biggest machines, whoever paved over the most ground, whoever could kill the most enemies, whoever could own the most raw materials, they were the ones! Not just White people but consuming people.

"But," thought Jesse, "consuming isn't a strong enough word for them. People-Who-can't-stop-eating, that's what they are. They'll eat each other, they'll eat everything in sight. They'll eat the whole earth and go on looking for other earths if they don't die first." And for the first time in his life, literally, Jesse thought about the old Indian prophecies in a favorable light. Most of them predicted the end of this world because of greed. The idea had repelled Jesse but now he wasn't so sure.

"Maybe we will all have to die because the White people, or some of them, are so evil that they cannot be changed. Maybe that's the Creator's decision. Evil will destroy itself. They will eat themselves up, in the end. But unless we can do something all these beautiful things and all the good people will have to die too."

He felt sad again. "But then, if all the good people are so indifferent, or apathetic, or lazy, or complacent, maybe then they're really selfish, too self-centered to try to save the world. So maybe they're not so good either. Maybe most of us are just letting the rats rule the world and we don't care all that much."

At that point Jesse prayed and he especially prayed for all the people, red, white, black, yellow, all colors, who were suffering in order to help the earth, the humans, and other creatures. He thought of Gandhi and Martin Luther King and Eleanor Roosevelt and Mad Bear Anderson and other people he knew about. He thought of the old Indians trying to help with their prayers, ceremonies, and suffering. He thanked the Creator for the world and all the beauty in it. Then he walked down the mountain in the dark to seek the companionship of Antonio Chavis. He didn't want to be alone any more that night. And he was hungry.

As Jesse crossed the desert far below the mountain he remembered an Indian song:

In circles
circles
sacred circles.
Running on a sacred
round
earth.

He felt better when he reached the ramada. Antonio was expecting him. The beans and meat and coffee were still hot and there were tunas, already brushed, for dessert. The fire was low now but the coals were bright and friendly.

After eating, Jesse said to Antonio, "Do you remember that ancient Mexican song of Nezahualcoyotl? The one that goes:

I foresaw, being a Mexican, that our
rule began to be destroyed.
I went forth weeping that it was to
bow down and to be destroyed.
Let me not be angry that the grandeur
of Mexico is to be destroyed.
He who cared for books wept,
he wept for the beginning of the
destruction."

Antonio paused in the midst of working on a carving he was making. "Yes, I remember it. Nezahualcoyotl foresaw, the Spanish conquest, ten years before it happened."

Jesse then told Antonio about his thoughts, especially those on the mountain. "What does it mean, Antonio? We see so many things of beauty destroyed. We see good people defeated. We see the greedy ones win. We see Indians helpless to do anything. Yet you seem happy and contented. Atomic bombs, Hiroshima, the Nazis, rednecks down South, the...I don't need to go on. You know what I mean."

Antonio was silent for a time, staring into the coals of the fire as if to seek an answer there. Then he held up his carving and said, "You see this. This is the answer."

"What? Your carving?"

"Yes, my carvings and your carvings. Thousands of carvings. Millions of carvings. Or only one. It is all the same."

"I don't comprendo."

"Well, there's another old Mexican poem that goes:
Not for always on the earth,
Only a little here.
Although being jade it shatters;
Although being gold it breaks;
Although being quetzal plumage it tears,
Not for always on the earth,
Only a little here.
So you see, not only are our lives short but even the things that we create, the carvings, the songs, the buildings, the tombs, or whatever, they too will only exist a short time, from the point of view of the universe. Nothing material will endure in the same form forever, not even these mountains which are looking at us tonight through the darkness."

"Where does that leave us then?" asked Jesse. "Is it a waste of time to try to do anything good? Maybe I should try just to get rich and have an air-conditioned gold-plated Cadillac and sleep with as many women as I can and, well, is that all?"

"You yourself, Jesse, have also heard another old Aztec saying that goes:
Those of the white head of hair, those of the wrinkled face, our ancestors,
they did not come to be arrogant,
they did not come to go about looking greedily,
they did not come to be voracious.
they were such that they were esteemed on the earth:
they reached the stature of eagles
and jaguars."

"What does it all mean, Antonio?"

"To me it means that our destiny is to do things which elevate

53

us, not in the sense of getting rich or powerful, but which elevate us ethically and spiritually."

"Our destiny is to live in dignidad.

Our destiny is to live con respeto.

Our destiny is to introduce into our lives un gran calidad. Una estatura de calidad. Quality, character."

"We say it is a 'quality cigar.' We mean it has something that other cigars don't have. The same with people. And it's that quality that we must seek. You can also call it autenticidad, authenticity, trueness, realness, being an eagle and jaguar.

All we can do, Jesse, is to live our own lives with absolute care, with discipline, so that we attain the highest stature, in terms of quality, that we can. We cannot live the lives of others.

Jesse, you may be able to influence people by the examples of your own life but you cannot make a greedy man an altruist. You cannot make over other human beings. But you can take command of your own life. It belongs to you. You can either live it as if it truly belongs to you or, like a lot of fools, you can make-believe that it belongs to others and let yourself be pushed and pulled about by every little whim or fancy.

Our lives belong only to us, but in the manner in which we use ourselves we can either be a joy to other creatures, a person of honor and beauty, or a sorrow, or even a brutal fiend. It is up to each of us. We have that freedom.

Some people pretend that they don't have any freedom. The truth is they don't have freedom, but not because of anyone else. They don't have freedom because they don't want any. To be free one must be mature, one must accept responsibility for oneself. Many people want only to be children. They want candy all of the time, only it's boats, and sports cars, or big houses, or excitement, or dope or liquor or sex. Do you understand? We have only this short life to live. We all must die in a short while. You too, not long after I go, you too will have to leave this wonderful world. So be it!

Everything material that we create, that will have to go too, sooner or later. My carvings, made of wood, will not last long either. But is it worth doing? Absolutely!

Nothing good is in vain. Everything of beauty that we try to create is worth our efforts, even our suffering. Why is this so? Let me put it this way. Suppose that I just sat around, moaning and groaning over my old age, or just watched TV, or went down to the cantina and drank cerveza? What then? I would most likely already be dead! At the very least, I would do nothing worth doing, nothing worth leaving behind. I would not create one single drop of beauty. I would have no dignity, no quality, no authenticity. I would be, as they say, un cero!

But when I carve I work lovingly with the wood. I help the wood to realize its potential. I bring out its inherent beauty of line, form, and texture. The wood and I, we are friends, we work together. I help the wood and the wood helps me.

Now those are acts of love. They are also acts of creating. Creating, bringing something new into being. Maybe too, when people see this pieza de madera they will enjoy it also. So pleasure has been given. Maybe thousands of people might get harmless pleasure from a little carving. So is that not wonderful?

My joy in creating beauty. The wood's joy in becoming beautiful. The people's joy in seeing it. The love I have for the wood. The love the wood has for me. All of these things are immaterial. Now that's a good word. To some it means unimportant because it is spiritual, emotional, feeling, not hard, solid, and physical. But they are wrong. Such joy affects us physically, transforms our bodies and affects everything around us.

But all of this is in the realm of the quality of one's actions. And that's all that we have. We own nothing else. We don't even own our own bodies. We have nothing but one thing – the quality of our lives.

One's life is short and it consists of only one thing – the quality of one's acts. That's all you have, Jesse, and that's enough.

It will take you an entire lifetime to become an eagle and a jaguar. Isn't that enough for anyone to think about?"

Jesse was quiet for a long time. He looked off into the darkness and then at the stars, so bright and numerous in the desert sky. He could feel, as in the canyon, the immensity of time and it dawned upon him that those stars had been shining just the same for millions of years. Doubtlessly, they would go on for millions of years more.

"Antonio, I don't really understand. Something seems to be missing. What do you mean by the quality of one's acts or the quality of one's life? I guess you would include everything that we do, how we behave, and all of that – but what about our thoughts, dreams, prayers?"

"Yes, that is all part of it."

"Okay. But what about quality – can't there be good quality and bad quality?"

"By quality I mean the same as character or nature. One could say 'it is the character of one's acts or life that is important' or 'it is the nature of one's life,' and so on. Hombre, what I mean is that a beautiful woman, beautiful body only, has nothing if she is vain, or shallow, or without humility. She has nothing because the beauty of her body is not her own anyway. It is a gift of the Creator and is not her own doing. So she cannot take any credit for her body. But what she does with her body, with her mind, with her life – that she can take responsibility for. And it is on the character of her life that she will be judged, not on her purely physical beauty."

"Is it like this?" asked Jesse. "Suppose that I have been given the gift by the Creator being able to draw. I cannot take credit for that gift but I am responsible for its development, for its perfection, and for what it is used for. If I choose to draw advertisements to sell some product that nobody needs then that would be one kind of life. But if I use my art to create beauty or to help people understand the world better, then that would be something else. In either case it would be the nature or the calidad or quality of my actions, of my life, that is important. Is that right?"

"To me, that is true. You see, what is the difference between an Emiliano Zapata and a, well, let us take Adolf Hitler. Both were very energetic, both worked very hard for what they believed in, both became very popular leaders with millions of followers, and both were probably very intelligent although I must admit it is hard for me to concede that Hitler was truly intelligent. Let me say that he had a very active mind, full of lots of ideas, mostly bad, but some good ones too. Anyway, Zapata had the mind of a country Indian. He was humble. He didn't want to be a leader. He didn't want to impose his will on other people. So he dedicated his life to the selfless liberation of the campesinos. If he had a flaw, it was in not understanding that the revolution would be meaningless unless the society was truly democratized. He didn't understand politics. Nonetheless, his character was good. He was spiritual. He respected others. He tried to do good all of his life.

Hitler, on the other hand, was an incomplete person. He needed to be worshipped by others. He had no humility and he created one of the most arrogant, brutal systems of murder the world has ever seen.

So you see we must judge others, and ourselves, by what we do. By the character of what we do.

Nazi Germany has been destroyed. Its' monuments and statues and conquests are all gone. Zapata's revolution has also been destroyed, since the wealthy classes and corrupt politicians still rule

Mexico. Now all that is left is the character of these men's lives and the character of their influence on other people's lives. The one is a nightmare of pain, suffering, and brutal inhumanity. The other is a caress of unselfish love and noble self-sacrifice."

"So when you talk about character you are talking about reaching a high level of acting and thinking, going on a good road," commented Jesse.

"Sure. All the old Indians talk about the need to follow a good road, the Red Road of the Sioux, the Good White Road of the Delaware, the Pollen Path of the Navajo, the Peyote Road, they are all the same, and they are very much the same also as the road that Jesus followed. It is that kind of a road that takes you up, that takes you along a path where the character of your life is one that can be described as beautiful."

You told me that Black Elk talks about how it is the meaning and the understanding that gives power to what we do."

"Yes, and also that peace comes to us when we realize that the Great Spirit is at the very center of the Universe and that center is in each of us," added Jesse.

"Well!" announced Antonio. "We have not answered all the questions of life, and no human ever will. But Jesse, do not be discouraged. Each one of us has so many gifts that we cannot even begin to bring them to a stage of perfection. Each one of us has so many challenges to face, so many choices. But I am convinced that if we choose a good road, a road of sincerity, of beauty, of humility, of meaning and understanding, that then our lives will have not been lived in vain."

Jesse ate some cold tortillas and beans, drank a little water, and went out into the desert to lie on his sleeping bag beneath the stars. He was transfixed by them for a long time, but then, as if compelled by an unseen force, he arose and prayed to the four horizontal directions and to the sky and the earth. Finally he prayed directly to the center, to the Creator, asking for help.

"Grandfather, help me. I am
ignorant.
Grandfather, help me. I am
a poor boy, pitiful here before you.
Grandfather, help me to understand
how to live.
I am thankful for everything you
have given me.
I thank you for this wonderful,

mysterious world.
This world is so good, but the
people who live on it are often
so bad.
Wichemi, Help me! Help all
of us. Wicheminen.
Wanishi! Wanishi, moxúmsa!"

A snake, a sidewinder, came crawling by. Jesse sat on his bag, very still, and let it go on.

He crawled into his bag and listened to the coyote up on the hill, singing, and he fell asleep with beauty all around him.

Red Blood

Chapter Six: School on the Docks

Jesse got a job with a trucking company. A friend helped him get into the Teamster's Union and while waiting for a chauffeur's license he started working in the warehouse and on the loading docks. It was hard work at times but gradually he developed the art of throwing a box into just the right position without having to walk up to the stack and straighten it out by hand. It was kind of like throwing a football just right, laying it in there deftly, almost effortlessly but it took a while, and many misses to perfect. Of course, you didn't do that with all the boxes.

The loading jobs also provided time to talk. Jesse's crew-mates were an interesting group. Some were working their way through college, others were going to load or drive trucks the rest of their lives. Most liked to talk. They were inveterate political analysts, experts on sex, enthusiastic practical philosophers, and just plain bullshitters on just about any subject.

One thing Jesse liked was that they didn't just want to tell dirty jokes or Jewish jokes or deal with that kind of trivia. Oh, there was one or two who kind of moved from group to group oozing with obscene stories but those guys were not very popular. Everybody thought they were kind of obnoxious, and the truth was their jokes were boring as well as pointless to anyone who is either getting enough sex or who likes women. "Dirty joke tellers are almost always women-haters, and sexually screwed-up or just plain frustrated," one dock philosopher commented to Jesse. It seemed true.

Jesse developed his closest ties with an open-minded White college student studying at a junior college, an older White guy of radical political leanings, a Mexican kid from Jesse's high school, and a big, heavy set Ponca Indian who had played semi-pro football and had bummed around the country as a jack of all trades.

They didn't always get to work together and they didn't set up an exclusive group, but usually two or three would team up on a truck and, in between loads, during slack time or on breaks, they would sometimes convene for practical jokes or deep philosophical discussions.

The Ponca, Big Ed, had been a boxer at one time and he did look like he could handle anybody. Not only was he tall but he had a big chest and shoulders to match, and a large belly that hung out above his belt-line. He moved, in spite of his bulk, with a cat-like agility and a kind of dancing-rhythmic swing, a swagger of sorts. He always seemed to be kind of floating loose, swaying, gesturing.

Big Ed was always playing practical jokes. When Jesse first came on board he was a little scared of Big Ed. He wasn't used to the way some western Oklahoma Indians joke all the time. But after a while he realized that being kidded about his nose, his ears, his intelligence, his lack of sexual experience, his dropping boxes, were Big Ed's way of seeing what kind of a person he was – it was a way of establishing contact. Jesse managed to keep his cool at first and then later to come back with suitable wisecracks of his own.

Jesse was a good talker but mostly he learned from his friends. They respected the quickness of his mind but it was the others, for the most part, who had the experience.

Billy Tiger was one of the greatest talkers. Of Black and Seminole ancestry on both sides of his family, he was as tall as Big Ed but had a more solid, pillar-like build and a round head. Built like a stevedore and of reddish-black complexion, Billy was full of stories and editorial comments about Oklahoma. One such tirade was set off by a joke Big Ed had made at the expense of a White Okie co-worker who preferred not to hang around with Jesse's 'cosmopolitan' friends.

"Do you know what an Okie is?" said the Tiger. "Why, a real Okie is half-Black and half-Indian, maybe with a little White thrown in."

"Indians are never Okies. They're just Indians."

"Those people you call Okies out here in California? They're not Okies at all. They was from Mississippi, and Tennessee, and Kentucky and Kansas. They just stopped over in Oklahoma for a generation on their way out west."

"No, to tell the truth, they wasn't even from Mississippi either. They was really from Georgia, the Carolinas, and Virginia. They just kind of camped out in Tennessee, Kentucky, and Mississippi for a time."

Big Ed nodded, and added: "Whenever the Indians leave a place, y'know, the land is still good – young, fertile, rich, but after a generation or two these English-Scotch-Irish people, they just wear it out, make it into dust. That's why you get those dust bowls, and worn-down red clay hills. They just can't stay very long, so they keep movin'. Always wearing out the land."

"That's right," said Billy. "That's why the real Okies is Red and Black; the White don't really count. Ain't many of them who are blondes that's for sure!"

"It's a funny thing about them White Okies or whatever you want to call them," said Big Ed. "Some of 'em are real scrawny and pasty lookin', like they gonna blow away or just die right in front of you. I guess they don't eat right, or somethin'. But the funny thing is they get better jobs than Indians, or Coloreds, more money, but somehow they still look funny-unhealthy lookin'."

"You must be talkin' about the poor Whites, cause some of them rich Whites get plain fat," responded Billy Tiger.

"That's true, but you notice most of them still don't look healthy. Now, look at Avery here, and Ron, they're both White but they tan, they don't just turn red around the neck, and they look healthy enough considerin' that they're White." Big Ed laughed, poked at Avery and Ron, and everybody laughed.

Avery was a Marxist-Socialist who had some kind of advanced education. He probably could have been a college professor except that his radical views had exiled him to manual labor. Anyway, he seemed to prefer physical work to a desk job. Known usually as 'the Doc,' he was always explaining Marxist theory and introducing ideas like 'proletarian solidarity' and 'class struggle.'

"You men shouldn't talk that way about poor Whites. Their physical condition and their nutritional deficiencies are a direct result of two things, modern capitalistic exploitation and the south-ern-style feudalism they came out of. They've been kept in igno-rance by a system of class exploitation which has used them as pawns against the Black population and has simultaneously deprived them of any of the rewards. Eventually the poor Whites and Blacks must join together to overthrow capitalism and feudal-ism."

"Well I'll tell you one thing. Those poor Whites and the Coloreds sure ain't comin' together very fast!" said Billy.

"Yeah but listen here, some of 'em – the girls – sure chase after Indian boys. I've had a few – no, more'n a few – come after me, an' some of 'em good, too. But I don't like hillbilly music, so I couldn't stand it," remarked Big Ed. "You know, I hate to yodel." They all laughed.

Ron, the White college student, broke in. "You know, it's a funny thing, but opposites do attract, like they say, law or no law. I have to admit it – anyway I've told you before – I really like non-White girls. I don't believe in communism, Avery, but I do like the idea of proletarian solidarity as you call it. That means to me bein' able to take out the kind of girls I want to – red, brown, black, yellow, you name it."

"Why don't you do it now?" asked Jesse. "What's stoppin' you? I take out different kinds of girls."

"The truth is he's afraid of real women," shouted Billy. "He likes to talk about brown girls, but if he ever got in bed with one, he'd be scared out of his wits! They'd be too much for you Ron. Amigo, they'd wear you out in a day or two and you couldn't even lift one of these here little boxes let alone read a book."

"He might forget about his books altogether, once he saw that black fluff of heaven between two brown legs!" suggested Max, the Black student.

Avery would usually try to steer the conversation back towards intellectual topics and sometimes the others would join in for lengthy tours de force, but then Big Ed or Billy or someone else would need the relief of a laugh and they would steer the talk in a humorous direction.

One thing they all agreed upon, even Doc Avery, was that they all liked to listen to or contribute to, anecdotes and treatises on the female sex. But each approached the subject from his own cultural background. Big Ed, Jesse, and Art Villa liked to listen, and sometimes they contributed a little, in a general sort of way. But like most Indian men, North American or Mexican, they never discussed their experiences with any particular woman beyond some very general expression. "Hey, how was your lady last night?"

"Real good. I think I'll take her out again, if I can."

Jesse never liked to talk about girls he liked in such a way that they would become a commodity, a thing. Most Indian men were like that. Maybe it was because they respected women, or just because of some deep-seated reserve.

Some of the Whites and Blacks, though, liked to talk about every woman they knew, even their wives occasionally. They didn't seem to hold back anything, some because of the desire to brag, some just to fascinate the listeners. On the other hand, Billy Tiger was willing to talk about girls of different nationalities he had known in the ports of the world in the past but he grew reserved when it came to his current love-life.

It was a great education for Jesse, about everything from boxing to the horse races, from presidential elections to the crops grown in Guanajuato (where Art Villa was born), from scientific socialism to how Indians lived in the old days. A few subjects, such as religion, had to be approached cautiously since some took it seriously, others were indifferent, and Avery was an avowed atheist. Nonetheless, even this subject could be dissected so long as one did it with one or two others, rather than with the whole group.

Avery, the revolutionary, had married a Black woman when both were members of the Communist Party but they had split up when he left the party in disillusionment over the Soviet invasion of Hungary. Later, he had married a younger Black girl who was not much of a socialist but who admired his intellect and seriousness. They had only one child because Avery was afraid of raising mixed children in a racist society. He always tried to live at the edge of the ghetto or in mixed neighborhoods because there were less hassles that way. He couldn't live in White neighborhoods (and didn't want to anyway) but he also couldn't live in totally Black areas because of the way first-generation mixed children were often treated. So he and his wife, like a lot of Indians really, were always on the fringes.

Jesse and Billy Tiger disagreed with Avery. The Tiger had a Filipino-Hawaiian wife he had married in Honolulu. A terrific looker, she had literally overwhelmed Jesse on the occasion of his first meeting her. She represented for a time Jesse's ideal of a woman, beautiful yes, but more than that, supportive, nurturing, self-confident, and open. She loved her man and was a good match for him, strong and tall like her Hawaiian ancestors, but statuesque and exotic also. She and Billy had lots of children and wanted more.

Billy said, "Damn it Avery, you're too timid. You should have lots of kids-maybe a dozen. Then they can help each other. Teach 'em how to fight, how to stand together. Sure it's tough for Brown kids but you're making a big mistake 'cause your boy is all alone. He's going to have it harder. One is no good – a whole gang is what you need.

"Someday, that's what I want," added Jesse. "I'm going to have a lot of kids, and they're all going to be proud of what they are. I'm going to teach 'em how to talk Indian, if I can, and other languages too. I really like my brothers and sisters and they helped me a lot. You know I would have been lost if I hadn't had them around."

"One of these days, Doc, we're goin' to have a non-White majority in this country and then we'll see some changes," said the Tiger. "Now you know I can take care of myself. Plenty of White cops and sheriffs have tried to beat me up but they usually end up with the broken bones. But I want more than that. That's just defense, you know. I'm not fool enough to believe that you can get what you want just defending yourself. That's why we've got to have lots of children. They'll have more children, and then we'll have a regular army of fighters. Only then will things change."

"Listen" he added, interrupting Avery's response. "I'm half-Seminole, you know. Now my people always had to fight. You've heard of Osceola? Now, there's a true American hero, not a fuckin' slaveowner like General George! Well, my people fought like hell for years and years. And those Seminoles in the Everglades, they're still legally at war with the United States. And another thing, we kept fighting in Oklahoma, in different ways. One of my ancestors, Wildcat, led a big bunch of Indians and Blacks down to Mexico more than a hundred years ago, just to find freedom from those White sonofabitches. So I know."

"Maybe you're right," responded Avery "but Marx teaches us that the international proletariat must become self-conscious and realize that ethnic differences are just tools used by the capitalists to preserve their profits. That's why they can get us to fight in their goddamn wars. Just wave the flag and play some patriotic music and we're all willing to go out and die for the bloody robber barons."

"We have to stop thinking in terms of White and Black, or Indian and Filipino, and so on," continued the Doc. "We have to worry more about educating White workers than in having more Brown babies. The capitalists can corrupt non-Whites too you know, look at South America and Japan. Nationalism is a curse. The class struggle is what counts."

Big Ed, who had been listening silently, now chimed in. "Avery, you're crazy. You mean well, I know that, but you are truly crazy, out of your mind. Are you really trying to tell me that you can take a White cracker-redneck and make him into part of some kind of color-blind worker's movement? Stop, let me finish!

That is so much bullshit! They haven't changed and they won't change. I've heard this socialist bullshit all my life. It's been going on for a hundred years or more and it has always been anti-minority, always led by Whites who want to make sure that they control their lily-white labor unions and little – what do you call them? – oh yeah, vanguard parties. 'Vanguard!' That's a good word, but they're just a bunch of wild-eyed nuts. They go down to Oklahoma or

Mississippi they're going to get killed by their fuckin' White working class masses!

Listen! Another thing. You're okay Doc, you listen to other people. But most of the commies I've seen don't listen to anybody. They think they know it all. They're just as conceited and big-headed as any other White jackass."

Avery responded, "Okay, that's true, I realize that now. But there's no reason why minorities can't lead the proletarian movement. You can be the organizers. If the Blacks would work for socialism instead of civil rights, and if the Indians worked for a classless society instead of trying to keep these reservations – concentration camps are what they are – then we could get somewhere. What are civil rights worth in a capitalistic society?"

"Now wait a minute," said Jesse, finally jumping in. "Reservations are bad only because a big White bureaucracy runs them. And the BIA is a socialist bureaucracy, run by college-educated anthropologists and sociologists and social welfare types who think they know what's good for Indians.

Another thing. They're bad because the Whites have taken so much land away – just give us back some of our land and give us our own self-government and we'll be okay. Reservations are our homelands you know. They're nations with the rights of any nation to self-determination."

But Avery had a response. "Jesse you're wrong. The BIA may be bureaucratic but it is not socialistic. It is controlled by capitalists who want to get every possible bit of profit from the reservations. That's why the land keeps disappearing and why dams are built to flood the land, and so on. And another thing, in a capitalistic society your leaders are going to be bought off, corrupted. Self-government will just be an illusion. Your own people will rip you off."

"But the White people who run the BIA and the Bureau of Reclamation and all those other agencies are not just capitalists," said Billy Tiger. "They are also White and by that I mean that they have a culture that is arrogant and imperialistic. I think you White socialists would be just the same. Don't they build dams in the Soviet Union? Don't they relocate people in China. If your socialists decided that they needed uranium from the Navajo Reservation wouldn't they get it, just like it's being gotten now?" said Billy Tiger.

"Avery, the Tiger has hit on the crux of the problem," said Big Ed. "Your ideas are okay except for one thing. You have forgotten about the way people think, the way they act, their values. Most the White people in this country are restless, aggressive, materialistic, and conceited. Adopting Marxist slogans doesn't change them, any more than Christianity. Hell, they don't believe in any of that crap. They just go ahead and get what they want. That's why your commies are so dogmatic, inflexible, and arrogant. They're part of the same way of thinking. I sure as hell would not trust them to decide what should happen to Indians!"

"Religion is the opiate of the masses," said Doc. "Christianity is just a trick of the capitalists to keep the poor Whites and Blacks hoping for the promised land when they die, while the rich rip them off while they're alive."

Jesse jumped up. "Avery, you are off the track. Why can't you say the same about marxism. Socialism is just a trick of the vanguard to keep the poor workers hoping for the promised land of equality while the party bureaucrats rip them off every day. And listen, Christianity, or some of it, may be used to keep people under control but Christian churches are very different from the old Indian religion. Native worship can't be an opiate because it's not run by anybody but the people themselves."

Doc interrupted. "But you have lots of superstition and magic and medicine-men or whatever. What makes you think that doesn't have the same effect?"

"Wait a minute. Indian medicine is not superstition. I feel sorry for you, Avery. When you get sick you're going to have to go to some White rip-off doctor who'll cut you up and you'll die anyway. You can't go to an Indian doctor because you have no faith, so you couldn't be cured. But I've seen many cures. I know what I'm talking about," said Big Ed.

"The problem with you, Doc, is you don't know nothin' about Indian religion. It's a free religion. We have to find our own way. Nobody controls us, nobody tells us what we have to do. The holy men, they just point the way that's all."

Avery tried to interject something but Billy Tiger roared in, "I never have seen a medicine-man or an Indian doctor or a road chief who had any money at all. They're all poor, just as poor as everybody else. Christian preachers, yes, they get fat and sassy, but the medicine men they're totally different. Remember, our Indian churches are simple; we build them ourselves, that don't cost nothing but hard work. Indians don't spend no $50,000 or $100,000 on buildings, no way!"

"Okay, maybe so. But Indian society according to Marx is a primitive stage of development, preceding feudalism. In order for society to progress we have to pass from the stage of tribalism to bourgeois society and industrialism. Then, at that stage, and in feudalism too, religion becomes oppressive. So then socialism has to eliminate religion," lectured Doc.

"Avery, you are somethin' else," said Big Ed. "Why should we believe what some bird named Marx thought about Indians? Did he ever see any Indians? Did he ever learn from any Indians? No. He was a middle-class European Jew who believed every fuckin' bad thing he ever read about Native People. Now how can you have a real philosophy based on somebody else's bullshit?"

Jesse added: "Remember, Doc, when you said that religion is an opiate to keep the Blacks under control? Well, then how do you reconcile that with the fact that the Black church has helped colored people survive through all of these years of slavery and Jim Crow. And what about the Black preachers and church members who are right now risking their lives down South?"

Time went by fast on days such as that and everybody enjoyed the stimulation derived from argumentation. Working men in those days were not stupid, and neither were non-White workers. They read labor newspapers, they listened to the radio, they went to radical lectures, they heard preachers on Sunday, or medicine-men any day. They thought on their own as much as anyone else did. Not all of them, of course, but enough so that you could get a group together in almost every factory.

Jesse had increasingly become interested in politics. Virtually all of the students at Harding High had been pro-Kennedy in 1960 and all of the Indians at the Indian Center, hating the Eisenhower-Nixon termination policies, supported Kennedy-Johnson, at least verbally.

But a couple of years had passed and Jesse was no longer an unquestioning supporter of the first Irish Catholic president. Indians had waited expectantly for some signs of change but the same old faces ran the BIA and termination was still the controlling policy.

Jesse complained to his friends on the dock: "You know, Kennedy appointed a task force to study Indian affairs and not one of the members was an Indian? W.W. Keeler, a vice president of Phillips Petroleum was the only member with any Indian blood and he's the Principal Chief of the Cherokees, appointed by the president. Nothing has changed at all. Now Kennedy has appointed a Whiteman, a defeated politician, as Commissioner of Indian Affairs. What do you think, Big Ed?"

"In all my years I've never seen it get better. Democrats or

Republicans, it don't mean a damn thing. I didn't expect much would happen."

Max interjected, "Well, Black people are sure disappointed. Kennedy has turned his back on civil rights. He is full of beautiful speeches but that's all. We can't live on promises while the FBI stands around and allows the rednecks to kill people."

Villa added, "We had a strong Viva Kennedy campaign but all we got out of it was one lousy appointment in the Department of the Army I think. Mexicanos just got fooled again."

"I told you guys that Kennedy was just a super-ambitious smooth-talker. Hell, he was created by the media, or let me put it this way, he knows how to use the media to make himself look like something he's not. He wants you to think he's an urbane, sensitive, sympathetic president that you can trust. But that's just a TV image. He's really after power, just like Nixon, and he's owned by the same big corporations. Didn't he try to invade Cuba? Isn't he getting us involved more and more in Vietnam?" asked Avery.

"Well, I still think he's better than Nixon," commented Ron. "Hell, Nixon got money from Chiang Kai Shek and had a big slush fund and all that shit, or so I hear. Besides, I like the Peace Corps. Kennedy has done some good things."

"I admit his speeches are good," responded Jesse. "But we can't live on speeches. A lot of Indian children are dying every day because of poverty and no medical care. What do I give a shit about those good speeches? Has he returned one acre of land to Indians? No, goddamit! The BIA is still selling Indian land to Whites in California and leasing it to Whites everywhere else. No, he's a complete failure, so far."

"And he always will be," said Avery. "You've got to realize that he's part of the wealthy power-structure that rules this country – big corporations, oil companies, coal companies, uranium companies – they paid for his campaigns. Do you think he's going to give Indians even so much as forty acres? Hell no, the land is needed for mining companies and White cattlemen! The capitalists want to break up the reservations, open them up to more exploitation. They don't want any more land going to Indians, that would be stupid!"

"Kennedy may not be as bad as you think," interjected Billy Tiger. "What if he were to do something radical? He just won by a few votes."

"But what's the difference? A president is still president. With a flick of a pen, he can return lands to the Pit River People; he can give Blue Lake back to Taos; give the Papagos some of their lands back. A lot of it is land White people don't need. And Papago life-expectancy is seventeen years! With a flick of his pen, he could do a lot of good and it wouldn't cost him but a handful of votes," answered Jesse.

"That's not the point," responded Avery. "The point is that even desert land may have minerals underneath it, or it might have timber, or water. So why give it back to the Indians?"

"Hell, that don't make any difference. Even if the Indians had it, the BIA would turn right around and give it away for next to nothing. So that's no issue," asserted Big Ed.

"Why give it to the Indians if the BIA is going to give it away again? You see, that's just it. Either way Indians and other poor people are not going to be allowed to own anything. Let me give you a different example: People that own stock don't have to pay any income tax on their first $100 of income, right? But you have to pay tax on all of your savings account interest, you see? Rich people get a big tax-break when they buy apartment houses, don't they? They get to depreciate everything and then they get half of their gains tax-free anyway. Do you get that on your house, hell no! The tax laws are written for the rich. Has Kennedy changed that? No. Will he? No. And there's a helluva lot more poor and working class people than there are Indians. But he just shows his teeth, looks handsome, calls for them to 'do it for your country' and they just fall down and roll over with joy. Mark my words, friends, they are accumulating as fast as they can, getting richer everyday. So much for patriotism!" concluded Avery.

"You're probably right," said Ron. "I read somewhere how General Motors, Standard Oil, and a big tire company set up this dummy corporation to buy up all the streetcar lines in the country, like here in L.A. Then they tore up all the tracks and sold their own buses, gas, and tires to the dummy companies. Now all we've got are these stinking buses, and smog, smog, smog! And now that nobody wants to ride the buses, General Motors and Standard Oil want to sell them to the public. Then we'll have to use tax money to buy their damn buses and all!"

"Yes, and the different public utility commissions all give their approval while thousands of miles of rail lines are torn up. They must be getting a lot of bribe money," added Max.

"You better believe that the capitalists are always at work, night and day, to make money. That's all they're after. They don't care about smog. They don't care about public transit. They don't care about anything except profits. Someday, you'll see, after the cars get too crowded on the streets some guy will come in and propose a new subway or a rapid transit system. The capitalists will be all for it because they'll get to build it. They'll make big money off of replacing what they destroyed in the first place. That's why capitalism is a deadly system. It can never be reformed," concluded Avery.

"Well, the revolution's going to be a long time coming," said Big Ed. "As long as the majority of White people believe in General Motors and hate Indians and Colored folks there ain't no hope. It's that simple."

"Hey, this is depressing me," said Ron. "Let's talk about something good. Did you see that new waitress down at Dan's Cafe? Notice how she leans over to take your order? What boobs!"

Red Blood

Chapter Seven:
Ripples in a Brown Revolution

Jesse heard the door slam, followed by angry-sounding footsteps on the stairs. Then a bedroom door shut with a bang. He looked at his sister Ladell, but didn't say anything. Ladell stared out the window for a while. She said, "I guess I better see if she's okay."

"I'll come along," responded Jesse.

They went up to Cary's room and Ladell knocked on the door. "Go away. I don't want to talk," was Cary's answer.

"I've got to get something," lied Ladell, as she cautiously opened the door.

Cary was laying across her bed, still dressed in her "job interview dress" as she called it.

"You need to talk to someone. What happened?" asked Ladell.

Cary sat up and motioned them in. She really wanted to talk anyway, to 'get it off her chest.'

"Well, it's hopeless. I failed again!... I'm 'overtrained.' How do you like that?

I had two interviews today. One guy took one look and said he'd already found a secretary. The other said I was just too qualified, that his job wouldn't suit me. I would be dissatisfied, he said.

I guess I was a fool! The dunce of the class of 1957! I should have stayed with art, painting pictures on the boardwalk, or something like that...

Why did I go to secretarial school? All that waste!... Look at me... I learned typing, filing, dictation, shorthand, office machines...and all for what? No one wants me as a secretary and I'm 'over-qualified' to be a file clerk. What's wrong with me? Do I have B.O? Does my breath smell bad? Do I look funny or something?"

Jesse and Ladell merely listened, giving Cary a chance to cool

71

down, to ease her frustration.

"Maybe I should have gone on to college to study art. That's what I wanted to do. But if they won't hire an Indian secretary how could I expect to be an artist? I guess I'll get a job in a laundry. At least Indians are known to be able to wash clothes!"

"Maybe if you keep trying you'll find something," said Ladell. "Don't give up. You're very good and sooner or later you'll get a chance to prove it."

"I'm going to try the Bureau of Indian Affairs and if I can't get a job there I will try a laundry," responded Cary. "The BIA has opened a new relocation office on South Broadway. Maybe I can at least get a filing job. I don't think I'll tell them everything I can do."

A week or so later she did get a position with the Bureau, processing and filing relocation papers.

At first, Cary was happy to be working. Gradually, however, Jesse noticed that her enthusiasm had diminished and that she was moody again.

"I'm getting to where I hate to go to work," she said.

"It's terrible, Jesse. I can't believe it!...These Indians are being brought in from Arizona, New Mexico, and even the Plains states. They are so poor. Many can hardly speak English. Most can't read signs even. They don't know anything about city life at all, even things like traffic signs or how to ride on buses.

The people at the BIA treat them very rudely...callously. They get no real counseling and they're always having problems because the Bureau puts them in rough neighborhoods.

And the jobs! Low wages, working in sweat shops or what-have-you. Yes, laundries! That's the most common for the women....So many of them turn to alcohol or they just go home.

I feel like an evil person! I do what I can but I'm just a clerk. I can't bawl out the counselors or the big-shots! I'm helpless...I don't know what to do."

"Don't the people know what they're getting into when they agree to be relocated?" asked Jesse. "I mean, they must have some idea."

"I don't think so. They're promised a better life, that's all. They're not told about all the problems. I mean, the BIA counselors don't have to live in flats in rough neighborhoods, with no furniture, and with all of the temptations, all the crooked businessmen, and the loan sharks you find in poor areas. So maybe the counselors don't have any idea about what to say anyway. Not many would come if they knew the truth."

"Maybe it's a plot to get rid of Indians," said Jesse.

"Don't say that, Jesse! I feel bad enough already," sighed Cary.

Jesse and Ladell decided to help Cary find a better job. They started watching the classifieds and discussing what might be a good place for her to try. One day Jesse saw an ad for positions at the Los Angeles City College and several secretarial jobs were among them. Jesse offered to drive Cary out there but she wouldn't go at first. She could not face further discouragement.

But one morning Jesse and Ladell announced that they were taking her there, that Cary had an appointment scheduled for afternoon and that they had already phoned the BIA with the news that she was ill. Cary was furious at first but, true to her nature, she was soon overwhelmed with appreciation for their concern and their love. So she went and she got a job as a secretary. Life changed for Cary then. She started taking evening classes in art and, after saving some money, enrolled as a full-time student.

Ladell was more of a problem. Tomboy that she was, and very dark brown and Indian-featured, Ladell just barely made it through high school. The last two years, after Cary had graduated, were especially hard ones because she became fully conscious of racism and teacher antagonism. Worst of all, she learned full well that most of the minority males, especially Mexicans, favored light-skinned females. Most of her boyfriends were actually Filipinos or Whites because they seemed less prejudiced than the Mexican boys.

Lots of dark brown girls, whether Indian or African, run into a lot of trouble in a racist society. Even if they have 'nice' or 'White' features, the darkness of their color causes them to be passed over at an early age. All too often they come to believe that they have to 'put out' in order to be popular. Sometimes they get hooked on dope or liquor.

Even Jesse noticed that everywhere and in every way possible White newspapers, magazines, movies, and TV favored light-skinned women, usually White blonds. But the most devastating thing of all was that the Black magazines almost always used models for their ads who were essentially light-brown mixed-bloods. And the Mexican popular magazines were just as bad, favoring light-skinned brunettes with fake orangy-blonde hair. Jesse often wished that someone would have the nerve to publish pictures of dark-skinned beauties! But the best they could do was to feature an occasional exotic Eurasian or some other light-skinned type. The truth was that the big-shots didn't think that dark-brown women could sell a tube of toothpaste no matter how beautifully they smiled with pearly-White teeth, and no matter how dark-brown skinned the audience might be.

So Ladell had a hard time. The rest of the family was supportive and told her she was beautiful. She was, of course, but she didn't know it. Ladell sincerely believed, for a time, that she was dark and ugly.

She managed, though, to get through high school without becoming pregnant but what was she to do after that? Cary, who was lighter, had had a hard time of it, and anyway Ladell was not about to become a secretary.

She managed to get a job working in a bakery, helping to pack crates full of sweet rolls, but she soon became tired of that. Jesse tried to talk her into going to college to become a forest ranger or a national park ranger but that seemed impossible, both because of her color and her sex.

For a time she held on, supported by her family ties and a dynamic love of life. But after Cary got started in college, she became depressed, not that she was jealous of Cary. It was just that she didn't see any way that her interests, her dreams could ever be fulfilled. The contrast was too great. And so she got married, Indian-style, to a Sioux from South Dakota who had been relocated in L.A. He was not a bad guy, the Lakota, he just couldn't hack it. Within a year he was gone and Ladell, with a baby boy, was left on her own.

It was at this time that Jesse, now 17, began to realize what had been happening with his sister. He thought that she was one of the most beautiful women he knew but now he realized that she thought otherwise. Jesse also had always admired her vitality, strength, and drive, but now he became aware that all of that had been blunted and he hadn't even really noticed.

The family brought Ladell and her baby home, as Indian families usually do, and she was made to feel welcome in every way. And Jesse began to spend more time with his sister and his new nephew. He liked to play with the baby, becoming something of a father (as uncles often do anyway). But more than that he tried to share some of the things that he had learned from the old people, from Antonio Chavis, and from books on racism and Indians.

Jesse didn't yet understand everything about the effects of oppression. He didn't really comprehend why his beautiful, talented sister should feel so negative about herself, but he did realize that she had not had the chance that he had, to go back to Oklahoma by herself or to drive out to the desert to stay with Antonio. Always a tomboy, she had been forced to assume a girl's role after puberty and that had restricted her and made her more vulnerable, perhaps, to the personal doubts created by racism. So, as soon as he could, Jesse took his sister and nephew out to the desert and he shared his ideas with her at every chance. Antonio, understanding much of what had happened, was very helpful as well.

The rest of the Rainwaters were around to help too. Cary loved the baby, Elisa loved the baby, Andrew loved the baby, and they all loved Ladell. So they were a good household, actually made richer by one. No, not just by one, because they had all learned something about how they needed each other and that added something extra as well.

Andrew Rainwater was getting older and he couldn't work as hard as he used to. Jesse didn't want Ladell to have to work right away or for Cary to quit school so he went to work extra hours and began to contribute to the family pot. That made him feel good. He was needed. He was getting to be a man.

Ladell began to change. Her old brightness began to return as she went hiking with Jesse and Cary or sometimes other friends. But most of all it was Antonio Chavis, out in the desert, and Jesse's dream.

Jesse told Ladell about a new dream he had. The two White Europeans he had heard before were talking, but this time it was about something meant for Ladell to understand. In the dream one Whiteman said:

"The Brown Americans and the Black Africans are to be our servants and slaves. Everything that they have is to belong to us, even their bodies. Their very women we will take whenever it pleases us. And when they are no longer beautiful we will cast them aside and take others. And they shall all work for us and do our bidding."

"But how can we make them do that? How can we make them willingly accept so terrible a fate?"

"It is easy. They are a different color from us. Generally, they are darker than we are. So in order to set things in proper order, as everything must be well-ordered in this life, we shall establish the rule that lightness of color is supreme and destined to rule. We shall ordain that light is the color of God and that dark is the color of the Evil One, that White is the color of purity and superiority and that brown is the color of filth and abomination.

We shall tell them that they have been made dark because of a curse of God, because God is displeased with them, and that in order to gain favor with God they must obey us. They must kneel down before us and forget everything that they have ever known before."

"But will that be enough? Will they believe these inventions of ours?"

"They will believe. We will prove it to be true. We will remake the world so that it is true. Lies can be transformed into truths easy enough; all that is needed is repetition and a system of rewards. We will reward lightness and punish darkness.

We will reward each person according to how much he resembles us.

We will establish a color grading system. White will be 'first,' light brown 'second,' medium brown 'third,' dark brown 'fourth,' and black-brown or black 'fifth.' But we will also give grades for the shapes of noses, for the color of the hair, for the color of eyes, for the width of lips, for body build. The final rank will be a composite of all these but color alone shall count for half.

A person will carry these grades with them all their lives. No amount of achievement can change them except in very rare cases where we might have to give a higher score to a dangerous man in order to keep him on our side.

Each class of persons will be known by different names, such as mestizo, mulatto, half-breed, quadroon, high yellow, bright mulatto, cholo, zambo, and so on. Each class will be made to be jealous of every other class.

Families will be divided.

Tribes will be ripped apart.

And they will forget even the names of their nations.

Only castes shall remain, and we shall be the highest caste and we shall rule forever because the others will hate themselves and hate each other too much to ever unify against us."

"But how will you make them hate themselves? They don't hate their own color and features now."

"There are many ways. Our men will take their women, the most attractive ones, and produce children. These children will be of different shades. The lighter ones will be favored. The father will show esteem and affection according to the degree of likeness to him. And he will train the mother to do the same.

Generation after generation this will be repeated. Hundreds of variations in color and features will be produced but always, over and over, light will be rewarded, darkness punished.

Before long it will not be necessary to even worry about it. The slaves and servants themselves will do it all for us. They will punish themselves if dark and favor themselves if light.

Thus it is that one can arrange to rule forever. The conquered ones will hate each other. The lighter castes will carry guns for us and will willingly kill their darker relatives. But if the light ones ever give us trouble, then we can recruit soldiers who are dark. They will gladly kill the near-Whites who, by then, they will thoroughly hate."

"But you know as well as I do that these dark women are often very beautiful, and the men handsome as well. How can we keep our own White men and women from becoming so besotted with them that they might elevate them to a high status, out of foolish love-worship?"

"That will happen but we must separate love from caste. High-caste men will always have the right to lie with dark women. After all, such things cannot and should not be stopped. But the dark woman must always retain her caste. She must not be allowed to rise in status. She must be a concubine, never a legal wife or if the priests ever insist on the latter, then she must still be treated as an inferior.

We will ordain forever our system of machismo, male rule, so that the man will always be superior to whatever woman he is with. White women will never be allowed to associate with dark men.

Now, in this way and by these means, we can utterly destroy the Red Nations, utterly destroy the Black Nations, and give birth in their place to a race of White-red-black mongrels of a thousand hues who will do our bidding.

In the end they will do anything to be like us and to curry our favor. Those who do not attain the proper way of thinking will be mercilessly pursued and destroyed.

Finally there will be no resistance. We will have become Living Gods, and we will rule the people of color for all eternity!"

The horrible nature of Jesse's dream shocked Ladell. But the shock was greatest precisely because the horror was real! It had really happened – in Virginia, in Massachusetts, in Mexico, in Brazil – it was horrible because it was true.

But Jesse's vision had the desired effect. For the first time in her life Ladell was able to separate the subjective from the objective. Up to that moment she had always dealt with her darkness of color as a subjective, personalized thing. It was she who was dark. It was she who was unattractive. She was the guilty one. Somehow she must be at fault. It was her personal, subjective problem, no one else's, just hers.

But now Ladell realized that her status as a dark brown woman arose, not from a subjective condition, but from an objective system of racism and colonialism. Her degradation had been planned. Her inferiority had been artificially created. Her subordination was indeed part of a scheme, a terrible insane scheme to make her a psychological slave forever. She was the victim not of her own failures but of a system.

Now that's something that one can deal with. One can fight a system – it's outside of you. But one cannot fight oneself.

Ladell was fortunate. She had been able to cross that magic line, that line of personal liberation that all oppressed people have to cross if they are to be free, that dangerous line that colonialism always tries to hide more than anything else. The schools had thoughtfully tried to prevent her from knowing that such a line even existed. Her family was only dimly aware of such a line. But she and her brother and Antonio Chavis, with the help of the within-seeing which comes from the Great Mystery, together, they had found the line and now she could begin to cross it.

A new Ladell. Brown is beautiful, Black is beautiful. The sounds of chains breaking!

Not everyone finds it easy to understand these things. So many forces, all around, serve to lead people up blind alleys into psychological swamps.

Jesse's older brothers, Andy and Dewey, but especially Andy, had spent their early years in Oklahoma. This gave them the potential advantage of remembering something of Lenápe culture but along with this went the actual memory of hard times, poverty, and Oklahoma's strangely ambivalent (one could say warped), attitude towards things Indian.

Their experiences in the army were not very positive. Andy was wounded in Korea and spent some time in a hospital afterwards. Dewey did not actually experience combat and he spent two drab years in routine barrack's life. Both of them developed drinking habits and lost a sense of self-direction. For several years they had a hard time getting any sense of purpose, although Dewey was helped along by a cute Chamorro girl he had met and married on Guam. She saw him through his ups and downs. Finally he used his G.I. benefits to enroll at L.A. Trade-Tech, trying out various trades but finally settling on printing lithography.

Both Dewey and Andy kind of avoided the rest of the family during their 'drinking days' but Dewey's wife, Alicia, often came over to the house with their children. Later Dewey moved close by, feeling better about himself, and he and his family spent a lot of time visiting Andrew, Elisa, and the rest. Jesse and Dewey had chances to talk, and gradually Jesse came to understand something about army life and the sense of alienation developed in many Indians by the military.

Andy was a harder case. As the eldest son he had a built-in sense of responsibility. This only seemed, however, to make him feel extra guilty about his drinking and about going around with girls he never wanted to bring home. He also had a negative sense of self, similar to Ladell's but compounded by becoming alienated from the people he loved and who loved him. He tended to seek out White girls like so many insecure Brown men and that was unfortunate because he tended to have poor judgement when it came to girls. Possibly, because of his drinking, he tried to avoid anyone resembling his mother or sisters. Whatever the reason, he tended to associate with shallow, sharp-tongued women who kept him partying, fighting, and following the car racing circuits. He didn't visit home very much.

Later, after a serious auto accident and a period in jail for drunk driving, he turned towards religions that might help him re-order his life. A White woman who was a follower of the Jehovah's Witness group kept visiting him and finally they were married. He joined the Kingdom Hall and was able to stop his drinking and hold down a job, thanks to the discipline of a sect which supplied rigid guidelines for life.

Andy and his wife, a pale, rather plain woman named Doris, visited the Rainwater family on a few occasions although firm ties were not established. Doris was sincerely interested in converting the entire family; that was her duty in fact, but Jesse and the rest, although polite, were too critical and skeptical.

Jesse read the Watchtower literature and tried to understand what motivated this religious group. He was impressed by their dedication and their apparent absence of skin-color racism. On the other hand, he couldn't get excited about Middle Eastern-European ideas about 'kingdoms' or about religious philosophers who argued endlessly over which parts of the Christian Bible they wanted to emphasize or interpret. He never could understand how those who talked about the 'literal interpretation of the Bible' never took the entire Bible 'literally' but were always picking and choosing, interpreting and explaining away whatever didn't agree with their particular pet doctrines.

Anyway, it all seemed so foreign and strange, compared with the simplicity and beauty of Indian religion. But then, it was an easy road, with every turn worked out by someone else. Andy seemed to need that kind of security so Jesse never argued with him. Maybe it was the right road for Andy.

Jesse, of course, was not so sure about his own path. He thought about going to L.A. City College like Cary but a far greater urge was to travel, see the country, and learn more about the Delaware language and ways. He also wanted to visit his Houma relatives in Louisiana and see what the other Rainwaters were like. Most of all, he wanted to do something, in some manner, to help Indian people but he was not sure what that could be. During this period he read a lot of Indian newspapers, visited the Indian Center quite often, and went to political meetings. New ideas were beginning to spread throughout the Native world, prompted primarily by the increasing activity of people called 'traditionalists.' In New York State, around 1957, the traditionalists of the Iroquois Six Nations Confederacy had come out of obscurity to oppose New York State plans for taking reservation lands. In turn, the Six Nations' people had established contacts with other groups, such as the Miccosukees of Florida, the Hopis, and the Pit Rivers in California. Jesse read about their beliefs and was much affected by them. He also knew about the goals developed by a big conference of Indians held in Chicago and he sometimes read publications of the newly-formed National Indian Youth Council.

Occasionally some speakers passed through L.A. and set up meetings. Jesse went to one where some pretty radical ideas were being put forward by Jim High Eagle of a group called Original Americans United. High Eagle said, "Who are the Americans? Are they the White people of the United States? No, they are not. All the people living in North America and South America are equally Americans. The Yankees or whatever they want to call themselves have no right to steal the name of this land, a land stretching from Alaska and Greenland to the southern tip of South America.

But of all the people living in the Americas today only those who have Indian blood have an exclusive and prior right to the name of the land. The White Anglos say that Mexican Indians, descended from the ancient Aztecs and Mayas, are not Americans. They want to Americanize them! Now isn't that a joke? But it isn't funny because it's part of a scheme to steal our land from us, to divide us, and to make us into foreigners in our very own country. The White people want you to believe that 'American' Indians are different from Canadian Indians and Mexican Indians. They want to destroy our sense of racial unity. They want to divide us to control us better."

Jesse listened intently because High Eagle was directly addressing some of his major concerns, some of the things that had long confused him.

"We have to develop ties with our brothers in Peru and Bolivia and Canada. We have to forget about the BIA's full-bloods, half-bloods, eighth-bloods, and so on. We have to forget about what our blood is mixed with, whether it be White, Black, Chinese, or whatever. What is it that makes us Indians or Native Americans? Is it our White blood? No. It is the Native blood that counts, not what it is mixed with.

We are one people. Let's get it together!"

High Eagle's philosophy appealed to Jesse, not only because of his own racially mixed ancestry but because he had long seen that most Mexicanos were really Indian. He also knew many part-African people like Billy Tiger and Antonio Chavis who had as much 'right' to be an Indian as he had. It had always troubled him that, of all the peoples he knew of, the Indian nationality was the only one whose membership was being determined by an agency of the U.S. Government!

Jesse realized, however, that High Eagle's thinking was not popular among a lot of Indians who were under direct BIA influence. Only those who had gotten away from the Bureau or who, like the traditionalists, had an ideology which rejected the U.S. Government and its programs, only those kinds of Indians were prepared to accept Mexicanos, Red-Black People, and Canadian Native People as direct racial brothers. And, of course, since so many Mexicanos wanted desperately to be Spanish or White and since Red-Black people were constantly being told that they were Black by both Blacks and Whites, for all of these and other reasons pan-Indian racial unity was a hard path to follow.

In company with Max, his Black friend from work, he also went to several Black rallies. One of them in particular made quite an impression because a Black preacher-turned-radical gave a rousing speech on how the Whites had distorted Christianity to suit their purposes. Among other things he said: "When you look at pictures of the people in the Bible what color are they?"

"White, all White!"

"Yes, White! Old White men with long beards. Some of them even have blue eyes and light brown hair! Now, what is the truth?

Have you ever seen pictures of Arab people, of the people of Arabia, Palestine and Egypt? Have you ever met any? Well, let me tell you they are not blonds or blue-eyed White people. Many of them are as black as any of us here and most, the vast majority in fact, are brown people with black hair and dark eyes. And let me tell you a secret. You promise you won't tell anyone?"

"I won't tell!"

"Lots of them have curly hair, kinky hair, frizzy hair, wooly hair, you name it, they've got it!"

"That's right!"

"Now let's dig a little deeper yet! The ancient Jews wandered from Arabia into Egypt and we know that they married people living in Egypt. Now, what did the Egyptians look like? Were they White?"

"No, not White!"

"They were always a brown people. All of their murals, the painting in the tombs that have been found there, they all show them as reddish-brown people of various shades and they show them with frizzy or curly hair. And among the Egyptians were many Ethiopians and Nubians of black color, sometimes as kings and rulers.

Now let me tell you something else. The bible says that Moses' wife was a Cushite woman. Where was Cush? It is what we now call Ethiopia! So Moses' wife was a Black woman. How about that? Did you ever see any drawings showing Moses coming down from Mt. Sinai to meet his Black African wife?"

"No, never!"

"The Jews who went into the land of Canaan were not a White people. They were a mixed people just like their Arab relatives, just like the Egyptians and probably just like the Canaanites and Phoenicians as well. They were probably not very different from the Egyptians who are living today.

Now, it is from that stock that Jesus and his parents, Joseph and Mary, came. Jesus was a Galilean peasant who spoke the Aramaic language. He wasn't a Greek. He wasn't a Roman. He was a middle-eastern Jew of a very mixed racial background.

Jesus, my friends, was a brown man! He probably had pronounced Semitic facial features. And he probably had curly hair. Maybe it was even frizzy! He could have looked like a lot of you sitting in this church right here today!"

"That's right. Amen."

"One thing's certain. He was no blue-eyed, brown-haired Whiteman! We have been lied to and it's about time that we bring Jesus home where he belongs!"

Later Jesse was to hear even more radical sermons but this one made an impact because he could still visualize in his mind the mass produced 'portraits' of Jesus in which the man of Galilee had medium brown straight hair, blue eyes, white skin, a brown beard with golden shades in it, and a northern European nose. What if Jesus had a 'Jewish' looking face with 'oriental' eyes and a prominent nose? What if he was very brown from his biological past as well as because of working in the sun as a carpenter? What if he really had curly or tightly curled hair? Would the Whites reject Jesus if they saw him as he really was, or would they become more tolerant of racial differences?

That same evening when talking with Cary and Ladell, Jesse had a idea. The idea was prompted in part by posters he had see depicting great leaders of Black history. Why not a series of Indian posters? And why not posters of Jesus as he really was, and of Moses and Mrs. Moses?

"How are you going to draw Jesus as he really was?" asked Ladell.

"I don't know for sure, but I have an idea. I've seen lots of photographs of the people who live in Galilee today, as well as in Egypt and Arabia. Of course, they're lighter today due to a lot of Greek, Roman, and Crusader intermixture, but maybe I can find a good brown Arab face and use it as a model."

"That sounds exciting Jesse. Maybe I can help. We can go into the poster business!" said Cary.

"It's something that's really needed," interjected Ladell. "I want to see posters of all the great Indian heroes, and Mexicans. It could be really helpful for our people."

"Some could be photographs, of course, if we can find them. Others can be drawings. Some will have to be black and white but maybe others can be in color," said Jesse.

"Let's check with Dewey. He can tell us what it will cost and maybe he can help with the printing," commented Ladell.

As they got deeper into the project they all came to realize the importance of research. How do you locate photographs when you don't know where they are housed? And more importantly, how do you find out about Indian heroes when your education has denied you knowledge of any but a few of the most famous?

They began to realize that it was a long-term project and that they would all have to do a lot of reading before they could know how to go beyond Sitting Bull, Geronimo, and Crazy Horse. Nonetheless, they did make rapid progress. Together they found the small but valuable library of the Southwest Museum with a warm, dedicated librarian who took a personal interest in them. With her help they examined the museum's photograph collection, discovered private volumes with old pictures and learned of the Smithsonian's collection in Washington, D.C. Jesse also went through Frederick Webb Hodge's Handbook of American Indians, making notes on little known Indians of great significance, including Delawares like Tammany and Black Beaver.

In the meantime Cary had started drawing pictures of Jesus and Moses and Mrs. Moses based on a composite of actual Middle-Eastern men and Ethiopian women. Two-thirds of the way through the summer of 1963 they had four posters ready to be printed: Jesus, Moses and Mrs. Moses, Black Elk, and Geronimo. Ladell then took over the business side of the project and with Dewey's help the posters were printed in a small initial run. They had used up almost all of their savings but within a couple of months the gamble had paid off. Black church members bought the religious posters in large numbers and the Indian ones sold rapidly both at the Indian Center and at local pow-wows.

Jesse, finished with high school the previous June, decided to drive back to Oklahoma to go to college in the fall. Cary planned to continue her art studies at U.C.L.A. So the poster business was left to Ladell to manage. She was truly excited about the venture, both because of the challenge it offered and because of its content. A new door had opened for her and, with mother Elisa helping with her young child, she was now able to enroll part-time at City College in business courses as well.

It wasn't a big venture, of course, but Jesse and his sisters had hit on a useful form of mass education, and not with just the photographs or drawings either. The text for each poster had been as carefully planned as the picture. Jesus was called by his real name "Yeshwa," with Jesus in parenthesis, and, with the help of several Indian friends, the Indian posters were bilingual in English-Sioux and English-Apache, respectively.

But Jesse wasn't ready to settle down to anything steady, no matter how useful or profitable. He wanted to get away from L.A. and away from home. He wanted to travel and to study.

And so, in late summer, he set out in his newly-acquired used station wagon loaded down with camping gear, drawing supplies, and several hundred posters. His first stop would be Antonio's place and then, after that, Oklahoma.

RED BLOOD

CHAPTER EIGHT: OKLAHOMA DAYS

Jesse decided to enroll at the University of Oklahoma in Norman. He had debated about which college to go to but the smaller teacher's colleges looked pretty unimpressive. He finally picked O.U. because it was the only one offering any courses on Indians.

Before classes started Jesse had a few weeks free. He used them to visit his Delaware relations north of Tulsa and then to wander about, going to pow-wows and dances. In the Muskogee area he decided to visit some of his father's relatives, especially an uncle who had married a Creek freedman lady with very African features. Jesse knew that many people avoided their colored relations but after his good friendships with Billy Tiger, Antonio Chavis and other Afro-Indian 'breeds' it seemed like a pattern that he ought to break.

The uncle, Benjamin Rainwater, was older than Jesse's father, so he had by then a whole crop of grown-up sons and daughters. A sister, married to a Cherokee freedman, also lived in Muskogee, so Jesse soon discovered a whole 'mess' of first and second cousins scattered through the region. Ben and his wife Clara were very happy to see Jesse and treated him royally. A family gathering was arranged so that all of the cousins and in-laws could meet Jesse and look him over.

And they were beautiful people. Dozens of cousins of different shades of yellow-brown, red-brown, and ebony-brown, of different sizes and ages, of different kinds of hair, of different facial features-but most of them pretty or handsome in the way in which Indian-African-White mixed-bloods so often are.

Jesse's mind reeled at the procession of exotic Polynesian-looking, Filipino-looking, Egyptian-looking, never-to-be-duplicated-anywhere-looking girls, boys, women, and men that he met. The older people also interested him with their stories of an aspect of Oklahoma history totally ignored by virtually every book that he had ever (or would ever) read.

Gradually Jesse came to realize that both White and part-Indian authors had chosen, for reasons of their own, to almost completely ignore the very existence of several hundred thousand Indian-Black mixed-bloods. And here he was, right in the middle of a crowd of such people, his own flesh and blood, surrounded (he was told) by a city, the majority of whose so-called 'colored' people were actually the descendants of former citizens of Native republics.

Jesse listened with great interest to the stories of the old ones. He also was fascinated by the chatter of the younger people, by their accents, and by their smiles, body movements, mannerisms, and interests. He was struck by the 'Indianness' of the older generations, while the youngest one seemed to be much more 'colored,' yet different from Black people he had known in Los Angeles. It was clear that some vast undocumented cultural transformation was taking place but Jesse was simply overwhelmed by the complexity of it and could only store data in his mind for later reflection. 'Integration' and 'civil rights' had begun to appear in Muskogee, but many restaurants still did not welcome people of part-African appearance. Muskogee had never been as bad as some of the smaller cities of eastern Oklahoma but the era of segregation and Jim Crow was, nonetheless, well-remembered even by the younger children. That process of segregation had served, in effect, to force Jesse's Red-Black relatives in a Black direction because they had to attend 'colored schools,' go to 'colored' sections in the parks, and so on. Quite naturally, the fact of being part-African or 'Black' had acquired dominance in their lives, a dominance which all but erased the significance of being part-Indian for the younger kids.

So while the older generations still acted and thought like a mixed people with a more or less Indian way of speaking and behaving, the younger ones were drifting towards the mass culture of Black Americans. But, as Jesse noticed, there was still a strong tendency to marry people of part-Indian blood or of the so-called Louisiana Creole type. Few of Jesse's in-laws by marriage were lacking in a claim to Indian blood, no matter how African or White their physical appearance.

Jesse really enjoyed his visit in Muskogee although he had a few nervous moments when he felt White people or Indians staring at him as he accompanied his cousins on a tour of Bacone College or when they went to a formerly segregated park. This 'nervousness' weighed on his mind. He could erase it intellectually but emotionally it was hard to wipe away a feeling that he was violating 'the Oklahoma code' by publicly associating with other Brown people (some lighter than he) who happened to have tightly-curled hair or African features.

Jesse left Muskogee with a feeling of sadness, sadness to be saying goodbye to a wonderful group of kinfolk and sadness that most of them might never be able to participate in their Indian heritage, not only because of prejudice but also because they themselves had developed religious, musical, and behavioral preferences quite distinct from the Indian world.

In any case, registration at O.U. abruptly thrust Jesse into the Whiteskin's side of Oklahoma life. The 'controlled madness' of selecting classes, paying fees, taking tests, and filling out forms was bad enough but on top of that Jesse had to face the crowds of White students, secretaries, professors, clerks, and officials with very few brown faces to be seen and those entirely among the students.

The Indian students seemed to be mostly freshmen too, and their hair was cut short and they were generally dressed exactly like their White counterparts. The girls were all dolled up to look like Jackie Kennedy or some White movie star. Jesse teamed up with a couple of guys, western Oklahoma Indians, and they went around together. He was assigned a dorm room with a Choctaw and a Cheyenne-Arapaho, but the Choctaw didn't seem to want to associate with Indians. He was quite light-skinned, although dark-haired and dark-eyed.

The atmosphere at O.U. was a shock to Jesse. He had come back to Oklahoma to be around Indians and to be immersed in Native culture, much as someone might go to Paris to be exposed to French ways. But he discovered that which he should have already known but didn't – that O.U., in general, was a school self-consciously repudiating the Indian and Red-Black heritages of Oklahoma. In fact it was, in many respects, a school trying to repudiate all of Oklahoma except that the sheer cultural impact of thousands of White Oklahoma-born students made that tendency somewhat unrealistic.

Jesse discovered that Norman was a Whiteskin's town and O.U. was their college. The Indians who attended were expected to act as White as possible. If, in their private lives, they participated in Indian pow-wows or went to Forty-Niner dances, that was their business but it had nothing whatsoever to do with the mission of the University which was to expose them to Chaucer and Shakespeare, to Mozart and Beethoven, to pep rallies and queen contests, to big-time football and formal dances, to the history of White societies, and to the reasons why they should be grateful that the White people had taken Oklahoma away from the Native nations.

The Indian students at O.U. were usually the products of twelve years of White Oklahoma or BIA education, so most of them could not conceive of protesting. Completely and utterly passive, the thought of trying to change O.U. never entered most of their minds. So they conformed, as best they could.

Drop-out rates were very high, especially among the more tribally-oriented Indian students. They tried to conform but at the same time the cultural dissonance in their lives forced them to go to off-campus Indian gatherings as often as possible. There they often got drunk, forgot to come back to school, and gave it all up.

The Indian students who had already accepted the superiority of White society tended to become super-conformists at O.U., trying in every way to repudiate any evidence of Indianness. The lighter ones sometimes simply disappeared from view.

Jesse tended to hang around with the western Oklahoma types, simply because they were the more Indian, physically and culturally. But their passive acceptance of the BIA and of injustice in general, and their tendency to use alcohol as a 'solution' to cultural conflict, as even a 'badge' of Indianness, was difficult for Jesse to accept.

For a while, though, Jesse fell in with them, traveled to Forty-Niners and Hand-Game gatherings, drank quite a lot, and tried to understand what made them tick.

He saw a pretty medium-brown-skinned girl at one such event, a student from campus. She came up to him and said, "My name is Pauline. I've seen you at O.U."

"My name's Jesse. I'm Delaware. What's your tribe?"

"What ya know, I'm Delaware too, also Caddo and Wichita. Would you like to dance around?"

"Sure would!"

"I'll show you what Anadarko girls are like! You want to find out?"

"Yes, Pauline I sure would."

As they went around, Indian-style, Jesse felt the warmth of her body, and the slight pressure of her breast on his elbow, a pressure which increased as they danced longer. That dance was followed by another and then came a break.

"I liked that Jesse. Now let me see, I need a drink! Do you have any wine stowed away somewhere? If you don't it's all right. I know where we can get some."

They ended up going to Jesse's car with a bottle purchased from an Indian who specialized in selling liquor at dances.

"I'm a good time girl, Jesse. I like to have fun. My grades are okay, ya know, but I'm really not too keen on that college bullshit. It's just somethin' I want to do to get ahead of the game. I'm really a Forty-Niner girl!"

"Why did you decide to go to O.U.?"

"I don't want to be poor, that's it! I don't want to live like most Indians do. I want to get a BIA job, or something like that. I want to have what White people have but I want to party like an Indian, ey! How 'bout that!"

"Sounds good if you can handle it."

"I can handle it, Jesse. And I can handle you, too."

"I believe it."

"Let's get serious. Stop fooling around, Jesse. I like you. I like what you got for me!"

They had been kissing off and on, between swigs of wine. Now she pressed against his body and rested her hand on his leg, moving it gradually so as to touch his pants above his penis. Meanwhile, Jesse was following her lead by cautiously touching her breasts.

"C'mon Jesse! Don't you like me? Stop pussyfootin' around! Rub me like you mean it!"

Jesse had some experience at necking but he really had never been out with a young woman who was ready and determined to go all the way. Nonetheless, he had a condom which he had learned always to carry just in case.

"Jesse, let's drive off somewhere private-like. Not too far! But somewhere we can do it, and soon!"

So Jesse moved his car some distance away, on the other side of an out-building. And there they got into the back seat and made love. It was the first time for Jesse and he didn't do too well, what with messing around with the condom and being inexperienced.

"Keep going Jesse. Damn you! Keep going. You're getting little! I could have had another one – if only you would have kept going!"

"Sorry. I just couldn't hold it any longer."

"Oh well. I had an orgasm before. But I coulduv' had a second one, a really great one. But that's all right Jesse. I'll teach you. I'm a great teacher, you'll see!"

So Jesse was initiated into the world of sex by a girl whom he liked but didn't love. He didn't expect that they would be philosophically compatible but sexually they hit it off right away.

Pauline was active in the Native life at and surrounding O.U.

Most of it was non-political and there were a lot of social cliques and petty rivalries. Nonetheless, since 1961 when a big Indian conference had been held in Chicago, some of the students had became involved in the National Indian Youth Council and they tried to bring some kind of activism to O.U. Indian life. Jesse agreed with much of what the NIYC stood for and he sold posters to help the cause. Nevertheless, he did not feel completely comfortable with the NIYC group.

One of the 'angry' spokesmen for the 'militant' minority was Fred Bear, a Pawnee from north-central Oklahoma. He had gone to the Chicago conference and had later hitch-hiked to Gallup to help plan the organization of the NIYC. A good speaker and thinker, he was also a heavy drinker, a rough and tumble bar-fighter, and a steady kidder. Unlike the average Indian student, who tried to act White at least around O.U., Fred and some of his friends (though not all) wore old jeans, cowboy boots, and acted in a rude and abrupt manner. What bothered Jesse was that while they were not White middle-class acting they also didn't act like traditional Indians. Their models were really the 'bar-room Indians,' with whom they seemed to identify because of a sense of oppression and alienation from both the White and Indian worlds.

Fred identified as an 'angry Indian nationalist' but what did that mean?

Jesse asked him what he thought about the disappearance of Indian languages and the old culture. Fred said, "Forget about all that culture bullshit! That's just something the anthros use to keep us penned up like zoo freaks for them to poke at. Jesse, worry about Indian people, not Indian culture. Right now the tribes are controlled by old men who just sit around and do whatever the BIA wants. Nobody does anything. Everybody just sits around waiting for something to happen, and the same old clique runs things in the same old way."

"Well, what do you really want to do?" asked Jesse.

"We're going to shake them up. We want to organize the youth and then go back to the tribes and elect new people, young people, to office. We want to take over and then we'll get some changes."

"It sounds hard," said Jesse. "If the BIA is so strong, won't they just spread rumors about you? Won't the people be afraid to vote for younger people, especially ones labeled militants? And won't the same pressures exist after you take over, I mean from the BIA and White society?"

Fred looked blankly at Jesse, as if Jesse were too dumb to waste his time on. "Man, there's a lot of dirt-poor, knocked-down, beat-up Indians out there just waitin' for somebody to organize them. They'll vote for us! And the BIA? We'll take them over too. We'll get our own people hired in top jobs and take over the bureaucracy."

"Some of the traditionals are talking about nationhood and tribal sovereignty, even independence from the U.S. What do you think of that?" asked Jesse.

Fred looked puzzled. "I don't know. The traditionals are kind of crazy. They talk about religion and prophecy. I don't think they have a chance. We're stuck with the BIA, I guess, so we might as well use it. There's money there, and programs. We need to take them over. How can we have nations in Oklahoma when we don't even have reservations? Our allotted land is all mixed up with White holdings."

"It seems like true liberation would include nationhood and the revival of our languages and cultures. After all, what good is power if it's just power to do what White people do?" asked Jesse.

"Jesse, all that is dead or dying. Look around! These Indians are either drunks like me, angry militant drunks, or drunks like Billy Pool, White social-climbing drunks. We speak English. We've got to use the Whiteman's tools. We've got to master his system. We've got to get rid of poverty and create jobs. That's the way we have to go. You worry about starving in Indian. Most people would rather eat good in English!"

"Okay, so you see the tribes as some kind of corporate structure that can deal with social and economic problems, not as nations. I may not agree, but I can accept that concept. But what about Forty-Niners and Hand-Games? You seem to like them as well as the next guy. And you dress like a country Indian. What does that mean?" queried Jesse.

"I'm not against all Indian ways. I have been raised that way and I enjoy them. Besides, that's how you meet other Indians and organize them. You can't organize in a suit and tie! And I dress the way I feel. I identify with the country Indians, and I like to dance and pick-up girls, ey!...Listen, dancing and gambling and drinking are all that most of us have, that and fucking, so we have to have that. But it's not something you try to promote or protect or preserve. It's just there. It's part of us."

"I'm pretty dumb, Fred, about a lot of things I mean. But it seems to me that your culture is a new pan-Indian thing which is unhealthy in a lot of ways. The old traditional ways and the Peyote Road help to keep families together and lead people in a spiritual, ethical direction. The give-aways and all of the sharing are good. They help the people. Maybe the people are too passive when it comes to politics but that could change.

On the other hand, the pan-Indian culture you seem to promote kind of revolves around alcohol. You seem to actually want people to drink. You made fun of me and dared me to keep up with you when we first met. Every time you have a dance or whatever you always have a lot of liquor. It seems like you won't accept people who don't want to drink or jump from girl to girl.

Hey, let me finish! You haven't had much luck with eastern Oklahoma Indians and a lot of the more traditional western ones stay away too. I think you're hurting your own cause. That's all," finished Jesse.

Fred sat quietly for a minute. Then he commented: "Jesse, I'm going to die a drunk. If I'm going to organize these lumpen-proletariat Indians then I've got to drink with them. Besides I'm one of them. Aw, hell! It's the Indian way, Jesse, so that's all there is to it."

Finally Jesse said: "Well, I support all of the NIYC proposals, as far as they go. I guess they're just not radical enough for me. I see most of you – not you personally, but some of the other leaders – as the alienated children of Christianized Indians who are already in power. You're rebelling against your own parents and grandparents but you don't know enough...no, that's wrong, you don't have the freedom yet to junk the Christianized, BIA system altogether. You just want to take it over.

Maybe you're afraid of the traditional ways because they're so hard. You don't have long hair, and neither do I. It's hard to have White people put you down all of the time as a dumb old full-blood blanket Indian.

But anyway, it's the old traditionals who are the real source of Indian liberation. That's the direction I want to go in....But I'm not putting you down. You're a good speaker and you've got a lot of know-how, and guts. I just want you to know that I can drink, and I can dance, and I can gamble and I can support NIYC but I'm looking for something deeper. I don't want to just change the BIA. I want to eliminate the need for it altogether. And I'm tired of seeing Indians die from booze."

So Jesse and the NIYC people got along all right even though they disagreed on many things. The truth was that the NIYC types were often preferable to the upward-climbing 'BIA brats' who were common at O.U., or the near-White types who were ashamed of everything except their BIA scholarship checks or claims case money. Jesse tended more and more, however, to hang around with a few of the quieter Indians who were proud of being Indian but who didn't fall into the extremes of hard-drinking or social climbing. They were few in number and many of them, like Jesse, were studying art.

There were a few Black students at O.U., although ten years earlier there were none at all. Jesse, out of curiosity, went to a few of their meetings on campus. They were surprised to see him and some seized on his visits as a portent of a possible Black and Indian civil rights coalition. Jesse told them frankly that he came only as an individual and that they would get no support, or at least no public support, from other Indians.

He was intrigued to discover that the Blacks at O.U. possessed a distinctly 'national' conception of their history, identity, and destiny. In no sense did they see themselves as a distinct Oklahoma People of Color with a multi-racial heritage. They did not seem to be aware of the rural Red-Black people nor were they aware of Colored people who could speak Creek, Cherokee, or Choctaw. The Black students defined themselves in terms dictated by Ebony, Sepia, and the NAACP, the Southern Christian Leadership Conference, and SNICK (the Student Nonviolent Coordinating Committee). After a time Jesse realized that most of them were urban Blacks from Oklahoma City, Tulsa, or Guthrie who had very weak connections with rural Oklahoma in any case.

Jesse's Indian acquaintances reacted variously to his going to a few Black meetings. The more traditional the background the less the reaction. The more marginal or White-oriented, however, made it very clear that they didn't like 'nigras' and didn't want anything to do with them or their struggle. Jesse became a 'suspect' in their eyes, more dangerous than an ardent NIYC radical calling for the picketing of some BIA office.

For many of the O.U. Indians the idea of "associating with Blacks," however innocent, was the most terrifying thing that they could think of. One of Jesse's friends, a Seminole-Creek artist named Rufus Wildcat, helped him to understand what the hostility was all about. Rufus was older, had travelled some, been in Korea, and, as it turned out, was a distant cousin of Billy Tiger (Jesse's old friend in Los Angeles).

"I hear you been getting a lot of attention from the moccasin telegraph lately," Rufus had remarked. He didn't add anymore, waiting for Jesse to respond if he wanted to.

"Yeah" said Jesse. "I even had a fight with Pauline. She

screamed at me for going to a Black student meeting. I wasn't going to go to anymore, but after that I just had to go again. It's no big deal you know. I was just curious. That's the way I am. But I'll be damned if any clique of White racist Indians can tell me what meetings to go to."

"So now you and she have broke up, I hear," commented Rufus. "That's putting a lot of pressure on, isn't it? Woman power, ey!"

"Oh it's all right. She's nice but we don't see eye to eye on a lot of things. She's prejudiced against Mexicans and Colored People and God knows what else. It strikes me as being kind of dumb to be so down on dark skins when you're not Snow White yourself," asserted Jesse, in a disgusted tone.

"Well, Jesse, I recall you talking about racial grading systems and I thought your ideas were pretty accurate. But like a lot of college professors you didn't apply your theory where you should have, right here at home and in your own life."

"What do you mean, Rufus?"

"Well, many years ago the Whites told the Indians: 'we like you better than we like the Blacks. We don't like you as well as we like ourselves, of course, but your color is more like ours and your hair is not bushy, and you've got lots of warriors so we are gonna treat you better. We want you to catch all the runaway Black slaves that come your way. We'll pay you for them. Above all, don't mix with them because then we might think that you are Blacks too.'

So some of the Indian tribes started selling runaway Blacks. Then later they started getting slaves of their own but they didn't treat them like slaves. They treated them real good and even mixed with them. After a while the Creeks and Seminoles and other tribes fought wars with the White people so naturally they got to where they didn't much give a shit what the White people said. That was when they really started mixing with the runaway Blacks and the ones who were supposed to be slaves. But at the same time the tribes were mixing with Whitemen who brought in White ideas. Some of their light mixed-blood descendants brought in slaves and really tried to set up plantations. So the Indian societies began to split apart, at least in the South. Still they held together, even after they were forced to move to Oklahoma."

"But what happened? You had the full-bloods who, if they had slaves, treated them like kinfolk and intermarried. Then you had Red-Blacks who were like full-bloods. Then you had light-skinned rich mixed-bloods with lots of slaves and big farms. Some of these, like one old Creek I've heard of, had eight or more wives, most of them Black, but by and large these White half-breed Indians tried to keep the slaves in line. Still there was a lot of mixture."

"Of course, the Seminoles were different when we were back in Florida. We adopted the Red-Blacks and runaway Blacks and, luckily, we had very few White half-breeds to make us prejudiced. But here in Oklahoma, even we have gradually picked up prejudices too.

Anyway, the Whites started taking over Oklahoma and they told the Indians: 'Hey, you better watch out. You got an awful lot of colored people in your tribes. A lot of them are part-Indian and your people are marrying with them so fast that pretty soon you'll all just look like 'nigras.' You know how we treat 'nigras.' We're going to raise the Jim Crow flag over this land and the coloreds are going to have to go to separate schools, ride on separate railroad cars, and crap in separate outhouses."

Rufus laughed and Jesse chuckled too, even though the absurdity of it all was increased by the fact of its utter realness.

"So the Whites said: 'We need you Indians on our side. You own a lot of land and oil that we want to share in. You have a lot of pretty girls that we want. Lots of you are almost White anyway. So here's what you must do. You must split your tribes apart. Don't have nothing to do with any Indian who has kinky hair. Chase all those freedmen out of your country. We'll help you. And if you're good and don't have nothing to do with the niggers we'll give you a special place in Oklahoma society. Those of you that are real light, we'll let you act and be like White people. Those of you who are Indian-looking, we'll treat you okay if you try to act just like us.'

But the White people also said, 'It's hard to be a Whiteman. You've got to learn how to steal and cheat and how to be rough and aggressive. So we're going to teach you. But you can't learn how to be White just in school. We're going to steal from you and cheat you and treat you rough, for your own good, so you'll learn how to be like us.'

But then they said over and over again, clear up to the present day. 'Don't forget that you're better than Negroes. Don't ever go around with them. If you do we'll start treating you just like them, so don't forget. The flaming crosses and the lynchings will be for you too, if we start thinking of you like 'nigras.' So beware!'

And that's what a lot of these Indians been doing ever since. They been be waring!" concluded Rufus.

"I see what you mean. So a lot of Indians are really threatened by Colored People because they fear they'll become less acceptable to White people," mused Jesse.

"Sure. You have to remember that there are counties in western Oklahoma, north-central Oklahoma, and even in the east where an Indian boy can't go to a high school dance with a White girl and where the only White women Indian men can usually get are trash or whores. And the upper-class Whites are real cautious when it comes to associating too closely with Seminoles or Creeks because of the mere suspicion of African blood. In some of the worst areas Creek mixed-bloods try to pass themselves off as part-Cherokees in order to avoid that suspicion. I've got a cousin who married a White woman and she thinks he's a Cherokee mixed with Italian because he's got very curly hair!"

"I guess a lot of Indians here are super-sensitive about who they are related to then. How does this affect the cultural situation? I mean does this make them want to go White as much as they can?" asked Jesse.

Rufus pondered the question, making a few brush strokes on a painting he was working on. Yes and no. Some – the ones who are from BIA or Christian families – they try to go White, of course, if they're light enough, or at least they try to be as acceptable to Whites as possible. But a lot of others find a kind of protective refuge in Indian culture."

"What do you mean?"

"Well, if it's better to be Indian than Colored then Indian culture, especially public pageants, pow-wows, queen contests, parades, and the like, offers a public demonstration that you and your group are truly Indian and not just a brown people who, in many cases, are as dark as a lot of Blacks. It also differentiates Indians from Mexican farm laborers, who are generally of similar color. More importantly, our White business people and chamber of commerces have come to really appreciate pageants. So real Indians are a valuable resource, especially when the oil wells dry up."

"Cash register Indians!" remarked Jesse. "But maybe it's better than having them trying to destroy everything Indian....I don't know, though, maybe it also corrupts Indian life."

"It does that but it also has helped to build a certain pride, so I guess it isn't all bad."

The two friends grew closer as the year went on. Jesse eventually told Rufus about his father's background and the Rainwater relatives, as well as about his Delaware side. It was then that he learned that Rufus also had Red-Black kinfolk including Billy Tiger. All of this served to draw them closer together.

One time Jesse said, "There must be a lot of part-Black Indians who want to participate in Indian activities. How do they do it?"

"They stay close to home, or where they are known. If they go to pow-wows or ceremonies with relatives or where they are invited it's all right. But they don't go to gatherings in strange places and usually they don't go around Anadarko or western Oklahoma. They don't want to go anywhere where they might get insulted or even thrown out. So fear of being embarrassed keeps them close to home."

Jesse took a drink and thought out loud: "It really pisses me off to see all of these light mixed-bloods, who want to be White anyway, parade around as Indians when other people, with maybe more Indian blood, are forced to kind of hide out just because they are part-Black."

"Well it's going to take a long time to change that Jesse. A lot of Indians are just beginning to be proud of being Indian so the idea of getting them to accept Black blood is a long way off."

"Yeah, but maybe we as artists can do something about it. How many paintings actually reflect Indian history? We could paint pictures of the period of the past hundred years, for example. Some of them could be of racially-mixed Indians and Black Indian citizens," mused Jesse.

"Hey, we are supposed to produce flat two-dimensional paintings for the White tourist trade. How are you going to paint things that White people won't buy? How are you going to get a show, let alone make a living?" asked Rufus.

"So we're cash register Indians too," remarked Jesse, almost to himself.

As the year wore on Jesse found himself growing more and more alienated from Norman. The atmosphere was so overwhelmingly White and so schizoid, a weird mixture of rural Oklahoma White fundamental Protestantism, conservative to right-wing political ideology, and college-town academic subculture. On the campus one could escape, to some degree, the Bible Belt-conservative atmosphere of the state, but the moment one stepped off campus, picked up a newspaper, or turned on the radio one was reminded that it was Billy Joe Hargis and Oral Roberts, not Shakespeare or William James, who dominated the minds around you. Most Indians tried to insulate themselves from this atmosphere but it was impossible to escape completely.

Even the most nationalistic and traditional of Indians, if they understood English, could not totally escape the constant religious and secular propaganda. When one allowed the radio or the TV set to enter one's home one opened the door to constant cultural brainwashing. And even if the traditional Indians disagreed or intellectually resisted in certain areas of thought, they were often defenseless in others. After all, the Whites were so powerful, so successful, so stridently insistent, so persistent, and so unanimous in their opinions (or so it seemed), that many Native Americans felt that there must be truth in what they say.

Little wonder that Oklahoma Indians took to drink, or gave in and dreamed of White rebirth, or tried to hide, or developed supersensitive, self-denigrating personalities, or hated Negroes, or hated Whites, or both, or hated Indians, or erected a complete Native culture around them as if to live in a world of White non-existence.

Anyway, Jesse was disappointed with his classes, except for art. The courses were taught in much the same way as his high school ones had been. It didn't matter that a professor might say, "everybody in Oklahoma has some degree of Indian blood." It was just a bullshit lie. It didn't mean anything more than to say, "everybody in Mexico has some Indian blood" or "everybody in Peru has some Indian blood." The fact of the matter was that it didn't matter because the Indians were still treated like dirt or were ignored or were to be changed whether they liked it or not.

The truth was that most of the Whites with a little Indian blood, just like their counterparts in Mexico or Peru, didn't act any different than Whites who had no Indian blood. In fact, if anything, the 'thin-bloods' made things worse by getting control of tribal councils and speaking 'for' Indians. The traditional Indians, especially in eastern Oklahoma, usually had no voice.

Jesse found that many professors, whether part-Indian or not, had little understanding of the history of Oklahoma or of America because they accepted, without question, the great myths of 'manifest destiny' and the desirability of White victory. They might feel sorry that so many Indians had died on the 'Trail of Tears' but, after all, it had to happen because otherwise there would be no Atlanta or Chattanooga or Birmingham or Jackson. If the 'Sooner' hadn't swarmed into Indian Territory there wouldn't be any Oklahoma City or Norman or O.U. The professor might not ever have a job, so his fate was linked with the success, and defense of, imperialism.

But often the professors didn't even see that. Some just thought it was a jolly good adventure of cowboys, squatters, Texas Rangers, and wildcat oil men. These told lots of anecdotes and loved it all. Jesse did manage to take a history class from a sympathetic professor, and that helped a great deal.

Still it was good to escape from all that. Indian get-togethers provided one form of relief but Jesse gradually grew tired of them. For a change, he went with Rufus to visit Seminole people in the Wewoka area, he looked up older Indians, Shawnees and Kickapoos near Tecumseh and Shawnee, he visited Delawares near Anadarko, and looked up some cousins in Oklahoma City.

On one of his trips he went to a Shawnee peyote meeting, not too far east of Norman. The meeting was held on a farm owned by a Shawnee-Seminole family and the beauty of the place attracted Jesse. A creek wandered through the land; there were lots of birds and rolling hills covered with clumps of trees that provided a restful atmosphere. The family consisted of an older couple, an unmarried son, and a granddaughter, younger than Jesse, with a child but no husband.

Jesse started visiting the family regularly. He liked to talk to the older couple, he enjoyed the country atmosphere, and he found the granddaughter very pleasant. The Big Deer family let him set up a camp along the creek, a hundred yards or so from the house, where the stream made a bend around a little hill. Jesse slept in his car when it was raining or cold and slept out of doors otherwise. He always brought the family some food and a gift or two every time he came.

Grandfather Big Deer was a full-blood Shawnee while his wife was Seminole with some slight amount of African blood, to judge from her extra wavy hair and somewhat broad nose. They spoke Shawnee and Seminole-Creek, as did their son Rolly. The granddaughter, Ramona, was a dark brown girl, rather tall and somewhat slim. Her face was beautiful indeed, with large round eyes and high cheek bones. Her beauty was enhanced by long shiny-black, wavy hair which she never cut. Orphaned when quite young, Ramona had been raised by her grandparents and she, in turn, helped to look after them. She was reserved and shy with strangers but in her own milieu she was both outspoken and lively.

Jesse enjoyed being in Ramona's presence although it only dawned on him gradually that his visits were as much to be near her as to be in the country or to learn the Shawnee language. When he found himself transformed into a carefree, happy, ecstatic mood by the mere act of getting into his car to drive to the Big Deer place, and when he found himself singing the entire way, with no recollection of the passage of time, and when he discovered that his heart fell to the ground on one occasion when she wasn't at home, then he comprehended that Ramona had grown to be an important part of his life.

For a long time, though, he treated her like a sister or a close cousin, partly out of respect for her family but partly because he was in awe of her. Even though she had a child, a little girl, he somehow didn't know how to initiate anything with her. So he just let things take their own course.

RED BLOOD

CHAPTER NINE: CHITTO HADJO COUNTRY

Ramona Big Deer had attended Oklahoma public schools for a time but her dark color had often prejudiced the teachers against her. In her area most Indian pupils had a hard time anyway but the darker ones suffered most of all. Ramona was glad, therefore, to go to the BIA schools for the balance of her education. Many teachers were still prejudiced but at least she was not singled out all the time.

She had natural talent that under more favorable circumstances might have resulted in her becoming a great poet or a famous artist. Instead, what little encouragement she received was designed to push her into the narrow confines of what the BIA art teachers considered to be 'Indian art' and her writing was largely neglected. She loved to run and excelled in the girl's athletic program but again her potential was never realized. She became pregnant before graduating from high school and returned home to have her baby. From that time on she helped her grandparents and worked part-time as a motel cleaning maid when she could get transportation.

Jesse made a strong impression on her. He was a warm brown color much like her grandfather and he had clean-cut, handsome Indian features. He was taller than her, just under six feet, and had a medium energetic build, well-developed but without excess muscles or fat. More than that, Jesse impressed her as a sensitive, intelligent young man who had a seriousness of character she liked. She was, however, put off by his being a college student and an 'artist' (however humble he might be about his accomplishments). It seemed to her that he would never be seriously interested in an uneducated 'backwoods' girl like herself but the more often he came, and the more he talked with her, the less shy she became. Gradually Ramona got used to his presence and just acted like herself which, unknown to her, delighted Jesse.

This state of affairs went on for some time, until the blossoms had already fallen from the fruit trees. Ramona had often told Jesse of her interest in running so he challenged her to a race along the country roads and around the fields. She was out of practice but so was he. Jesse had always liked to run but he had never pushed for great distances, whereas Ramona had run for miles as a young girl and had fine, muscular legs (made all the more attractive by that fact) and good lungs. No doubt, she was the better of the two but Jesse managed to keep up once he got past the critical point of aching sides and a tight chest. They worked up a heavy sweat and then walked for a while to cool down.

Jesse touched her arm lightly and said, "You're a good runner. I'm glad you can get ahead of me."

Ramona asked why and Jesse replied, "Because it gives me a chance to watch you move, to watch your body. You really are a beautiful girl. Maybe the most beautiful I've ever seen. Will you get mad at me if I tell you something?"

"I don't know," she laughed. "How can I tell ahead of time?"

"Well, you know I like you, so don't get mad. You can hit me if you want but I have to tell you. You have the most beautiful behind..."

Jesse didn't get to finish because Ramona took after him, punching wildly but laughing at the same time.

As he was back-tracking Jesse finished, "I can't help it. Your behind looks so good when you're running. I just wanted you to know why I was dropping back every once in a while."

Jesse felt that the tide had turned, that a change had come, that he couldn't go on pretending that Ramona was like a sister when every thought of her caused an excitement which charged throughout his entire body. When she caught up with him he grabbed her loosely, letting her half-hearted punches land on his chest while he peered into her eyes and smiled.

"Come close, I want to tell you something." She didn't move closer but she did stop hitting. He pulled her close to him and whispered: "I can't lie to you Ramona. I'm crazy about you and must have you. Either that or I'll have to stop seeing you. Your behind really got to me...." She started struggling again, but he squeezed her tight. "And I can smell your body up close and I have to have you closer yet." He kissed her and then asked, "Do you like me? I mean, do you like me as a man?" She half-smiled at him, looked at him with her big doe eyes and whispered, "I like to watch your behind too, and your front. Does that mean I like you like a man?"

They joked around a little and Jesse said, "I think I love you Ramona. I'm not just kidding."

"I never have been kidding, Jesse," she replied. "I just never thought you'd get around to wanting me. I thought maybe you only liked college girls."

Jesse laughed and said, "I've been in awe of you because you're so beautiful, so – I can't think of the words – just so wonderful a woman, built so nice, with such a good mind and good personality. Don't worry about college. You can go to college someday, if you want. Anybody can do that nowadays – but to be a fine person, that's not so easy."

Soon they were kissing and their ardent need for each other manifested itself in the strongest possible way. Still, they put off consummating their newly-confessed love until later. They both wanted, it seems, to begin the deeply satisfying adventure of dis-covering the secrets of each other in a gradual way, postponing love's climax until the darkness of night when Jesse's campfire could reflect off their brownish-golden bodies.

Afterwards, Jesse lay back, with Ramona's scent on his lips, her naked body beside him, and his hands still touching her, absorbing her warmth. Then he turned again to look at her, so dark mahogany-colored in the darkness, with reddish-golden touches where the firelight danced, and with her hair loose and fluffed out around her shoulders. He kissed again her breasts, warm-brown, dark-tipped and full. Then he turned to touch softly with his lips her long legs, dark, smooth, finely shaped, soft to touch. For a time he paused just to let his lips lightly roam over the hair between her legs and then, bit by bit he kissed his way up her mid-section, to breasts and then neck, ears and lips.

"I just want to eat you up — consume you. Consume you with my eyes, my nose, my lips, my ears, with all of my senses. Make you part of me."

"I like to do the same, Jesse. I like to look at you. It's like study-ing. I want to study you carefully, all over, and absorb you, like my eyes and my mind are out there touching you, bringing you in — inside of me. Can you feel it? I can see you like to study me, Mr. Student! Well, I like it too!"

"Ramona, I can't look at you enough. There's a million little things to discover about you, things that I want to know about, from your beautiful athletic feet to your soft, gorgeous hair."

After that Jesse practically moved on to the Big Deers' place, fixing up his camp better in the process. The dormitory room at O.U. was almost abandoned and Jesse spent as little time as possible on campus. He continued to study for his classes but his only motive was to prove that he could succeed.

He wanted Ramona to understand who he was so on two different weekends he took her and her daughter to visit his Delaware kinfolk near Bartlesville and his Rainwater relatives in Muskogee. She was well-liked by all of them and, in the traditional Indian way, accepted them on their individual merits, and liked them in turn.

Gradually Jesse felt more like his old self. He now could associate with people more of his own temperament, stay away from cliques and gossip, and spend a lot of time outdoors. Still more importantly, Ramona's love fulfilled him in a way he had never known before and his many cousins helped replace the gap left by his brothers and sisters. He also was able to do some drawing and he helped both Ramona and several cousins to learn a few basic techniques.

But as summer approached, Jesse had a lot to think about. His original plan had been to travel to Louisiana during the summer to visit the Houma people. He also had an ambition to retrace the movement of the Delawares from Kansas back to New Jersey. Now, however, he knew he would not be returning to O.U. One year was enough. So what was he to do? If he didn't go to school he would probably be drafted and he hated the thought of spending two years in the army. On the other hand, if he did go to school he would have to pick a place and get accepted.

And what about Ramona? He loved her very much but her grandparents needed her and he didn't make enough money to support Ramona and Melinda, her little girl. If he didn't watch out he'd be trapped in Oklahoma in some crappy job.

Jesse was so tired of college that he put off making any new applications until it was too late. Meanwhile, he spent his spare time building a ramada at the camp, a stone cook stove, and putting up a big double hammock for sleeping. He also painted and sketched, did a lot of running with Ramona and together they visited friends and relatives as before.

In Muskogee Jesse met an old Red-Black freedman named Marshall Grayson who was close to ninety years old. His mind was absolutely sharp and his memory was superb. Grayson was one of those true folk historians, like people used to have, with literally the history of Oklahoma in his mind.

Jesse and Ramona began visiting Mister Grayson frequently, a convenient thing to do since he was the great-grandfather of some of Jesse's in-laws.

At first Jesse just listened, but then he began taking notes. Grandpa Grayson told about the days before the Secession, when his ancestors had all lived together in the Arkansas District of the Old Creek Nation. Some had been Indian slave owners and others were slaves or free Red-Blacks. The slaves in his family were often related by blood to the 'owner' and actually had it pretty easy, basically just paying a sort of rent but working on their own.

"The thing that really brought us down, that ruined the old Indian Territory — you know what it was? I'll tell you, it was when the tribes got a lot of White half-breeds and let White people come in to lease the surplus lands."

"What did the Whites do?" asked Jesse.

"Well, just to give you one example, let me recall to you how the Seminoles used to be part of the Creek nation. But the Creek half-breeds and the intermarried Whites, they objected to the way the Seminoles treated the Blacks so free and easy. As a result they split into two nations but since the language was the same it was hard to tell one from the other.

The Secession came and the White half-breeds joined up with the White Texans, the true Indian's hated enemies. The fullbloods, Red-Blacks, and slaves who could all joined up with the Union side, fighting under the leadership of old Opotholeyahola." Grayson raised his voice, "We were abandoned by the Union soldiers, but the Union Indians fought hard anyway. Still they eventually had to escape on another Trail of Tears, this time to Kansas, up on the Arkansas River. A lot of them died and suffered up there, but at least they were free, my own grandpa died up there, so I know."

"Did the government ever make up for that?" asked Jesse.

"Well, yes and no. First off, the government treated most of the tribes worse than they treated the White secessionists. I mean they never took any land away from the White rebels, you know — I guess that shouldn't surprise anyone. Ha, ha. Who ever heard of the U.S. taking any land from White folks, ha, ha."

"But they did take land from the Indians," said Jesse.

"They sure did! Took away about half or more of the Creek land, and so on. It didn't matter that half the people had been loyal to the Union side. They all lost anyway, although later on in 1867 or so they got paid — the loyal Creeks I mean — for some goods lost on the way to Kansas."

"What happened to the slaves and Red-Black people?" asked Ramona.

"They were freed, of course, and the government signed treaties that gave all the colored citizens their Indian rights. It was only right, anyway, cause they mostly had Indian blood anyhow. Most of 'em spoke Indian and they had suffered just like the fullbloods, and even before that they had had to sweat to make the half-breeds rich. So it was only right. They had earned their citizenship, that's sure.

The Creeks and Seminoles were all right. They treated the freedmen pretty good and elected some to the national councils, but the Cherokee, Choctaw, and Chickasaw half-breeds were sore losers. They had a lot of White people living with them and were more prejudiced."

"Do you think that the Red-Blacks and the Indians would have gotten along all right if they had been left alone?" asked Jesse.

Grayson thought for a while and then said, "I believe they would have, but right away the Whites started trying to drive a wedge between the different kinds of citizens. After the Civil War, the agents made up a list of all of the part-African people and tried to keep them from getting any payments for land. Then their list was used thirty years later by the Dawes Commission. If your folks were on that list, then they classified you as a freeman even if you had Indian blood or had been free before the war.

Still, in the Creek nation at least, fullbloods and so-called 'freedmen,' they sided together and supported Isparechee for chief. The White half-breeds didn't like that and sometimes they wouldn't count the votes from Marshalltown district, where a lot of Red-Black people lived, because they were all for Isparechee. So they fought on – you know about the Green Peach War, don't you? Well, it even came to blows, but the half-breeds they usually kept control because the government was on their side.

Isparechee tried to save the Creek Nation but the government was bound to divide up the nation's lands and let the Whites take over. All this time Whites and 'states' people, colored people from other parts of the country, were coming in, mostly Whites. They squatted on land or married Indian girls or rented from the half-breeds. They got to be a majority that way. There were a lot of out-laws. No law and order to speak of. Lots of 'em were no-good Whites from Texas or Arkansas. Some were half-breed Cherokees. A few were Red-Black guys like one Cherokee-Black guy I saw once who spoke Osage too. The Creek Light-Horse Militia tried to keep order but too many restrictions were placed on what they could do.

Anyway, by the 1890s the Whites outnumbered the Indians and colored citizens almost two to one. They couldn't stand the fact they couldn't vote or hold office. You know what I mean? They were land crazy. We call them Egana-nok-salgi, people greedy for land. But on top of that, they couldn't stand to be second fiddle to Brown people, simple as that.

So the government moved. They broke all the treaties and said 'you're going to have to enroll and take allotments.' At first they took a roll of everybody, in 1895 I believe, but then the Dawes Commission was given the power to do it their own way. The government took over the nations, took our schools away, and left our national council powerless. Then this congressman from Kansas, Curtis, who had helped steal money from the Kickapoos, passed an act giving them complete authority to allot our lands and to terminate the tribes forever. That was 1898 as I recall.

Isparechee, the chief, refused to go along but the half-breeds elected Pleasant Porter and he gave in. I believe he later regretted it.

So in 1899 the Dawes Commission started enrolling everybody. But they did it in a bad way. They made two rolls, one for 'citizens by blood' and one for 'freedmen.' That was so they could divide us up, make us jealous of each other.

Most of the people were unfamiliar with forms or couldn't read that well, maybe not at all in English. But the rolls were in English and the people spoke Creek mostly, or Euchee. So they didn't understand, and the officials all spoke only English.

Who was to know what roll you were being signed up on? Well, the truth is that you were put on whatever roll they wanted to put you on, no matter if you had Indian blood or not. If you looked Colored they just put you on the freedman's roll because that way they could get rid of you later, and the grafters could get your land easier.

If you look at one of the freedmen's enrollment cards today you can see that there is no place for degree of Indian blood. They just assumed that they didn't have to record any degree of blood for Colored citizens, so now today lots of people can't get any Indian benefits because there's no way of proving your degree of blood. To me, that was wrong, but like so many other bad things it was just done!

Of course, there were many Indians who had African blood who got on the 'citizens by blood' roll but they did it because they had influential friends or relatives on the national council...or because they hid out and and nobody saw what they looked like!"

"Didn't the people try to resist?" asked Jesse.

"Yes, thousands of fullbloods and others hid out. They refused to give up their treaty rights and Indian status. But it didn't matter. They were rounded up and thrown in jail, or half-breeds were hired to go out and get their names, or the Dawes people used the 1895 and earlier rolls to track them down.

The worst deal was that half-breeds and White grafters went out and signed up as many people as they could, but they also got them to sign papers they couldn't read that sold away their lands. The fullbloods and Colored people didn't know they were doing that. They were lied to, tricked, beaten, scared, and sometimes the grafters had to forge their marks anyway."

So from Grandpa Grayson, Jesse and Ramona learned something of what had gone on in the 'formative' days of the state of Oklahoma. Jesse decided to produce posters of Chitto Hadjo, Redbird Smith, Jacob Jackson, Eufaula Hadjo and other leaders who tried to save the Indian nations, as well as of Isparechee, Opotholeyahola, and earlier resistance heroes.

At a later session Jesse learned how the Whites had used every 'legal' trick conceivable to fleece the allotees of their lands and how the Ku Klux Klan had arisen later to terrorize Red-Blacks and other Colored people, to drive them off their homesteads and force them to move to the cities or out-of-state.

"At first the allotments were restricted. They couldn't be sold. But in 1908 they removed all restrictions on anything except a forty acre homestead for the half-bloods. If you were three-quarters or more your whole allotment was still restricted. You can see how, by not recording any blood-degrees for the freedmen they now could get their land easy-like.

Anyway, restrictions didn't stop them. They took over the children as so-called guardians, they pushed through bills making fullbloods incompetent so they could get their land, and they did everything else you can dream up. The courts were all crooked, of course.

You can see what happened. The Whites got all the good land. All the level areas, the river bottoms, the farmable land, the oil land, they got all of that. The freedmen were cleaned out first because a lot of their land was just exactly in the areas the Whites wanted. I think it was planned that way.

The fullbloods were given land back in the hills. That's what some of them wanted while others just had no choice. Anyway, what

Indian land is left is in the hilly areas even today.

The Red-Black people and the freedmen, they're almost all in towns today, like Muskogee, Okmulgee, or Tulsa. Except for a few places they couldn't stay in the country, the Whites were after them all the time, cheating them or burning crosses, whichever worked best. And, of course, lots of them didn't see the value of holding onto land when they could get a little money and move into town.

Lots of freedmen are gone now. They're up in Kansas or out in California. Oklahoma is just too hard to bear, for a lotta people I mean."

Jesse also learned how, after 1907, it became illegal for Indians to marry persons who were part-African even if they were cousins. Grandpa Grayson told him of many couples who avoided that restriction by going up to Kansas to get married, but even so life was hard. Many Indians who were part-African went to BIA schools and were regarded as Indians so long as they stayed in government schools, but they could not transfer to Oklahoma public schools unless they went to a 'colored' school. Many of the more successful Red-Black people, and there were some, sent their children to private schools or colleges in Kansas. Others went to Langston University, a Colored college in Oklahoma named, ironically, after an Indian-White-African mixed-blood from Virginia.

After finishing his courses at O.U. Jesse and Ramona took off with Melinda for a time, going up to the Tulsa area to attend a Delaware funeral and visiting around. They met several militant traditional leaders who were active in the Indian spiritual unity movement, including Mitchell Crow, a medicine-man.

Crow was an active leader in the Creek stomp dances and ceremonies. He lived a very simple 'fullblood' life, out in the country, with a wife and children who spoke very little English. He often visited friends in Tulsa and other towns, giving talks and healing people. Many Indians were discouraged because of the loss of the ancient knowledge and all of the changes in their lives, but not Mitchell Crow. He said:

"It is true that many of our tribes have lost their ceremonies and even their customs. But how did they get those things in the beginning? They didn't always have them. No, the Creator gave them to us in visions and dreams. That is how we got our ways.

Why can't we dream new dreams? Why can't we seek visions again? Nothing is truly lost. If we have the desire and are willing to sacrifice and suffer, to pray and ask for help, we will get what we are seeking. Someone will dream once again how to conduct a ceremony. So it can be brought back. The same with our treaties. We must never give them up. Even if the government and the BIA Indians scoff at us and call us dumb fullbloods we must keep going on.

Many suffered for our treaties. I've read that as late as 1915, 2,000 Creeks were refusing checks from the BIA. Many have lived in poverty rather than agree to be an allotted, terminated Indian. I know, and you know, how much people needed that money, but it was blood-money and they turned it down.

We must stand on our treaties. They are all that we have. If you are not a treaty Indian you are a government Indian and that's no Indian at all.

You know that the 'Certificate of Competency' which the government is very willing to give you says that you are now a competent person and no longer an Indian!

So we have to remain 'incompetent.' If we become 'competent' we have to become a non-Indian.

That's the way it is. You must either stand as a restricted treaty Indian or be a 'competent' non-Indian.

We will stand on our treaties. They thought in 1898 when they broke the treaties that we would give up, that we would disappear. They thought in 1907 when they refused to create the State of Sequoyah and created Oklahoma instead that we would give up, that we would disappear. They thought that when they published those so-called 'Final Rolls of the Five Civilized Tribes' that we were finished.

Well, it hasn't happened! We don't believe in those 'Final Rolls.' We have our own roll, a roll of people who still want to be Indians. And for us the treaty is our charter, our constitution. We know who we are. We will outlast them. And we will rebuild our sacred ways.

Right now in Washington State the people are fighting for their treaty rights with the fish-ins. Right now in Oklahoma the traditional Cherokees are organizing. Right now in New York the Six Nations League is asserting its treaty rights.

All over Indian people are awakening. This is a time of hope. There will be much suffering yet, but the White society is on its last legs. A new day is coming and my heart rises up to the sky thinking about it."

Truly, it was remarkable but Jesse had seen it often. Within an hour or two of Tulsa or Muskogee were hundreds, even thousands, of traditional Indians who looked, talked, and lived like 1907 had never happened. They stubbornly spoke Creek or Cherokee or other languages. They suffered from poverty because that was a price they had to pay. They voluntarily let the White society flow by without getting enmeshed in it.

Jesse felt good thinking about that, although he also worried about TV and other changes. Would the Indians survive another fifty years? Anyway, Mitchell made him feel good. Ramona liked him a lot too, but then she spoke both Shawnee and Muskogee-Seminole so, in a sense, she was already there. She didn't need to be 'converted' but, nonetheless, Crow added insights to her understanding.

Ramona's association with Jesse had a considerable impact on her self-image and aspirations. She had come to realize that an inquiring mind could learn a great deal and that, in fact, it was a real sin to allow one's mind to vegetate. She also came to appreciate what art might do and what it could mean.

She liked Jesse a lot, maybe even loved him. But she had become convinced that she should not get 'attached' to any man until she had developed herself as a person. She had too much experience as a single mother and motel maid to want to remain an uneducated person any longer.

"I want to go back to school, Jesse. I want to get my high school diploma and then go on to college or art school. Maybe I'll go to the institute at Santa Fe."

"What will you do with Melinda?"

"I'm going to talk with my grandparents. Maybe they can take care of her for a while, but mostly I want to get their advice. They have a lot of wisdom. They will know which aunt or cousin might be able to take Melinda for a while, although I've got my own ideas too, of course. I might be able to keep her with me too, if I can get financial help."

"Well, I want to go back to school someday but not yet," said Jesse. "I guess I may get drafted pretty soon. I don't know quite what to do. I think I love you, Ramona, but I'm not able to help you out much, financially I mean. I'm just not there yet."

"I know, Jesse. You need time to get your life sorted out too. I don't want you to have to go to work as an unskilled laborer or as a truckdriver or whatever. You've got too much talent to just work at any old job. And you sure don't have to feel any obligation towards Melinda and me!"

"I don't feel an obligation! What I feel is love, I mean I care! Hey, why don't you and Melinda come out to Los Angeles to live with my parents. You can go to school there. You know, I've told you about Cary and Ladell. They would help you too."

"Thanks, Jesse, but I don't want to be a burden on your family.

It's not like you're my husband already! I'm your girlfriend, I guess, but we haven't made any long-term commitments.

Besides, I want to find my own way. I want to prove that I can do it. Then we'll see! After I've got my diploma, then if you're still interested, we can make a commitment. Also, I don't necessarily want to be too far away from my family. Santa Fe is far enough, but L.A. would be too far, can't you see?"

"Well, I'm going to help you out as far as I can, Ramona. If I get drafted into the army I'll give you my car. You'll need something to get around in."

Ramona did get to meet Jesse's parents because they drove back to Delaware country that summer. Everybody got together at Jesse's grandparent's place. Andrew and Elisa Rainwater both liked Ramona and Melinda and the feeling was mutual. Later Andrew and Elisa also stopped at Ramona's grandparent's farm to meet the Big Deer family. Jesse was also very pleased when the Rainwaters visited Uncle Ben in Muskogee, receiving a warm welcome (as Jesse had) from all of the cousins and in-laws.

Jesse had by then made up his mind. He would volunteer to be drafted so as to at least bring an end to uncertainty. He was told that he would be sent to North Carolina for training if he was sworn in at Tulsa and that he could select his specialty if he volunteered so he decided to do that. He hoped, in that way, to see a little of the east coast and meet some eastern Indians. Maybe the army wouldn't be so bad if he could see some new country and learn some new skills.

Jesse had arranged for Ramona and her uncle to take over the sale of posters in Oklahoma. Ladell was going to send a supply of the new Chitto Hadjo, Redbird Smith, and Isparechee posters as soon as they were printed, so that would help her out financially. With his car, and with her being eligible for BIA financial aid to go to school, Jesse felt that Ramona would be able to move forward without getting stuck as a motel maid again.

For two months Jesse and his fellow recruits sweated through boot camp under a hot North Carolina sun. Most of the Indian boys just naturally drifted together because there was a lot of tension between the Whites and the Blacks and they didn't feel comfortable with either group. Jesse was able to get along with everybody but he especially enjoyed learning about east coast Indians and swapping stories with fellows from different Oklahoma, Louisiana, Mississippi, and Florida tribes.

A little while later Jesse and several friends went over to

Robeson County to visit the families of Lumbee buddies and still later they visited the Haliwas near Hollister, the Waccamaws southwest of Wilmington, and the Cherokees near the Great Smoky Mountains. They usually went with a buddy who had a car and ordinarily it was a pow-wow or a dance that attracted them. Jesse always went with Lucas Fixico, a Creek friend from Oklahoma and Elton Grimes, a Rappahannock Powhatan and the only Virginia Indian in the unit. All three were serious types who wanted to see as much as they could of Indian life in the region.

In spite of local differences, the Native Americans of the eastern half of North Carolina greatly resembled one another. After a while Jesse got to where he could spot them on the streets, no matter how light or dark skinned they were.

Very wavy or even kinky hair was quite common among the eastern Carolina Indians and most showed a little African touch around the eyes and mouth. On the other hand, it looked to Jesse as if the majority had not intermarried with Blacks for many generations because virtually none looked like a first generation mixed-blood. Some were quite dark, darker than many people called Blacks, but their color was more of a deep-brown than a black-brown. Also the darker people's facial features were not African but more like a Caucasianized Indian look.

All of the Indians of eastern Carolina had been treated as Colored people by the Whites, and were the subjects of great prejudice. They had, however, supported their own Indian schools and the Indian Normal School (Pembroke State Teacher's College) in Robeson County. It was, though, the numerous Indian churches (usually Baptist) that seemed to be the focal point of their communities.

One of Jesse's friends told him, "The fact of the matter is that we don't really have tribes. We have Baptist churches-Black Swamp Baptist Church, Reedy Creek Baptist Church, you name it, we got it. The different families have been going to those churches since the Civil War – maybe before. That's what our lives are tied in with, that and our own Indian schools, and the few little bars that cater to Indians."

"What do the churches teach?" asked Jesse. "Are they different from White churches? I mean do they bring in some pride in Indian ways, Indian beliefs, or do they just use White hymn books, White bible lessons and so on?"

"Well, I ain't been to all of 'em, but I been to enough so I know they're all just about the same. The truth is the only thing Indian about them is the people, that's all. They just love to have White evangelists come to stomp and shout, and everything they use is from White folks, from one Baptist association or another. And the other kinds – the Methodists, Church of God – all of 'em seem about the same to me...No, there ain't nothin' Indian about them, 'cept the people."

"That's too bad. Don't they ever talk about the old Indian religion, about the Great Spirit, or about what White people have done to Indians?"

"No sir, not a bit. Jesse, I hate to tell you this but I don't know nothin' about Indian religion 'cept what I been taught. The preachers tell us that we was all pagans – real savages – heathens, before the Whites came. They say we prayed to rocks and stones and trees and didn't know nothin' about God. We was Devil-Worshippers, all goin straight to Hell. That's what the preachers say...

And as for White people... They pray for White people's souls that's all. They don't ever criticize them unless there's some big crisis and then they like to think it's just a few low-down crackers who are causing trouble...

Hell, them preachers worship White people more than Jesus if the truth were told."

"It sounds like the Indian churches have been a help, I mean like a center of community life. But it also sounds like the preachers will never let you go very far in the Indian direction. I guess they would be against any real revival of traditional tribes or culture."

"You better believe it, Jesse. Yes sir, no way we goin' to have any revival as long as the preachers and elders – deacons and all – run every community.

No, a whole lot of our people are Baptists first and Indians second. This is Billy Graham and Oral Roberts country, Jesse. What they say we believe! And if you go against it, well, you might as well just leave!"

"Don't some of the younger people feel differently?" asked Jesse.

"Oh, a lot of 'em turn away from the church for a few years, or maybe forever. But most of 'em that do that just hang around bars or race their cars around the country, killing themselves more often than not. What you gonna' do Jesse? Here it's either the church or liquor, or both. Ain't nothin' else."

RED BLOOD

CHAPTER TEN: EL SABIO

Twenty-two months after getting out of Boot Camp, Jesse was discharged from the army, no longer a boy. That he had become a disillusioned young man, was not due solely to what he had seen and heard about in Vietnam. It was also due to other dramatic events including the Canal Zone 'riots' of 1964 against U.S. rule and the illegal invasion of the Dominican Republic in 1965 by President Lyndon B. Johnson. This invasion, designed to prevent a democratic electoral victory by a candidate whom the U.S. did not control, disgusted Jesse because it reminded him of the so-called 'Indian wars' and made him look even more critically at the mess in Vietnam.

Also, it was the time of the assassination of Malcolm X, the Selma March, and the Watts Riots. All these things merged together with the war in Vietnam to form a tapestry of misdeeds of overwhelming proportions.

For Jesse the Vietnamese were too much like Native Americans. In contrast, the U.S. troops came to remind him more and more of the Indian-fighting army of the nineteenth century, with Black troopers thrown in just as they were in the wars against the Plains tribes and the Apaches. Moreover, he began to liken the Indians in Vietnam to the Indian scouts who were used against other Indians in the Plains wars. They were brave, worthy warriors, fighting for someone else's cause.

Of course, he had to keep his thoughts to himself. He used alcohol and marijuana to dull his mind. He felt like a mercenary for crooked Vietnamese politicians and generals. He wanted to show his support for the Buddhists who were giving up their lives for peace. Instead, he buried his feelings in beer and tried to smother his finer sensibilities with a litany of curses.

The first thing that Jesse did was to buy a used van. The second was to get some camping gear including a sleeping bag, cookstove, and lantern. The third was to buy a fifth of whiskey and a bottle of wine. The fourth was to take the liquor back and buy food instead.

It took a lot of courage to give the whiskey and wine back, but Jesse had resolved not to kill himself so soon after surviving in the military for two years. He had resolved to try to break the addiction which he had developed long enough to get back to Oklahoma to see his family and Ramona.

"I'm going to get a van and camp out in the woods. I'll get away from people. I'll cleanse myself if I can. I've always wanted to visit the old Delaware homeland and trace the route of the migration westwards. Maybe if I visit the Great Serpent Mound and places like that I can stop acting crazy. I don't want my mother to see me so crazy a drunk, an angry drunk. No liquor for me. Not 'til I get where I'm going."

He couldn't pray yet. He had stopped praying months before. He couldn't cry. There were no tears.

It was pleasant camping out in the fall through Ohio and Indiana. The campgrounds were empty and Jesse was alone most of the time, except for extremely bold raccoons and badgers. At night they scurried all around, over his sleeping bag, looking for food or just playing. He kept his gear in the van, out of necessity, but always shared a little food with them.

The great Indian mounds near Chillicothe deeply affected Jesse. He tried to pray on top of one of them and made a tobacco offering. But it was the Great Serpent Mound that impressed him the most. Who had built it? Probably not Delawares but maybe Shawnees. More likely, thought Jesse, it was made by the Euchees who used to live along the upper Ohio. A great people then, they were called the Tallagewi by the Delaware and figured prominently in the Walam Olum, the Delaware history which Jesse had read.

Jesse sat for a long time near the Serpent Mound, hoping that some knowledge would come to him. No one else was there and a soft breeze was blowing leaves all around on the ground and making music with the ones still in the trees. Jesse felt partially released and uplifted in some way, but no special knowledge came.

He then drove northward to old Delaware village sites on the tributaries of the Wabash and visited Tippecanoe where Tecumseh and the Shawnee Prophet had tried to revitalize Native life a century and a half earlier. Jesse studied the battlefield where the deceitful William Henry Harrison had staged his surprise attack and he then saw a cave where the Prophet had prayed. He spent a long time there and also on a rising field across the creek where the village had actually been.

The signs at Tippecanoe were, as usual, all pro-White and the village site itself was not even part of the monument. But it didn't really matter to Jesse, since he knew the true story. Still, it was a shame to see history so distorted.

Jesse's route then took him past the great Cahokia Mound in Illinois, which he climbed, and then through Missouri, passing several areas where Delawares and Shawnees had lived for decades. The first real freeze came just as Jesse reached northeast Oklahoma, but the reception he received from his relations was warm and he hardly noticed the approach of winter. He did see that his parents were older and his grandparents older still, but they all seemed happy and in good health. Andrew Rainwater had accumulated enough retirement and social security to retire, so he seemed relaxed and more at ease than ever before.

Jesse's roundabout journey had given him a little rest and the strain was gone from his eyes. He was able to remain civil around his relations, even though they noticed right away the loss of his youth, of his enthusiasm, of his spontaneity and lightness.

He was eager to be off to the southwest, to the Big Deer allotment. He knew from a letter written many months before that Ramona's grandparents had died and that she and Melinda had gone to live with an aunt in Oakland. Still he wanted to visit the place and to hear the latest news. Jesse had been a poor letter writer of late and none of Ramona's letters, if she had written any, had gotten to him.

An Uncle of Ramona was living on the Big Deer place, and he was glad to see Jesse. The old camp that Jesse had built was still intact and so were the memories. Thoughts of Ramona overcame him and he wondered why he hadn't written more often. Her spirit seemed everywhere. Driven, he ran along the trails they had followed, hoping to see her. Jesse was so desperate he would have phoned her but he knew she had no phone.

Jesse had intended to stay overnight but instead he packed up his gear and started immediately for California. He didn't really understand himself but for some reason he had to see Ramona. He also had to keep moving because a desire to get drunk was chasing him across the country like a spectre.

He pushed himself, driving hard, night and day, stopping to

sleep alongside the road when he became too tired to go on. When he finally reached Oakland, exhausted, he immediately set out to locate her aunt's house. Finally he found it in a mixed Chicano neighborhood but when Jesse knocked on the door a stranger answered. Ramona, Melinda and her aunt were gone. Where? No one knew.

Frenzied, Jesse checked with the post office and at the neighborhood stores. He inquired at the fast food restaurant where she had worked and everywhere else he could think of. No trace!

What could he do? Jesse didn't know anyone in the Bay Area. He called Ladell and Cary in Los Angeles but neither had heard anything. He checked at the Indian centers in Oakland and San Francisco, leaving letters but receiving no news. Desperate, he finally went to the police but they had no information.

Something had happened. They hadn't been gone long, but gone they were. The aunt had put her furniture in storage but the storage man had no address except for the local one and that of the uncle in Oklahoma. Jesse had just come from the uncle's so he knew they weren't there. But could they have passed each other on the way? Jesse doubted it. Anyway, he left another letter with the storage company and then sent another to Ramona in care of her uncle, just in case.

Jesse collected his thoughts gradually. He wandered around San Francisco, stopping at Indian bars and drinking a little. He imagined that he could control his thirst, maintain a level of balance. Finally, he broke loose enough so as to be able to move his van out of the city to a place where it wouldn't get looted or ticketed and towed away. Then he hid his money, except for fifty dollars, and took the bus back into the city. After that he hit the bars again and was more or less drunk for a week or so.

Jesse might have been badly beaten up or robbed or even killed. A Paiute woman named Betty, quite a few years his senior but still attractive and vivacious, took a liking to him and saved him for herself. She took him to her room, together with a supply of liquor, and they alternatively drank and made love together. When sober Betty was afraid of men, but when drunk she could perform great sex. Jesse had lost his interest in love-making and he too needed alcohol to release his libido, to let the juices flow once again. As a drunk he could have sex, he could cry, and he could talk about what he had seen.

Neither Jesse nor Betty remembered much of what had been said while they were drinking. But after the money ran out and sobriety intruded they took a new look at each other and decided that they had little in common, that some kind of ritual had been carried out but that it was over for now, although they could remain as friends. Jesse, with no change left, hitch-hiked out to where his van was parked and located his hidden savings. With that he got some grub and, after rechecking everywhere for Ramona, drove along the coast to Los Angeles, visiting Ladell, Cary, and his brothers. He saw Big Ed and Billy Tiger briefly but his emotional state was such that he couldn't stay anywhere long. So he drove out to Antonio Chavis' place in the desert, hoping there to find some relief from the depression which was weighing him down emotionally.

But as Jesse got closer and closer to Don Antonio's house he had a premonition of disappointment. Dread rose in his stomach and he sped up the van, worried beyond imagination. His fears were confirmed when there was no greeting from Don Pascual the Turkey, nor from El Sabio the dog or the geese, chickens or any other living creatures. Antonio's house appeared all right but there was no sign of life.

Jesse jumped from his van and examined the ramada and the chicken coop area. Not a living thing!

Remembering that Antonio almost never, if ever, locked his house, Jesse opened the front door and went in. There was no electricity. Gradually his eyes adjusted to the dim light and he was able to look around. Everything seemed in order. The house smelled slightly musty or stale, but nothing appeared to be amiss. Then Jesse noticed a white envelope on the kitchen table, an envelope with his name on it, written in Antonio's distinctive hand.

For a while Jesse just sat down at the table and closed his eyes. He was afraid to read whatever was inside the envelope. Antonio meant so much and he was to have been such a key part of Jesse's recovery or so he had hoped.

He got up and put a kettle of water on the stove. But then he remembered that it was a woodstove and hesitated. Finally, he checked the stove out, gathered up some kindling and started a fire.

Soon the water was boiling and he fixed some coffee. That calmed him and he was able to tear open the envelope, to find several pages on which Antonio had written:

Dear Jesse:
I know that one day you will come home again and that you will come to see me. At least I hope it will be so.

Sadly, I may not be too unhappy, since I will see you again someday soon. I have had to go down to México to visit algunos de mis parientes. These relations need my help and at the same time I want to see them one more time before I get too old to travel. Comprendes, amigito?

Tambien, I want very much to visit the shrine of Tonántzin-Guadalupe and Teotihuácan, the sacred city of the spirits. I have heard that the ancient Azteca-Tolteca spirit is reviving and that los danzantes are coming out more and more. I want to see that and to touch again the stones of those sacred places.

Oye, muchacho, I know that you've been through a lot. When I get back we will have mucho tiempo para tlatolear, para platicar. There is much I want to learn from you, even as I have a lot to discuss with you.

Oh yes, I have left my friend El Sabio, the wise one, with the neighbor in the green house. I am sure that El Sabio is lonely and would like to be with you, if you want him.

Una cosa mas, amigo, I am getting old, so if for some reason I don't make it back please take whatever you want but especially that carving of the wolf that I have made for you, Wolf Clan Man.

Adios

su compañero

Antonio

Jesse sat quietly for hours. His emotions were numb. Finally he managed to eat some cold food and to fall asleep.

The next day he shut up Antonio's house and went outside. His relief at knowing that Antonio was still alive was overwhelmed by his need to see him, to be relieved of his terrible burden of anguish.

He rested in his old place under the ramada and prayed, until his sorrow and the tears streaming from his eyes made him incoherent and unstable. Not knowing what to do, he wandered about the place and then rushed off into the desert in a condition of near hysteria. He managed to reach Coyote Hole, the canyon he had often gone to in previous years and there collapsed on the sand. He lay there for quite some time until he felt El Sabio beside him, nudging him. El Sabio was Don Antonio's oldest dog, the one that he couldn't give away. He had been waiting patiently but now he was there in the canyon, with Jesse.

It seemed as if he knew that Jesse needed help and that, therefore, his mission in life was now to run in that direction. Jesse hugged him and the two returned to Antonio's house, now a ghostly shell, silent and empty. Together they got in Jesse's van and headed off across the desert.

RED BLOOD

CHAPTER ELEVEN: JUAN GARCIA

Jesse finally went to sleep but it was a restless sleep, filled with many bits and pieces of imagery, none of which he could remember later – that is, except for one. By means of that dream Juan Garcia, the Indian of the O'odham Nation, entered into his mind, but he was a different Juan, no longer drunk, in fact stone sober. Juan was telling a story, a story that stuck in his consciousness even after he had awakened sweating, wet between moist sheets in the still dark room.

In his mind he could see Juan crouched as in his dream, in front of a huge Whiteman. It was the spirit of the evil side of the Whiteskin race and it had its pants down revealing an upright penis. But the horrible thing about it was that the penis was shaped like the neck of a bottle. And it changed colors – sometimes it was green, sometimes brown, sometimes clear glass colored like a fifth of vodka.

He could remember the voice, too, of Juan as he said, "The evil spirit of the Whiteman always has a hard-on. So he's always after something. He's always craving something, and what he wants he has to have. He will take it, no matter what, even a woman on her moon he won't leave alone. That's why he rapes the earth and digs deep into her, even in the wrong places and at bad times for her when she needs to rest, to recover. He won't let her recuperate or lie fallow to heal herself – he's after her all the time. And that's why he hunts animals in their mating season, or whenever he wants. The evil White spirit always has a hard-on, and he can't stop pushing on – gouging, tearing, digging, it don't matter. He doesn't love the Mother Earth, he just has this hard-on."

And then, as he remembered, the scene changed and the Evil

Spirit was talking to Juan. "Many Indian people have turned away from beauty. For them all the old Gods are dying. I, the White Spirit Power Supreme, I am the only God now. My cock always is hard and it must be sucked. You will suck it. Sometimes it will be a bottle of wine, sometimes of whiskey, or even gin. You must suck the bottle which is my cock, and that is the way you will worship me. Because of the pain I inflict on you I make you hate yourself and suffering, you sacrifice yourself to me. Thus I succeed."

"Now listen carefully," the White Spirit Power went on, "I am never satisfied. I'm always hard. When you suck on that wine bottle I will pour my sperm into your guts and eat you from the inside out. Only when you become the slave of my drug am I satisfied."

It was a horrible image, but Jesse could see Indian after Indian sucking at the Whiteman's liquor bottle cock, reaching out to touch his giant beer can balls, and dying, one after another, to give him satisfaction.

He could see stores, and bars, and whole buildings, full of Whiteman liquor bottle cocks, of all colors and sizes. And the countryside was full of them, standing upright like forests, where trees should have been. And the Indians were crazy – men and woman, boys and girls, BIA official Indians, tribal chairmen, Indians in old clothes, Indians in expensive suits – all of them crazy, with the bottle-cocks in their mouths, sucking and dying. And he could see many Blacks and White people, too, as the White Spirit's slaves. Many were prisoners of drugs, but it was just the same.

His mind reeled. He tried to suppress the images but he only succeeded in bringing back more of Juan's words: "Once upon a time, long ago, we were warriors, all of us, men and women. We worked together, helped each other, respected each other. But that's been gone for a long time now. The Whiteman taught us to be ashamed, to hate ourselves, to hate each other, and that's when we came to be his bottle suckers.

After we lost our self respect and our respect for our old Spiritual Ways, then when he had us pinned down on the ground, we converted. Groveling, with no meaning at all to our lives, with so much pain, he gave us a way to live. We now live for, and through, him. He tells us who is an Indian. He tells us that we are his Indians. We belong to him and only to him. And he gave us his bottle cock to worship, and also as a badge. You can always tell one of his Indians today – he drinks and sucks, he sucks and drinks, that's how you can tell. The White Spirit is very smart. He isn't 'good' you understand. He's very evil, but smart. He makes these Indians caress him and kiss his ass all day long and then they hate themselves more because of that and that way they need to suck more bottle cocks or do drugs just to get by. So he's very smart, as you can see. There's no use trying to fight him. You can't love him, but you sure can be afraid of him. But then, sucking his cock makes you forget all of that, so in a way it's a gift he's given to us, even though we're like slaves who have given up hope."

Jesse wanted to shut it off, but as nauseating as the images and words were, they seemed so powerful that he could not control his thoughts. Juan's voice kept returning, again and again.

"I guess there are still some old Indians, away out somewhere, or maybe in Mexico or South America, who are still like in the old days. I don't know about that. Around here even some of the medicine men are drunks, or are crazy about money, so like I say, I think the Evil One has won. Even the babies have White liquor sperm in them before they're born, since their mothers drink when they're carrying them in their bellies and give that liquor to the little ones. I was born that way, I guess, drunk. That's a kind of baptism that the White Spirit has given to us and it sticks too."

With an effort Jesse finally became fully awake. He put on his clothes and went outside. It was about five in the morning but still warm. Everything was quiet around the drab little motor court and instead of looking ugly, the stillness, the utter silence, and the darkness of night before dawn transformed it into a vague neutrality.

Jesse started walking and thinking. His dream must have meant something. Maybe it was a further warning to him to change his ways. He could see that it was true that Indians were just destroying themselves by drinking liquor. He knew he had to drop it himself.

Jesse wandered along irrigation ditches, out into the fields, smelling alfalfa and other crops. He sat down finally, beside a cottonwood, to watch the dawn in the east direction. He remembered how he had driven off with the old dog El Sabio and come to southern Arizona, visiting Scottsdale and looking up Indian artists. But even while he was doing that he also started drinking again and soon he stopped his own attempts at drawing. He visited camps of Papago, Pima and Navajo people working in the fields. He wandered from place to place becoming utterly depressed by the living conditions.

In a bar a Mexican labor contractor had boasted to Jesse about how he rounded up winos to use in the fields, how he kept them drunk with cheap wine when they weren't working, and how he had killed several people who tried to 'get smart' about not being paid wages.

The coyote boasted of kidnapping people to work, just picking them up and then not letting them go until they were buried. He bragged about how he could screw any Indian or Colored woman he wanted to, because he always carried a gun and, anyway, they would do anything for a little wine or some food.

Jesse had been hearing about how the little Indian babies were dying of malnutrition and he had himself seen the shacks they were expected to live in. So when the coyote kept bragging on and on about how he was proud of being a brute, proud of beating up winos and raping girls, Jesse just blew up. He had been drinking and he wasn't extra cautious. He shouldn't have blown up in that particular bar but he did.

The only thing that had saved him was that he attacked so suddenly, with such savage fury, that the Mexican coyote was caught off guard. He had been goading Jesse, that was clear, but when Jesse just sat there, looking straight ahead the coyote grew overconfident. Then suddenly Jesse had turned on him.

Jesse shivered a little as he recalled the incident. He had fully intended to kill the coyote, not consciously, but out of sheer fury. Anyway, before he could finish him off others in the bar had jumped in and attacked Jesse. Luckily, Jesse's anger was so great that he was able to defend himself pretty well and then, as he cooled down, a big Papago rose up and started swinging with a chair, hitting his attackers with shattering blows.

Then the Papago had grabbed Jesse and pulled him out of the bar, leading him at a fast run around cars, through fences, and out into the fields. They ran a long way and Jesse was almost sick by the time the Papago stopped to rest behind an irrigation levee. For a long time they lay there, breathing hard, until the Papago said, "Man, that's a bad bar to start a fight in. That Mexican you clobbered is a mean dude. He had lots of buddies there including the bartender. Worst of all, the sheriff's deputies are his friends. They're paid off, you know. He lets them rape Indian and Black or Mexican girls at his camps and gives them money too. So the deputies would have probably killed you or at least beat the shit out of you and put you in jail for years!"

"But, Christ, I'm glad you slugged him. I hate his fuckin' ass myself. But I been beat up and thrown in jail too many times to go after him voluntarily. Are you okay?"

Jesse was cut here and there, and sore in many places, but he had no serious wounds. He said, "I'm okay. But my van is parked near there. Luckily, not right in front but down a ways."

"We'll just have to leave it for now. We're in for a long hike, 'cause we have to avoid the roads. The deputies will be looking for us."

So Jesse hid out for a few days with the Papago, mostly on the Gila River Indian Reservation with a Maricopa family. Fortunately he had left El Sabio with his old friend Rufus Wildcat of O.U. days who by then had a small house in Guadalupe, outside of Tempe. Eventually, Rufus picked up the van for him and he and a friend brought it to where Jesse was staying. Then he and the Papago, whose name was Leroy Garcia, had driven on dirt roads to the Papago Reservation to stay for a few days with Leroy's uncle, Juan Garcia.

Juan was a wino, but he wasn't drunk all the time and, in fact, he had a brilliant, penetrating mind. For days he and Leroy and Juan drank liquor, lay around in the house or sat outside, and talked. It was at that time, while driving to get more liquor, that Jesse lost control of the van on a sharp, unstable curve, and turned it over several times. Fortunately, neither he nor Leroy or Juan were hurt, except for scratches and bruises, but the van was in bad shape.

Jesse was too disoriented to be sad about losing his van. The three of them just hitchhiked and walked to get more liquor and then went back to Juan's place. Later they towed the van to Juan's where Jesse just abandoned it after getting what he needed out of it.

Juan talked a lot. Even though Jesse didn't understand all of it at the time, parts reoccurred to him afterwards, sometimes in dreams, sometimes when he was awake.

Juan talked about what had happened to the Pima and Papago people. It was a depressing story because they had never fought against the U.S. and yet they were treated so badly. Sometimes he said, "There is no way to win. No way to win. They're too strong. All we can do is make babies and watch them starve. That is all we have left."

At other times, though, Juan's thoughts were very profound, although not always logical or coherent to Jesse. "We are running across the desert," he said. "We run for days and nights without stopping. Some fall and die. But we keep on running, always running forward, not stepping on any living thing. We run to the salt water of the gulf, run in the salt water, seeking visions. Our minds are in another realm, we are living on air alone. Visions come to us in the saltwater, in the ocean, and then we gather salt and run back home. Suffering for others, we bring rain. Suffering for others we bring salt. Suffering, we live."

He paused. "We were strong then, brave, and whole. Now we are fat, lazy, weak and afraid. The Whiteman has done that for us. Now all I can do is drink. I do not enjoy it. I would rather be running or planting crops. But for what purpose? Who cares now? The young people only want Pepsi and hamburgers. They don't care anymore. So I drink now. That is my profession."

One day Jesse had gotten up early and taken a walk. He saw a young girl bathing herself out of a bucket of water. She was naked but didn't see him. He sat down quietly and watched. Her bronze body was not fully mature but it was beautiful, streaked wet, shining in the dawn light. Jesse didn't move. After she had gone inside he got up, with an ache inside his body. Life was too precious to be wasted. One had to go on.

Juan and Leroy had not started drinking yet so Jesse suggested that they take some dried food, and go for a run as in the old days. It was strange, but on the spur of the moment, on a crazy whim, they did just that. They started out, to the south and kept going. Juan led the way. Slowly he trotted. Old and tough, he trotted on. Leroy, with too much fat, but big and strong, came next. Then Jesse.

It turned out that they couldn't stop. They had to walk part of the time but, as in a dream, they kept going. The sweat poured off them. They felt nauseated often. But somehow their bodies responded. Poisonous fluids came out through their skins. Weak, exhausted, they felt better.

So they kept going on. Villages were passed by except to get a drink of water. They slept under mesquites during the heat of the day. On and on. Sore muscles, blisters, but they kept going. They rested in one place with an old medicine man for two days. Then they were off again, veering to the east, running and walking to the top of sacred Baboquivari Mountain, where the rain clouds gathered to water the O'odham world.

It was grueling, torturous, painful. But their bodies grew stronger rather than weaker. They talked hardly at all. Mesquite beans and dried food replenished them. Water was their only drink.

On Baboquivari they prayed and sang songs. Juan knew lots of songs, songs about rain, beautiful O'odham songs. A cloud came. It was most unusual but it came from nowhere. It blanketed the peak and the three men were in the fog, mist all around. It rained on them. Juan took off all his clothes and the others did likewise. Their bodies were washed, cleansed, cooled, nourished by the cold rain.

For Jesse it was a monumental event. He made a vow then and there to let his hair continue growing long, to stop drinking, and to try to get back to his painting.

Leroy and Juan were also very much affected. When they finally got back to Juan's place they worked together to get rid of all the bottles. The house was cleaned up and everything was put in order. A sweat lodge was built.

Leroy said: "Uncle, I haven't felt like this in years. What has happened is good. You have a lot of knowledge. While you're still alive I want to learn as much as I can." The women of the family were all surprised and happy. Songs could now be heard.

Jesse had left then, and had gone to Rufus' place to see El Sabio. He realized that, in a way, it had been a mistake to leave El Sabio with a friend because the wise dog would have probably kept him from drinking again. In any case, the Wise One was very happy to see that Jesse was in one piece, woo-woo-wooing and licking him profusely. Nonetheless, he was happy taking care of Rufus' children and Jesse could see that he had a good place to stay for the time being.

So Jesse got a lift to the nearest Greyhound pick-up and took the bus out a ways, to avoid the crooked sheriff's deputies. Then he started hitchhiking and walking, sleeping wherever opportunity allowed. But after a couple of days he had become so hot and smelly that he had checked into a cheap auto court to get a shower and a good night's sleep. There it was that he had his dream about Juan Garcia.

Now here he was out along an irrigation ditch, watching the sun rise. All of a sudden he had an intense desire to get moving, to get out of Arizona, and on to Santa Fe, where he hoped to find out what Indian artists there were doing.

Jesse hurried back to the motel, gathered up his belongings, and set out along the highway. In a few days he reached Albuquerque and then, after camping out near Alameda, he went on to Santa Fe.

It was the spring of 1967. Soon floods of 'love children' would be pouring into San Francisco and the 'hippie' generation would be born. Jesse saw lots of them pass through New Mexico but he was not interested in their LSD, pot, or searching. Instead, he managed to pick up a job and spent the rest of the time examining Native art trends and talking with artists. Many were very helpful and Jesse saw that Native art was beginning to break away from stereotypical styles.

Nonetheless, Jesse had a lot of disagreements with some of the artists, especially around Santa Fe. As he told one fellow, "I really enjoy looking at the paintings. They do a good job of portraying the beauty of old Indian ways, and of animals, and ceremonies. But I'm still not satisfied. What I mean is this: there's no Indian artist up here like Diego Rivera. I don't mean in quality, I mean in purpose, message, conception. The Mexican muralists saw themselves as educators as well as artists and as being engaged in a political struggle. They saw art as part of the struggle to awaken and educate the masses."

An employee at the BIA Institute of Arts in Santa Fe really got angry at Jesse's statements. He said, "You're just a damn radical trying to cause trouble. We're trying to help Indians learn how to make a living. You can't sell political art! More than that, we're trying to show the positive side of Indian life. We want people to be proud and appreciative of the Indian heritage."

"That's good," responded Jesse, "especially since that's a new twist for the Bureau. But the truth is that those paintings are mostly pure myth. Almost no Indians live that way today. I've just been in southern Arizona where Indian babies die like flies and where the people are being treated like replaceable machine parts – if one dies, okay, get another. I'm sick of myth. Sure we need some beauty in our lives but we also need truth... I remember a painting one of the Mexicans did of a politician. On one side he's raising his fist and appealing to the Indian masses. On the other side his hand is in the pocket of a capitalist. Now that's what we need. How about a painting of a BIA man pretending to be a protector of Indian lands while he's busily promoting a dam to flood the reservation? Is that real? You bet!"

The BIA instructor was livid with rage. He felt personally attacked. "I know what you want to do. You want to stir up trouble. You want to get Indians to become dissatisfied. You're just a subversive."

Jesse laughed and said, "No, I'm not a subversive since I'm an Indian and I'm supporting my nationality. Besides, since when is it so bad to stir up trouble for oppressors who are stealing our resources and starving us to death? Man, that's total war. We are at war with the U.S. government and White society and we should have war art to serve our needs."

The BIA instructor got up and left but another artist remained and said, "Jesse, you've got some good ideas but it's going to be hard to get them across. Indian art is supposed to tell everybody about the beauty of old Indian customs as if they still existed. That's good up to a point. But when the myth serves to prevent any attention to the present, then that's a calculated strategy, you understand?

What I mean is that Indian art is political already, but it's the politics of trying to hide the brutal reality – sweep it under the rug! Now when you try to change that you're going to discover tremendous opposition. So just be prepared. That's all I've got to say."

One other artist added, as a parting shot, "Remember man, you've got to sell your paintings to White people and White galleries. Indians won't buy enough to keep you in underwear."

As the summer came Jesse visited Taos and many other pueblos and then headed west to Gallup. He wanted to see Canyon de Chelly and the Hopi villages, as well as explore the Navajo Reservation.

The drive to Gallup took Jesse back in time to other trips when he had passed through that city. He thought back to little Ella, the slim colored girl he had talked to on a Greyhound bus once, and he remembered the Mexican 'el Tejano,' Horacio Sotomayor.

While in Gallup, Jesse cut across some vacant lots to reach the highway leading to Window Rock. In one of them he saw a body. He went close to examine it and saw that he was too late to be of any help.

As he walked on his mind was agitated by the thought of how close he had come to also ending up that way, a dead Indian out in a field somewhere, or along some road, or in a ditch. He thought again of Juan Garcia's words as he passed a number of crummy bars with red eyed Navajos standing around. If only he could help them but there were so many, and he was just across the line himself. So he kept on moving, avoiding their stares, getting as fast as possible out of town.

Red Blood

Chapter Twelve: The Vacant Lot

It was a vacant lot. It wasn't really 'vacant' but that's what they call a place that doesn't have a building. It lay between the new superhighway and a cluster of run-down bars, stores and boarded-up houses. Weed-covered, strewn with trash and broken wine bottles, it reminded one of many Indians, rejects, wasted people, left to heal scars only to be scarred again, and again.

In the midst of the weeds, behind an old Ford sedan with no wheels or motor, next to a pile of broken up concrete on which a lizard sunned himself, lay Amos Billy. Amos' head was turned upwards and his vacant eyes, set in a pock-marked, wrinkled brown face, were staring but not seeing. He had died during the night, and still his ghost was hovering about, close by, unable to leave.

There are many Navajo ghosts in that part of Gallup. They cannot leave. They flow down the gullies and washes, they hang suspended in the bodies of wrecked cars, they haunt the wasted lots between the bars, and they cluster even under the bridges of the new freeway.

Gallup is one of those Indian death-traps that is also a soul-trap. The souls cannot leave. Hooked to the smell of wine and totally confused, these souls do not know how to follow the spirit-path to the other World. The humans who had these souls had lost the way, and their souls were lost too.

Amos Billy was killed by another Navajo. But that other Navajo will also soon be dead. His teeth are already rotten and even though he is only thirty his insides are already eaten mostly away. His liver will only last a few more months.

Amos Billy was already half-dead anyway. His soul often left him to wander about, lost, while Amos lay in a wine-trance. The soul knew it would soon be without a body, but it didn't find any place to go, so it came back as long as it could.

And along the freeway a haze rose, from the fumes of cars passing by. A fog, a yellow-poison fog, from the cars of tourists searching for Real Indians. 'Genuine Hand-Made Indian Jewelry.' The jewelry is easier to relate to, though, than Native People.

The tourists want to see Real Indians (but maybe not up too close). Funny! For over a hundred years they have been ordering their Bureau of Indian Affairs and their gospel missions to manufacture 'Imitation Factory-Made Indians,' winos, and ghosts!

Then they're surprised when they get, instead, angry hostiles ready to fight back!

RED BLOOD

CHAPTER THIRTEEN: TSEGI

The sun had lost it's power. Although still orange-red it was so low in the west that it's heat could no longer be felt except by putting one's hands on the rocks or pressing the body close to a stone surface.

The sun set twice on that day, first slipping behind a cloud. Then it was briefly alive again between the bottom of the cloud and a mountain rim. But the Sun-of-that-Day was doomed. It struggled to light up the sky still, using the clouds and vapors for mirrors to magnify it's weakening rays, but in spite of a magnificent display of pinks, reds, and yellows all across the sky, it finally plummeted to the other side, leaving a sense of void, a sense of sadness, a sense of losing a companion, a familiar friend gone at last.

High above the rim of Canyon de Chelly Jesse leaned against a wind-sculptured boulder and watched silently as Gishux, the day-Sun, left the world of the surface. An intense feeling had taken possession of him, a feeling which eddied about in the air, around the rocks, the yucca, and swirled up from the now darkening canyon just below. He felt the tingling magic of expectancy in his body and all around. Was something special about to occur? Or did this kind of magic always accompany the twilight on this rim above this Canyon of the Navajos, this Canyon of the Ancient Ones Who Came Before.

A fox moved slowly across the rim a few yards away. It didn't hurry. It seemed to know that Jesse was harmless. It almost seemed to want him to watch. He felt hunger pangs grow in his stomach but it was impossible to leave. In the daylight the deep, broad canyon had hypnotized him and hours upon hours had passed as every detail of the scene etched itself in his mind. The ancient cliff dwellings looked like little dollhouses erected in tiny little openings along the canyon walls. The ribbons of water way down on the sandy bottom, with clumps of trees and, here and there, a hogan or a horse. The ribbons divided, came back together, divided again in a pattern of effortless intricacy but one which challenged the mind to dare to try to absorb it, to understand it. And the sheer, smooth cliffs with pinks, and browns, and yellows, and tans, cliffs that beckoned across the chasm.

Could one fly across to one of those small holes on the opposite wall? What if one were tempted to float on the air like a bird, seeking out places ordinary humans could never reach except in dreams?

Jesse caught himself becoming mesmerized by the immensity of the canyon, the sky, the heat. He almost felt himself disappearing to become a part of that place, but he grew cautious, he stayed back from the edge, he prayed to Grandfather and to the Spirits of that huge Tsegi.

And thus he had spent the day, since the rising of the Sun, Opank, to now, Lawkwik, evening. He had not eaten at all, nor drunk anything, but until now he had not felt any need. The canyon was all that one needed – it nourished, filled to the brim, left no room for anything else.

Darkness fell gradually but when it came it was complete, like when the flap is closed on a sweat lodge. Then one can see only the red hot rocks in the middle of the lodge, and after the water is put on them for steam even that glow disappears.

There was no moon. Piske, it is dark, thought Jesse. I could go now. Yet I can't. I'm too much at peace. Maybe I'll just stay here and become a fossil. Then the White park rangers can show a slide of me every night around the campfire to tourists.

Jesse laughed to himself quietly. He could see lights in the distance, around Chinle and Many Farms, and once in a long while a pickup truck drove by on the road. Jesse had spent many hours in the back of such trucks, hitching rides from Gallup and around the reservation. Bouncing along, often with an old Navajo grandmother sitting nearby and usually a child or two. And when the wind was strong, or the truck slowed down on some arroyo-washed dirt road, the dust blowing in one's face in a smothering, choking cloak.

Gallup and the other border towns had depressed him, hurt him, the drunks and winos wandering aimlessly, the ugliness, the women and children waiting patiently, for what? The drab slums, makeshift houses, broken glass decorated lots, hot, exposed, bare, naked, and when the wind blows, fine dust.

He had gotten a ride from Gallup in the back of a big grey Ford pickup. "You want a ride? Climb in the back. Going to Fort Defiance."

"Thanks, I'll get off in Window Rock."

Along the highway the truck stopped to pick up an old Navajo couple, a man and a woman, both just walking along the side, not looking around. They sat next to Jesse, so that he could smell the liquor. Their clothes were old and dirty and their teeth were mostly gone. Skin not good, eyes kind of hollow, and Jesse was disappointed. He had hoped they might be elders who he could get to know a little and learn something from. The woman's eyes were not friendly, though, not warm, not hospitable. They were cunning — sizing him up. The old man just looked empty, drained, hanging on.

He tried to strike up a conversation after a while but all the woman wanted was for Jesse to get off with them at a run down bar called the Sagebrush, just at the reservation boundary. "Come and have a drink with us," she said, but Jesse recoiled at the thought. He knew she wanted him to buy the drinks, and maybe it would be okay but everything about her reminded him of a greedy person wanting only to take. She and the old man had no interest in him. Liquor was their only thought. He was just a dollar bill, or two, or even fifty cents.

And so they got off, walking back across a large dirt parking lot towards the white-colored, ominous looking bar with its cavern door. They didn't look back.

The old couple probably put Jesse out of their minds, what little of him had ever been there. It was harder for Jesse. They were to stay with him yet for a long while, haunting him like a pair of demons. It wasn't just poverty. They smelled of death, hurrying to death, wandering aimlessly to death, dying without meaning, a lonely old couple. Had they forgotten their children, grandchildren, great-grandchildren? Were they forgotten, already dead to their descendants?

Walking ghosts, liquor was their only family. Their descendants were bottles. Were they empty too?

Getting off in Window Rock, Jesse looked around, half-afraid that the old couple would pursue him, would soon appear. What am I afraid of, he thought? It is the old woman, she would do anything for a drink. No, It's more than that. She has lost her womanhood, all the nurturing female is gone. All that is left is a hard will that keeps her and her man going, a will pinned on getting the next drink.

I've got to escape from them, Jesse had thought, but not just from them, from Gallup, from the dead wino, from the drunks and dirty sidewalks, from the cavernous bars seeking victims.

As his thoughts returned to these things, Jesse became uneasy there in the dark on the edge of Canyon de Chelly. What if he ran into the old couple in the dark, on the road, eyes glowing yellow? They must be far away from here, he told himself but anyway his peace was gone. Forcing his body up after hours of sitting there, he carefully made his way between rocks and plants to the surface of the road. Eyes somewhat accustomed to the night now, with a billion stars providing some faint light, he moved along slowly.

Still he had to feel his way. A chill moved through his body and fear gripped him. Could he stay on the road? What if he walked right into a steer, or stepped on a rattler? Jesse started singing quietly. He stopped to look at the stars. He prayed silently. The feeling passed and he went on, sure once again, winding with the road down off the layers of the mesa to the little valley below.

Jesse had left his sleeping bag and pack in a clump of cottonwoods in a little side canyon. He had picked the place carefully so he could camp unobserved. Not having much money he had to sleep where he could, out in the open, whenever possible. A pile of rocks nearby gave him a sheltered place for his fire, where the low flames would be unseen by park rangers or by the owners of a nearby tourist lodge. But on this night, after groping through the trees in the dark, he was too hungry to cook anything. Cold food was good enough and besides, he had some cheese and salami that he had to finish up with crackers, before it melted and spoiled.

Resting back on his sleeping bag, against a tree trunk, with his stomach satisfied, he felt better. Cheese, salami and crackers made his cigarette taste good. He felt safe, protected, back in the trees, out of sight, in the total darkness where feeling with the hands, hearing and smelling were all that was left.

Red Blood

Chapter Fourteen: Loretta

Jesse found a good place to sit, where he could watch people passing to and from a trading post, a Chapter House, and a small cafe. In such places he would get out his sketch pad and try to capture the things he was seeing or, more correctly, the feelings he was experiencing.

A group of Navajo school girls came out of the store. They looked at Jesse with friendly, happy eyes, and then passed on, allowing sounds of laughter to drift to his ears.

He put aside his drawing pad and began writing a letter to himself, trying to save for another day the impressions racing through his mind.

"Beautiful Navajo girls. Skin so smoothly dark walnut brown, magically mountain honey-colored. Do you all taste as sweet as you look? No deodorants for Navajo girls, no strong smells to be erased, only smokey sage-juniper-piñon tinged aromas. Black, glossy-lustered soft hair streaming, cascading, falling, or wrapped proudly, on to the head. Why are high cheekbones so attractive? Why do they even make blonde European girls look better?

Navajo girls' eyes, Indian girls' eyes, all different shapes, some almond, some full and round, but it isn't the shape. Exuding from them is a warmth, a joy, a sheer pleasure in being an admired, free, proud, useful, skilled, nurturing, strong, independent, 'spoken for' woman.

Every Navajo girl, every Indian girl, is already spoken for at birth, before birth. The universe, the Great Creator, Changing Woman, the plants, the earth, Corn-Mother, all life, everything has made a place for the Native girl. Sensing her power, sensing her sexuality, sensing her established place as a creator and sustainer of life and of beauty, she walks in beauty, dropping as she goes petals of quiet laughter, blossoms of starlight smiles, and whole flowers of shielded sidelong glances.

To hear a Native girl sing. Not just vapid song from the front of the mouth. Deep and high, nasal, earth power singing, like the fado, or the flamenco in depth but sincere, open, without the decadence of corrupted civilizations. Gypsy beauty but pure and unpainted. Straightforward, arrow-sharp but soft, womanly. One could listen for days without awareness of time. Nights could fly by and one could grow old without caring, such is their power if they wanted to enchant that way.

When a Navajo girl grasps your belt and takes you to dance... To be with a proud, self-aware woman. One cannot use such a girl wrongly, unless one is truly deranged. They are too precious.

Navajo girls talking. Glottal stops and clicks at the end of words. Liquid flowing, not sugar water but some kind of melodious, dignified, powerful, soothing way of talking. Don't ever lose your accent, Navajo girl! If you do, I'll leave you. Don't ever stop talking in Navajo the way you do. Don't ever learn to sing sugary-empty. Husky-nasal voiced song, power-female talking, don't let it go.

Mother earth-female – upright walking, slim and full-bosomed, dancing, always dancing, running-dancing, walking-dancing, sitting-dancing, head up high, looking the world over, loving men.

Indian girls are man lovers. They birth men, they care for men, they are not afraid of them. Unabused, self-assured, esteemed, they can love fully. Traditional Indian men must be good too, sensitive to their women's power, gifts, they give too. But it isn't the women on my mind, wrote Jesse. It is their power-beauty that draws me.

Slight, small but they are not toys. They are not tanks either, with guns blazing like some other women. Real, authentic, filled with vital force of love itself, soft like wind but hard-carving wearing down rocks.

It is easy to fall in love with a Navajo girl, but is it fair to take her away? Shouldn't she raise more Navajo girls? If you take her with you, what can she raise away from other Navajos? Do you want to destroy that flow of generations – do you want to interrupt the very thing that grips you, brings it to a halt? Please, make sure that more Indian girls are made," thought Jesse. "Let them go on and on into the future, models, prototypes of womanhood after all the others have disappeared into the ocean of empty middle-class wives with its thrown-up waves of rebellious, man-hating feminists."

Indian girls could be changed, as Jesse had seen. Alcohol, poverty and hopelessness could create the cunning survivors of Gallup and the border towns, or the old ladies joining their men in connubial winoships. But in Window Rock and Fort Defiance Jesse had also met the products of BIA missionary training – hard, cold, bitter-eyed de-Navajoized ladies behind desks with their hair curled and done up in fancy World War II White styles.

Jesse had hated Indian women to do up their hair. How could they take their beautiful long black hair, reflecting the light like gleaming obsidian, and torture it with curlers or whatever to make it into something else? But the BIA and the missionaries taught them to hate their Indianness and long, straight black hair was one of the signs that had to be erased.

Still, that only made Jesse appreciate Indian girls more. If there had been no BIA, no missionaries, no hard-eyed White trader's wives, no corrupted Indians, then he wouldn't have thought that much about unspoiled Navajo girls. He wouldn't have appreciated them so much, at least not consciously, because there would have been nothing to contrast them with. And so even an evil has some value. At least it makes you appreciate the good that much more, that is, if you're still free enough to know the difference.

A few days later, Jesse got to go to a dance out in the country with a friend of his, a Navajo who had moved back to the reservation from Los Angeles. Fred Yazzie, a young man in his twenties, was sure of himself at the gathering and danced quite a bit but Jesse kept to the margins, listening to the singing and watching the other people intently but unobtrusively.

Every so often he would notice Fred dancing with a girl or talking with a group of men. Several times different men came up to Jesse and they would talk a little but the girls seemed to stay together in small groups except when dancing. Jesse looked at many of them but when they noticed him they turned their glances shyly away or laughed a little and talked with their friends. One woman, however, looked at him several times. She was, perhaps, a little bit older than most of the girls. Dark brown, with markedly high cheekbones; she lowered her eyes whenever he looked at her but, nonetheless, shot him veiled glances that told of her awareness of his interest. He called her 'Red Skirt' to himself, but she disappeared from view before he could get up the courage to walk over her way.

Disappointed, Jesse turned his attention to other portions of the crowded scene, until distracted by a hand on his shoulder. Fred was at his side, saying "You ought to go out there. Get in the lineup. There's a girl who wants to dance with you." He was grinning.

Jesse said "Are you kidding me? I'm scared to go out there."

"Go on. You got to. It's the rule. You can't just stand around all night. You got to make the ladies happy, Jesse."

So Fred kind of shoved Jesse out, and he went, not reluctantly but somewhat nervous at the idea of waiting to see if a girl would pick him as a dance partner.

He didn't have long to wait, though, as 'Red Skirt' came up to him, self-confidently but without boldness. "You have to dance or give me some money," she said as her hands grasped his belt. Her eyes frankly and good-humoredly examined him, carefully noting his reaction.

Jesse, on his part, was very pleased. "I sure ain't goin' to give you any money."

So they danced arm in arm. Jesse had learned the steps at pow wows but at first he felt very stiff compared with her confidence and her effortless movements. When the dance was finished he asked her to dance again and gradually he became more relaxed, becoming then increasingly aware of her body against his arm and of her hands in his.

"My name's Jesse. What's yours?"

"Loretta," she said. "I'm Fred's sister. We belong to the same clan."

"Did he ask you to dance with me?" queried Jesse.

"No," she replied emphatically, with a suppressed smile on her lips, "I asked him to get you out here so I could find out why you were staring at me so hard."

"I'm sorry, I didn't mean to look at you so, but you're very pretty and I just couldn't help it, Red Skirt."

"Red Skirt! Is that my name now?"

"Yes, that's what I called you, in my mind, when I was looking at you."

"You like me," she stated.

"Yes."

"I like you. What tribe are you?"

And so they talked and danced, losing track of the time and keeping together in between dances to show that they wanted to stay together. He could smell her body by then, and his arm sometimes touched her breast as they danced. His hands became sweaty and he was a little embarrassed but Loretta didn't seem to mind.

"You have a woman?" she asked.

"No, not now. I'm alone, looking for one though, if I can find a good one like you."

"I'm not good," she smiled. "I'm a bad woman. My nose is too big, face too thin."

"I'm not goin' to play any games, Red Skirt, you're beautiful so don't try to say things like that. I like your face, all of it."

She was pleased.

"You're staying with Fred, ey, but it's so crowded there."

"Yeah, I'll probably have to start camping out again. That's what I've been doing. Sleeping with the snakes and coyotes."

"How long you goin' to be around here? What are you going to do?"

"I'm not sure. It depends on what I find, if I get a job. The truth is, I want to find out about Navajo women. That's my secret mission."

"Hey, you'll never find that out; there's too much to learn, ey! But a good teacher would help. That's what you need."

"Can you recommend one?"

"Ey, there's an old lady I know, eighty years old. She's old and wrinkled and almost blind but she would be happy to teach you."

Red Skirt laughed. Many couples were drifting away now, going out into the darkness or disappearing among the trucks and camps. She took Jesse's arm and pulled him gently and they wandered off too, finally finding a place to sit beyond a juniper tree.

"I like you," she whispered. "You can stay with me if you'll be good to me, treat me gentle and nice."

Jesse kissed her and gently caressed her breasts. "I should tell you," she said, "I have two babies, two little boys. Maybe that would bother you."

"That won't bother me," replied Jesse. "I like kids. I just don't want a husband there."

Red Skirt smiled. "No, my husband's gone. I haven't got a man now."

And so it all fell into place. Jesse moved in with Loretta Begay in her little government built house in Chinle. She worked in the kitchen of the school cafeteria while a clan sister who lived nearby watched her children.

Loretta's husband had abandoned her, temporarily or permanently no one knew, and had gone off to find a job in Denver, people said. She was a high school graduate but that only meant that she had studied up to ninth grade work. She had learned to type a little but had ended up in the school cafeteria because she had no other skills and, with two babies, had no thought of going on to college. She really wanted to go home to her family out in another part of the reservation but since she had a job and the homeplace was over-crowded that was out of the question.

Loretta wouldn't have stayed in Chinle, however, if she had been completely alone. But she had her clan sister who lived nearby and some other relatives, such as Fred, who could be called upon for help in an emergency. Nonetheless, she deeply missed her family and home and often cried to herself at night when she felt depressed and lonely.

The school paid very little. Loretta managed, though, to send her family some money every so often and she saved what she could. Her dream was to save enough so that she could buy some sheep and a truck and move back home. She didn't like Chinle, especially where she was living. The government houses were square and poorly built. Hot in the summer, cold in the winter, with bathrooms that stopped working, and ceilings that fell in. There were no streets either, or yards, all erased long ago by cars and trucks driving wher-ever they wanted to. Everything was mud when it rained and dust when it didn't rain.

But the people survived and Loretta was one of them. She tried to beautify her house with what Navajo blankets and rugs she could afford to keep (and they could also be sold in an emergency). She had put up magazine pictures and a few photographs and, here and there, pieces of wood, herbs, knick knacks, and beadwork. Her fur-niture consisted of a few chairs, an old table, a radio, two mattress-es, and several packing crates used for books, magazines, toys, newspapers, and clothing.

Loretta usually cooked outside, on the shady side of the house in the summer, to save on fuel bills and because that was the way she had been raised. Having no refrigeration, she had to use mostly canned goods or dried food anyway. Still she had to go to the store almost every day because, not having a car, she couldn't carry much at any one time. She didn't really mind that since there wasn't much in the way of excitement in Chinle. Going to the store was a diver-sion, a chance to meet friends or to look over things that you might want to buy one day.

Loretta hoped her husband would come back someday but she didn't dwell on it in her mind. She thought far more about her fam-ily and her babies than she did of him. Other men had briefly known her but she hadn't found anyone she really liked until Jesse had lay down with her out there on the sand beneath the stars the night of the dance.

Loretta gambled, of course, when she let Jesse move in. He had no job. He had no money, so far as she knew. He would eat a lot of food. But like a lot of Indian woman she was not looking for financial support or middle-class security. That never occurred to her. Instead, she simply wanted to share her life, her body, her love, her nurturing with a man who would be kind and gentle and would share himself with her. What happened after that would be up to the future.

Jesse, for his part, was very happy. He fell in love with Loretta and their first days together were like a honeymoon. When she was away during the day he tackled the plumbing, borrowing tools to get the toilet and the shower working once again. He also repaired the ceiling and, after scouring the countryside for logs and pieces of wood, he built a ramada near the house and gathered rocks for a better fire pit.

Perhaps he felt guilty about living off a woman's labor. But so far as Loretta was concerned he repaid her many times over. The warmth of his body at night and his caresses were enough in themselves, but on top of that he played with the boys and eased her burdens in countless little ways. Jesse usually met her as she walked home from work and helped her carry groceries. He brought the babies along too, so that they could enjoy the walk.

At night, after dinner, he tried to learn Navajo. But every time Jesse tried to say something like "Dineh dish dintsa?" or whatever, Red Skirt would break into such laughter that he got discouraged. Jesse became convinced that Navajos have a secret desire to prevent outsiders from learning their language and that they use laughter to so embarrass the victim that he will give up. Nonetheless, he persisted since it seemed to entertain her and he knew, after all, that she liked him.

On their first weekend together, after carrying the laundry to a laundromat and returning the washed clothes to the house, they hiked up Canyon de Chelly loaded down with blankets, dried food, the babies, and Jesse's sleeping bag. Loretta had been up the canyon, so she was happy to show Jesse a place so important to her people's history. Jesse was elated to show her what he had seen and to learn from her what she had heard about the great Tsegi.

That night they camped together with only the darkness and the stars around them. The sound of running water and the breeze, high up among the cliffs and rocks, together made music for them and they were content. Loretta had not been so happy for a long time and even the little boys were positively affected by Jesse's attention and the new experiences they were having.

As Loretta cuddled the babies and stared into the fire, Jesse thought how wonderful she was. How nice it was to camp out with a woman who had been camping all her life, so to speak, who knew how to gather kindling for the fire, who knew how to stack the wood just right to get it burning, who knew how to cook with no utensils, and who knew how to love a man in such a way that he floated on a cloud singing, filled with warmth and tenderness, joyously becoming something wonderfully renewed at her touch.

In such a way the days and weeks went by. Jesse managed to buy some canvases and started painting. He got some beads and made a beading loom. Loretta was a good beader but she had given it up. Now she started again, working as Jesse painted. Jesse's ambition was to sell some paintings so that he could buy a sewing machine for Loretta. Then she could make clothes for herself and the boys. He also wanted her to develop her beading, sewing, and weaving so that she could better support herself if she ever lost her job.

During the day Jesse did a lot of walking, looking for wood, wire, and anything else potentially useful. As he walked about he also observed, learning a lot about the life around him. He saw how the Navajos, as vital and numerous as they were, were dominated by the White culture. The trading posts were run by Whites or half-breeds who acted like Whites. The signs were all in English every-where – road signs, business signs, government signs, even tribal signs. Even the *Navajo Times* newspaper was all in English. Who could read it, he thought. Who was it printed for?

The prices in the stores were terribly high, so he understood why everybody who could, drove to Gallup or other border towns to shop. It was not only an exciting diversion, it was also an economic neces-sity. The trading posts also had poor quality foods, lots of sugary cereals and other junk, and many times the corn flakes tasted moldy or stale. Used appliances, such as sewing machines, sold for almost as much as new ones in Los Angeles.

Jesse also observed how the White teachers and government officials lived in segregated compounds and took their money off-reservation. It was truly a colony, he thought, with everything, even the people, being sucked out by the colonizing society.

One day Jesse and Loretta hitched a ride together to Gallup in a relative's pickup. They sold enough paintings and beadwork there to buy a used sewing machine, some toys for the boys, and some fab-ric for making clothes. Jesse didn't get much for his paintings. He knew he was being cheated but what could he do? He was like any other Indian artist on the reservation, helpless because he needed the money, at the mercy of the White and Mexican curio shop owners.

Jesse decided then and there to try to find a way to sell his paintings directly to the tourists if he could. On the way home, in Window Rock, Loretta joined the tribal arts and crafts guild at Jesse's suggestion and got some wool for weaving.

Because of that, Jesse could also sell some of his paintings, using Loretta's last name, at the guild's store. Loretta had seldom been off the reservation, except to go to Gallup and other bordertowns, so Jesse planned next to save up money, get a ride to Albuquerque, and maybe buy a used truck or car there. Then they could go on a grand tour, visiting her home place and seeing a lot of things that were too far away to hitchhike to.

It took a long time but finally they had enough money, crafts, and paintings to take their trip. Loretta was on vacation so they had the time. Jesse found a used pickup in Albuquerque, with a camper on the back. Thus royally outfitted they drove north to Santa Fe where they visited the museum, galleries, and some of Jesse's artist friends. Loretta bought quite a few things and Jesse asked her, "Don't you think you ought to save some money? Just in case." Loretta looked at him with a sidelong glance and said simply, "My husband sent me a money order two weeks ago, from Denver."

She said nothing more, and Jesse asked no further. But it brought home to him the fact that she was a married woman whose man might well return one day. He also thought again of Ramona and how she was probably married by now, wherever she was.

Loretta was extra-affectionate towards Jesse after that and so they both had a good time, visiting Tesuque, San Juan, and Taos before turning west. They hiked through Mesa Verde and other ruins, although Loretta was nervous and refused to go into any of the old houses. "Someone might have died there," was all she said.

They drove to Shiprock and over to her family's home place, camping out as usual. Both very happy, they made love as ardently as when they first met and every evening around the campfire seemed so enjoyable, so relaxing, so free from worry that they hated the thought of returning to Chinle. Loretta's kinfolk were pleased to see her and Jesse was made to feel welcome. Still, he felt a little left out because many of the older ones seemed to speak no English.

When Loretta said she would like to stay for a while longer Jesse decided to drive back to Chinle alone. He stopped at Fred Yazzie's first and luckily so. Fred seemed a little nervous and said, "A few days ago I got a message that Loretta's husband was on his way back from Denver. He hasn't come yet, but I thought you'd want to know. He says, that he's sorry he left so suddenly but now he wants to move back. He's saved some money."

Jesse felt a churning in the pit of his stomach, but he said only, "Thanks for telling me, I'll go back and tell Loretta. You can tell her husband, when he comes, that she's with her family." Jesse then went to Loretta's house and packed up all his personal things, leaving nothing to cause trouble for her.

As he drove back out to her home place he made up his mind to let her go if she wanted to return to her husband. "After all, she doesn't belong to me. I don't own her. Anyway, it's best for the kids to be with their father."

Loretta was not surprised by the news. She said, "I love you Jesse. You been real good to me and my children. But I love my husband also and he's sent me money, so I know he cares about me. I think he needs me more than you do."

So Jesse turned away from her long black hair, her firm breasts, her warm brownness, her strength, her steady nurture, turned again to resume his wandering. He said only, "You've been good to me Loretta. I love you. If he's ever mean to you, leave him and come to me. Even if I have another woman, I'll try to help you out."

A few days later, from Gallup, Jesse phoned Lucas Fixico, his old army buddy in Oklahoma. It was the first time he had established contact with any friends or relatives for months (although he had sent a long letter to Rufus from Santa Fe before meeting Loretta and had also sent a letter to Ramona in care of her uncle and a copy in care of Ladell. But he had given no return address so there had been no replies).

Lucas was glad to hear from Jesse. He had gotten caught up in the "Indian Power" movement and was planning to go to the National Congress of American Indians convention that fall. He said, "Jesse, why don't we meet there. We can have a good time together." So Jesse agreed.

He drove south first, to Rufus Wildcat's place to pick up El Sabio. Now that he had a camper he wanted the dog with him, if El Sabio wanted to go along. The old wise one listened carefully, examined the camper, and decided that that was what he wanted too. So together they prepared to go with a bundle of Indian posters Rufus had ordered from Ladell. Jesse called Ladell on the phone but she had no information about Ramona, so he and El Sabio departed to the north, on the road once again.

RED BLOOD

CHAPTER FIFTEEN: INDIAN SUMMER HILLTOP LOVE

"Hey, when I got into this business I didn't have anything! I had a crummy education degree from a rinky-dink teacher's college, a good sun tan, and a loud mouth. Now I'm making twenty grand a year and picking up another five grand in per diem, airline tickets, and kick-backs. You can do the same, Jesse."

Art Little looked like a success. His hair was cropped short, his suit was expensive (not to mention his hand tooled cowboy boots and ponderous silver and turquoise jewelry). He was buying drinks for everybody and seemed to have a big wad of money.

"Yeah, I tell you. We're coming into our own now! This 'War on Poverty' and all of these new federal programs are literally shoving money our way. But to take advantage of it you have to be in a position to get a good piece of the action. My advice is for you guys to finish college. Get some mickey mouse degree, whatever, it don't make any difference. Then get yourself a job as a director of some program, or start out as an associate director in a larger project. It don't matter. But the key is – make connections. You got to have the right connections. Work with the people that really count, learn to play ball with them and they'll give you a run now and then."

"What do you mean, Art? I thought you had to submit proposals and meet guidelines?"

Art looked around the crowded, noisy bar. The room was full of conventioning Indians attending a National Congress of American Indians gathering. It seemed like most of the delegates were in one of the several bars in the hotel.

"Well, you know how things work here at the NCAI don't you? Everything's politics here," said Art. "You don't get elected to anything here unless you are part of a coalition, a political alliance.

There are all kinds of cliques – the Northwest tribes, the Plains, Oklahoma, the Southwest – they're the big ones. Success comes when several cliques get together and make an alliance."

"What do they do it for?" asked Lucas Fixico, Jesse's friend. "Just to be a big shot?"

"That's part of it. An awful lot of these Indians here have got real big egos, you better believe it. They carry their egos right out here – on the edge of their cuffs – always dangling for praise. But the real motivation behind it all is political power and that is spelled m-o-n-e-y!"

"What does the NCAI have to do with money?" queried Jesse.

"That's what it's really all about. First, there's jobs to be handed out. Then there's resolutions that might help one tribe but not another. Most of all, the BIA likes to make sure that it stays real cozy with the people who run NCAI, and the same with the federal programs. If you play ball with them, they'll toss big grants your way or, better yet, to your friends."

"Everything in Indian politics revolves around money. All these guys want is to get out of their dirt shacks. They want good houses, nice cars, fancy clothes. They want good-lookin' girl friends and nice soft beds to sleep on. Once they get a taste for that they'll never give it up."

"So where does the money come from? There's only one place - the Feds, because, you see, even tribal budgets are controlled by the BIA so every dime has to be approved. That's where you have to play ball."

"You mean, these tribal governments of ours are corrupt?" said Lucas.

Art laughed. "Corrupt, hell no! The money's there and it's going to go to those who can get it. The others are too dumb anyway, they'd just let it slip through their fingers. The BIA looks the other way, if you're on their side. Otherwise they manipulate things so you're soon tossed out of office."

"The BIA can get a tribal chairman defeated? What do they do, hold back on contracts or commodities?" asked Jesse.

"That's the ticket. They just lose the paperwork somewhere. And the people get the message."

"But how do they keep Indian delegates here at the NCAI from bringing all of that out into the open?" asked Jesse.

"Maybe most of them don't want it opened up," said Lucas.

"That's right," responded Art. "Most of these delegates here are just hoping to get their mouth on the tit so they're not going to do anything. Every once in a while, though, a rebellion starts. But they're easy to handle."

"How do they do that?" queried Lucas.

"By holding off on resolutions and other key issues until late on the last day, and by stacking the key committees. Most of these delegates start leaving Sunday morning, but the ones in control stay on and wrap it all up just the way they want it, late Sunday night. And, of course, they always hold the meetings in places like this where lots of delegates will just get drunk or sleep around with each other. The real work is all done behind the scenes."

Just then a hard-eyed, sharp-faced woman came into the bar. She spotted Art Little and came right over, and sat down at the table. Art did the introductions, "Boys, this is Daisy Ross, one of our most up-and-coming leaders. Daisy, meet Jesse Rainwater and Lucas Fixico. They're young but tryin' to learn."

Daisy tried to show a cordial smile but it was fleeting and seemed to only accentuate the tightness of her thin face. Jesse had heard something about her and it made him nervous to be so close. She was a chain smoker, a highly nervous person and she talked at length with Art about pending grants and contracts from agencies with alphabetical names like USOE, DOL, OEO, and, of course, BIA. Jesse and Lucas both felt like leaving the table but Art, noticing their fidgeting, told them to stick around.

Before long several other friends of Art and Daisy dropped by to join the conversation. Jesse learned more than he really wanted to know about wheeling and dealing. Later Art explained some of it to them.

"Daisy is a very smart woman. Tough and smart. She knows how to cuddle up to White people so they think she's the world's greatest Indian. She got herself elected to a tribal chair position. Now she's gotten herself appointed to a good position at BIA. Do you know what that means? Well, if you're in good with her she'll sign off on your budget and grants. If you're in bad, oh well, your paperwork might even get lost. The Whites haven't caught on to her and the Indians, they love her! She goes to bed with some, passes out favors to others, flatters some, and frightens the rest! Everybody thinks she has connections higher up in the BIA. The BIA thinks she is on the inside with the White House, and the Indians think she can protect their wheeling and dealing, so everybody plays up to her. She started out with with nothing but guts and a bluff, but now it's paying off. She helps me and I help her. That way we build an alliance – connections – that keeps us up on top of the pile."

"But Art, it sounds like, in a way you've given up on doing any good for Indian people. Like, I mean, you talk about programs as if they're just designed to generate money and jobs for Indians who are already middle class. I'm not trying to be critical, but what happens to the original purposes of the programs?" asked Jesse.

Art sighed and looked a little disappointed. "Jesse, I'd like to help the poor people as much as the next guy. But that's not what these programs are for. There are too many poor people and not enough money. You train a guy to be a welder. Okay. Are there any jobs? Well, maybe, but not where he's living, and so on. You know the story. But there are jobs, jobs for the people who run the job training programs, do you see? Anyway, I believe in building an Indian middle class, with money and education. Someday we'll have our own banks, and stores, and supermarkets, and hotels. They'll all be run by, or even owned by, a middle class. That's the way it's going, Jesse. You can't change it, so why not get on board?"

"I don't see too many poor people around here," said Lucas. "Everybody has their hair cut short and the ladies all have permanents. It must cost a lot of money to come to conventions like this."

"Yeah, that's true," said Art. "You have to have your hair cut and dress right, otherwise the Whites don't trust you. They think you're a militant or an old country Indian if you wear braids, so that's out. Let me tell you, they run the show because they control the bread. If you want a slice of that loaf you have to look like them, you have to learn to tell the kind of jokes they want to hear, and you have to agree with most of what they say."

"So that's why our commissioner of Indian Affairs filled his speech with jokes, one after another? I thought he was crazy, the first time I heard him speak," said Jesse.

"I thought he was a damn fool, a real ass," commented Lucas.

"Okay", responded Art, "but he makes the Whites sit back and laugh. He is numero uno, you know, and he's got a good salary. So what the hell? He makes the Whites feel good. They know he's no militant, so they put him in the top spot. That isn't so bad is it?"

"Yeah but what good does he do," said Jesse. "Under people like him we're losing millions of tons of coal at ridiculous prices, we lost water rights and power plants, and we aren't getting a damn thing back. What good does it do to be number one if you can't do any good for Indian people?"

Art looked around the crowded bar. He seemed to be getting the feeling that maybe Jesse and Lucas were not quite his kind of Indians, but he tried to sum it all up for them: "Look, the BIA is part of the U.S. Government. It doesn't belong to Indians. Where'd you ever get the idea that it's supposed to do something for Indians? That's bullshit. It does what the Interior Department and Congress wants. Don't you see? That's a given! It does what the Whites want. You can't change that but if you're smart you can go along with it and get something for yourself. The only, and I mean the only way the BIA helps Indians is by paying their salaries and giving out money to tribal governments, which also goes for salaries. That's all there is to it. Now, I want to give you a word of advice. Some of these militants think that they're going to change things. Believe me, it won't happen. Oh, I'm a supporter of all of them. I like to see the NIYC and the others raising hell. Why? Because every time the Whites get worried they cough up a little more money and you know who gets the money? People like me, we get the money. The only time the militants will get anything is when they get strong enough to be a threat, and then the key leaders will take nice jobs behind a desk. So I welcome the young rebels. More power to them. But I'm the one who's going to cash in the chips, not them. And you can cash in too if you're smart. So it's your choice boys. Get smart – cut your hair – put on a suit and tie, or get your head knocked in, for nothing."

With that pronouncement, Art got up and left. He was ready to move on to some other group, one where he could improve his connections or promote some new deal. Jesse and Lucas were relieved. They were tired of sitting in the bar with their soft drinks anyway so, after a piss, they started wandering around the hotel looking for acquaintances.

The lobby and halls were full of Indians milling around. By and large, they were different from the crowds Jesse was used to but they reminded him of a lot of the students he had met at O.U. and similar places, but grown up. Their colors varied considerably but the majority dressed like any group of conventioning Whites, especially Texans. The suits and ties of the men were often complemented by cowboy boots and hats, but otherwise, there was precious little unique about them. The women, often very attractive, and all dolled up, were very interesting to Jesse. What was going through their minds? What did it mean to be a typist for the BIA? How could you be a BIA teacher and keep your sanity? What did it do to you to be the niece, and ardent supporter, of a crooked tribal chairman?

Jesse and Lucas wandered over to an area where militant Indians from Washington State had set up a table. They were selling copies of their newspapers and seeking support for the treaty rights movement. Their appearance was very different from the other Indians since many had simple clothes and long, straight hair. A lot of the men and boys wore headbands. They, strangely enough, looked out of place in that national convention of Indians.

Jesse and Lucas started talking to them. "Are you getting much support?" asked Jesse.

A pretty girl with long braids laughed at him. "No, we are trouble makers here. We are an embarrassment to the Apples. They don't want to fight for Indian rights, they just want to kiss the Whiteman's ass."

"But it looks like you might get a resolution passed, supporting the treaties, so that's something," said Jesse.

"What we need is resolutions from every tribal council and a real show of united support. But the tribal councils are all afraid. They don't want to make the Interior Department mad at them." She paused, and then said, "Who are you? What tribe are you?"

Jesse said, "My name's Jesse. I'm Delaware and Houma."

She said "I'm Nisqually, Yakima, and Colville. My name's Mary."

"Are you staying here, in the hotel?" asked Jesse.

"Are you kidding? We've got a camp down at the Indian Center, in the basement. What about you?"

"We're sleeping in my car, over at a friend's place," responded Jesse. "What are you going to do for dinner?"

"I'm supposed to help cook over at the Indian Center, but maybe I can take off tonight. Are you offering to buy me a dinner out?" She queried, with a sliver of a smile on her pretty face. She was a dark brown girl with soft features and a good figure, accentuated by tight Levis and a sweatshirt. Mary was only a teenager but she was already grown up in her knowledge of men. Like a lot of Indian girls she was self-confident and experienced with the ups and downs of life. The fishing rights struggle had added an extra dimension to her character. Jesse liked her a lot better than he liked the well-groomed BIA Indians floating by.

"I'm getting tired of just going around with Lucas, my buddy here," said Jesse. "I've heard all of his old jokes and besides, he's not good looking. Maybe we can all go out together."

Lucas had been talking to another girl, a Shoshone-Bannock named Rita who had attached herself to the treaty rights group. She and Mary were acquaintances, so it worked out all right. They took off together to a little Chinese cafe a few blocks away. The food was good and the atmosphere was livened with anecdotes and jokes. Rita was one of those Indian girls who act kind of blase or indifferent at first but she turned out to be pretty smart and well informed. Mary was also quite intelligent and more openly outspoken than Rita.

Both girls were largely uninformed about the intricacies of dominant society government, economics, or politics but they were extremely knowledgeable about how such things operated at the day to day level on the reservation. They trusted no White persons whatsoever and they had no sympathy for Indians who compromised in any way. Jesse told them a little about what Art Little and Daisy Ross had been talking about. Rita's reaction was intense, "I would love to kill one of those son-of-a-bitches if I could. They have ripped us off so bad I could scream. Old people are dying and drunks get no help and young kids are committing suicide because of what they do. They're fuckin' parasites, blood suckers, feeding on other Indians. You know, I'll tell you something. I hate White people. I hate to be around them. I change completely when they come close. I just clam up because I'm afraid of what I might say. But I'll tell you something else. I hate the cock suckers that work for the BIA and the sellout Indians even more. But I don't clam up with them, I just tell them what I think."

"I feel the same way," said Mary. "When I was twelve a Whiteman tried to buy me for a lousy hundred dollars. My old man was half tempted to sell me too since he was flat broke and wanted a drink. But my mother and brothers ran that Whiteman off. The bastards have stolen all of our land, our rivers, our fish, timber, everything. Now all we want to do is get our treaty rights back and they try to kill us or beat us up – cops, game wardens, or vigilantes. It's rough to fight. We don't have any money. Lots of times there's no food. But everything's gotten better among us, except for a few sellouts. Even a lot of the guys have stopped drinking. We got more pride now, we're more together. I like that."

"Yeah, I've seen that at the traditional meetings, I've seen that together feeling," said Jesse. "It's good. That's the wave that's coming and I'm glad. I spent some time among some of these Indians who are trying hard to be White and they sure were a terrible bunch – jealous, gossiping, showing off – a bunch of drunks. Very cliquey. I never could figure any of them out."

"You mean at O.U?" asked Lucas.

"Yeah, mainly there," said Jesse.

"Well, man, as a Creek from way back in the hills I'll tell you, I never could figure out those Oklahoma Indians and I'm from Oklahoma. The Creeks are different, a lot of the eastern Oklahoma people are different. We've been neglected by the BIA for so long that most of us don't even know what it is. But some of these Oklahoma Indians, they are somethin' else. Hell, a lot of them seem to ooze BIA out of their pores. That's how they see the fuckin' world. I mean, it's hard to describe. My family, we're just Muskogee Indians and we don't ask nothin' from nobody. We don't care one damn bit about the BIA. But some Indians, they can't shit without getting the say so from some agent or superintendent."

"We got a long way to go," said Jesse. "A lot of our people have been raised to believe that the Whites are always right and that the BIA is like a great White Father, mean, ornery, crooked, and all the rest but still your father who you've got to honor and obey. They just can't bring themselves to rebel."

"Rebellion's easy in Washington," responded Mary. "The BIA has never done much for us and lots of us grew up never seeing a BIA school or even an office. We just lived out in the boondocks, fishing and logging. Besides, we all seen that the BIA was not willing to do one lousy thing to protect our fishing rights. Do you know, some of our tribes never even got reservations at all? Some tribes are not even recognized."

And so they talked on for a while. Jesse finally steered the conversation to a lighter note. "I wonder what Chinese women are like," he said. "I knew some at school but I never got to take any out."

"What kind of girls do you like, Jesse?" asked Mary.

"Girls like you. One's with bright eyes and..."

"Bushy tails?"

"No, just nice round ones," responded Jesse.

"I mean, do you like Indian girls best or White ones?"

"I'd be crazy to say White," laughed Jesse..."What about you, what kind of men do you like?"

"Strong ones. Indians, but not just any. Good looking ones, like you, and one's strong enough not to be sellouts. I don't like lushes, either. They beat you up too much...What do you do when you're not at NCAI conventions?"

"Well, I'm an artist, or at least I want to be. I also produce Indian posters to make a few bucks as well as help the movement, and I went to college for a year...Mostly I'm just kind of a wanderer, looking around, trying to figure things out."

"I just dropped out of high school. Couldn't stand it, staying in school with those rednecks while my relations were getting the shit kicked out of them. Then I lived with a guy, one of the organizers, for a while, but he got busted and left – they beat him up pretty bad in jail, so I don't blame him. Maybe I'll go to college some day. I'd like to be a lawyer so that I can throw some of their own laws up into their ugly faces! Do you think I can ever go to law school, Jesse?"

"Sure, so long as you got the desire and don't get tied up with too many kids first. You're smart enough, and your looks would win many a case."

Jesse leaned close and told her "You have nice eyes, big and deep and kind of mysterious, sort of like one of those rivers up in Washington. You're a good looking woman, and more than that, you've got strength of character. Personally, I always go for that."

Lucas and Rita, in the meantime, were carrying on their own conversation, and all four were finishing up their tea and eating fortune cookies. Satisfied, they got up to depart, now bonded together as friends, each different but yet the same. Some were more whole, some were more damaged by life, but all shared that common feeling of Indianness and what it implied. They understood each other and, to top things off, they liked each other.

There was a pow wow in the city, sponsored by the Indian Center, so the four decided to go there instead of returning to the convention. Jesse's camper was big enough for all of them and a bunch of posters too. He thought he could sell some at the pow wow. Mary, recognizing many of the posters and liking them, said she would help. She told him, "Your posters are great. I wish we had some like these up in Washington. What do the Apples think of them?"

Jesse replied, "They're scared to death of Geronimo holding the rifle, and some of the others they don't like because of the text. They don't like the one of the Black-mixed Indians from Ecuador, with the spears in their hands, or the one of Chitto Hadjo. But most of the grassroots people like them a lot."

The pow wow was a pretty big one, with a lot of out-of-towners present. For a while it went pretty well but later on the convention crowd, loaded with booze, began to get rowdy. Political enemies started to fight and would be lovers quarreled with jealous rivals. There was very little security at the pow wow and many of the older people and families left by midnight. Jesse, Lucas, and their friends kept out of trouble but it was often like tightrope walking between noisy drunks, many of whom were increasingly belligerent.

"Well, here are your middle class Indians," said Mary. "Drunk and noisy and angry. Either that or they're just crazy to get layed. I've never seen so many drunks. Money sure don't make 'em happy, does it?"

"Yeah, I'm getting kind of tired of it all. This is no way to run a pow wow. Why don't we take off?" asked Jesse.

Mary agreed, but it was a little harder to get Rita to go. She had by no means cured herself of an appetite for booze. Lucas had kept her dancing enough so that she was only a little high but, nonetheless, she was not anxious to leave since the booze had had the effect of making her largely immune to the noise and bad vibrations around them. Finally they got her outside and drove off.

"Where are we going?" asked Mary.

"I don't know, for sure," said Jesse, "but I feel an urge to get out into the country. I saw a good place the other day."

"What's out in the country? What have you got on your mind?" asked Mary.

"Just wait and see." Jesse drove out of the city to a place where a hill rose up above the surrounding countryside. He had noted the hill earlier, along with a side road that went off in that direction. The car bounced on the dirt road until he located a place to park, near the base of the knoll.

Jesse said "Okay here we are."

Mary got out but Rita said, "I don't want to go for a hike in the dark. Stay here Lucas."

Lucas stayed with her while Jesse and Mary, hand in hand, started up the hill. Jesse led the way silently, moving cautiously but surely in the moonlight. A vague trail led up to the top and Jesse could see well enough to avoid any hazards.

When they got to the top Mary said, "What a great view, in all directions. Why did we climb all the way up here, for the view?" She was poking Jesse, half teasing him since she really believed that Jesse had just wanted to find a spot where they could make love. Mary had already decided that that was what she wanted.

Jesse looked around in all directions, seeming to absorb the night into himself. He closed his eyes and let the light breeze caress him. Then he put his arm around Mary and said, "You probably gonna' think I'm some kind of fool, but here it is: I like you. I like your face, the shape of it. I like the way your teeth push out a little. If you were White, a dentist would have probably put braces on you and made them straight and plain. But now you're cute, in some way I can't describe. And your nose is a little irregular but I like that, I like the shape of your face. I like your long hair, and the way you braid it."

He put his hand lightly on her forehead, ran a finger down along her nose, and then rubbed the tips against her semi-prominent cheekbones. "And," he added, "I like the rest of you too. Your eyes are very powerful, and your lips too."

She had put her arms around him, expecting a kiss but Jesse backed off a little and said: "Because I like you I want to share something with you, so you'll understand me better...All good things come from the Creator. The Creator has done a good job with you, so I want to respect that. What I brought you up here for is so that I can share with you the gift of the beauty of this sky, and this earth, because there is nothing more important that I can give you. I'm discovering that I am a spiritual person, or at least I want to be. And I need to be out here on this hill for a while in order to clear my mind from all that boozing and noise we been in all day long. You may call me a fool. I know some militant Indians don't respect religion, just like the NCAI crowd, but that's all right. I get disoriented and depressed around those politicians and brown-nosers and I have to get out like this. Do you understand? Am I crazy to you?"

Mary pressed tight against Jesse and rested her head on his shoulder with her face against his cheek. "You are crazy, but crazy in a good way. Would making love to me help you clear your mind?" She smiled and kissed his cheek.

Jesse felt her body against him and a surge of warmth moved up through him. He kissed her on the forehead and then on the lips. "Yes, it will help me. But I just want it to be right because you're a beautiful person. I don't want it to be in the back of a car or in some closet. A beautiful person should live in beauty. Do you understand?"

It was a cool fall morning as the moon passed across the sky, shining its pale light on the hill where Jesse and Mary lay together. They didn't notice the cold nor the rapid movement of the moon. Across that chasm that separates human beings they attempted to reach, to reach out not just with hands and lips and toes but with heart and spirit and caring. Some people just try to reach out physically – just with the body, but it can't be done that way. Not that it doesn't yield a certain amount of pleasure; it's just that it seldom builds a bridge to another person by itself. Rustle of leaves, breezes blowing, caressing one's body, moon heat, mild and mystifying, lay there, listening to the world, feeling the solid earth.

Talking quietly, touching here and there, swinging around to try to grasp the meaning of all those stars, smelling her body, Pacific Coast smoked fish smelling woman, brown woman earthy warm, soft thighs, going home woman's womb smell between firm legs, sound of geese flying overhead, crossing in front of the moon.

Mary of the Salmon River, full-breasted Mary, young but ready,

Mary who's seen people die, Mary who's seen boys turn into drunks, Mary whose seen babies go hungry, Mary who has slept out on the ground for a third of her life, good Mary, young but ready.

Men, find good women like Mary and crawl back inside them, just for a little bit, to get renewed, to become healed, to have your men-wounds bandaged. She'll kiss them and make it better. But don't just crawl in by yourself. Let her crawl in too. She needs to go home for a rest just as you do. Women – brown women – are strong, made of good fiber – but they need healing too. Touch them, gently, with your smiles, laughs, eyes, spirit as well as with your body.

Gather up all those beautiful brown girls, millions of them, and hug them.

Can your arms reach that far?
Gather up those brown men and let them know you care.
They're all hurt, they're all wounded.
Love is the remedy.
Use your love like a medicine
Make people well.
Use your love like a remedy.
Make people well.
It's a sure-fire cure.
Make people well.
The true warrior dares to be gentle,
Makes someone well.

Jesse and Mary on a rising hill, whirling through space, without end, without time, without form, without shape. Spinning, spinning, spinning together, legs wrapped around each other, body sweat softly lubricating the flow, lying on the surface of a tiny spot of the tiny Mother Earth rolling around chasing herself in the sky. Jesse rolled over on his back and absorbed the sky with deep gasps of joy. The stars seemed within reach, just holes in a ramada roof, flashing, pulsating to a Forty-Niner beat. A night bird flew close by. They pulled the blanket up to wait for the dawn. Tired but drifting in an endless peace, floating on the earth's magic carpet, flying through space forever.

Many times couples hope that that moment of eternity will never end but it has to, like everything else. Spiritual in nature, it cannot be found in the physical sphere alone. Feelings in the gut surge up through the body, the skin listens and looks, the unseen world of awe and wonder presses in, a world bath. Did you ever take a shower in the world, bathed by unseen spirit particles? An orchestra of music rocks them on the hill, gently, from the belly up.

Jesse grabbed Mary and hugged her so tight it would have hurt except that she was in another sphere. Together, sharing that hill, making the ground feel good by laying on it lovingly. Hugging hard to try to squeeze into each other, to really tell the other that you care.

Wetness around now. Dew comes from somewhere to sparkle and dance for the pleasure of the sun's morning shafts of light. Little by little the stars flee before the oncoming waves of eastness. A new day has come, to look upon millions rising to peer through windows at drab gray buildings and roaring cars, millions with bad breath telling of unhealthy insides and bad thoughts telling of sick lives. But out on a hill without a name the sun found two whose eyes were smiling.

Truly those who are born again are born out on Mother Earth's caressing skin, in love, or prayer, or dawn happy joy. It's all there, outside of buildings, and it's all sacred.

Time is a healer, but love is faster.

RED BLOOD

CHAPTER SIXTEEN: RAMONA

In spite of the tribal officials in expensive suits, in spite of the self promoters, and in spite of the boozing BIA Indians, in spite of all the inconsistencies, Jesse could sense at the convention that a great change was taking place.

In 1966-1967, the Johnson administration had launched a terrible assault on Native People, involving the infamous Omnibus Bill which would have made Indian lands mortgageable, the giving away of mineral deposits at ridiculously low prices, and the appropriation of tribal water rights. The attack had the impact of forcing Indians to close ranks.

Now, for the first time really, the NIYC-style 'militants,' the Northwest fishing rights groups, the tribal council types, and the recognized national leaders were forced to act together. Even the latter were using terms like 'Red Power' and 'Indian Power.' The Johnson administration bureaucrats and arrogant 'planners' had succeeded where all else had failed.

Of course the true traditionalists were still too 'radical' for most of the others, but superficially, Indian people were united as never before. Jesse was glad to hear some of the young NIYC leaders talking in a nationalistic way. Some of them had matured a great deal, he thought. He especially thought that Clyde Warrior had become a very deep thinker but then Warrior had always been unusual, going to the South to work in the Negro civil rights movement for example. Warrior seemed to understand the true nature of colonialism, a concept many of his friends had not comprehended yet.

Jesse read some of Warrior's words: "Indians must introduce into this sickroom of stench and anonymity some fresh air of new Indianness, a fresh air of new Indian idealism, a fresh air of new 'greater Indian America.' How about it? Let's raise some hell!...This will not come about without nationalistic pride in one's self and one's kind."

Warrior also denounced those Indians who were being bought off with government jobs, a direct reference not only to Art Little types but also to some of his old NIYC comrades who still hoped to 'take over' the system.

Warrior emphasized that it was the 'system' that was the problem. "We Indians are beginning to see that the only way to change it is to destroy it. And to build something else." Most Indians, it seemed to Jesse, were not ready, however, to destroy the BIA. They just wanted to get it to do what they wanted, and to profit from contracts, grants, and jobs. So Indian unity was somewhat more apparent than real, after all.

Hanging around the edges were the Art Littles, cynically waiting to pick up the pieces from new programs created by the government in response to militant protests.

After the convention finished, Jesse was tempted to go with Mary to Washington. The thing that stopped him was bad news that he heard from a Delaware delegate. His maternal grandfather had broken a leg while trying to round up a horse and complications had set in. So Jesse said goodbye to Mary, promised to try to get up to Washington one day, and set out with El Sabio for eastern Oklahoma.

Something made him change course en route, however, and he drove down to the Big Deer farm hoping to find out from Ramona's uncle what had happened to her. He felt strange as he parked in front of the house, since the whole place seemed different. When he knocked on the door an unknown Indian face appeared and his heart fell to the ground.

"I'm looking for Rolly Big Deer or Ramona Big Deer," Jesse said in a voice that sounded queer, even to himself.

The woman responded: "They ain't no Big Deer's here anymore. Mister Big Deer died some time ago." She volunteered no further information and Jesse just stood there, shaken.

Finally, he asked: "Did you buy the place or are you renting?"

The lady replied: "Oh, this is restricted land. Can't be sold. We're just renting."

Jesse now saw a glimmer of hope. "Who do you pay the rent to. I'm trying to locate Ramona Big Deer and her aunt, Elsie Collins. They're friends of mine." He found out that the renters sent Elsie Collins a check every month in Oakland, California.

The woman also remembered having seen Ramona and Melinda but didn't know where they were. "I do believe though that they both went back to California with Mrs. Collins."

So Jesse at least had a new address in Oakland. That was something to go on. Finally, just as he was about to leave he turned and asked, "Mind if I drive up around the hill there. I used to have a camp there."

She said she didn't mind so he went to get in the truck. He had started the motor when the lady waved to him to come back. "What's your name, young man?"

"Jesse Rainwater," he answered.

"Well, I have a letter for you. Why didn't you tell me your name? I would have remembered right off."

Jesse didn't open the letter. He drove up to the old camp, gave El Sabio a chance to drink from the creek, and just kind of treasured the letter as if it were an object in itself, not something to be opened and read.

All kinds of ideas ran through his head: "Maybe Ramona is married. Maybe she has another guy. This might be a goodbye letter. I guess I have expected it anyway. I've had lots of other women so why should I expect her to still be single."

So Jesse sat down under the ramada, let the spirit of the old camp take hold of him. Finally he got up the courage to open the letter and read:

"Dear Jesse, I'm so terribly sorry that you came all the way to Oakland and didn't find us. We must have almost passed each other. Uncle Rolly was sick and Aunt Elsie and I both felt that we should go back to take care of him. When we got there he told us you had been there. I felt so bad! Uncle Rolly said you had gone up to the camp and wandered all over, so I went up there too. I could feel that you had been there, do you believe that? I really could. I almost expected to see you. Anyway, it was good to be close to you again.

Uncle passed away after a time and we have rented the house. I asked Mrs. Brown who will be living here, to give you this letter and the picture. The picture was taken of Melinda and me in Oakland. Anyway, we're going back to California in a day or two.

I've gotten your letters here at uncle's. I don't know where you are now but I hope our paths will cross again. I've just written notes to Ladell and to your parents. I will send my new address in Oakland to them as soon as we get a place.

In some ways it seems like years and years since I've seen you.

Jesse, I was sad not to see you after you got out of the army.

Anyway, I guess that by now you have your own life to live. I know the army bothered you. Maybe it takes a while to adjust to being out, especially these days. Everything is so upside down! And being separated for a long time changes people, I know. We were both very young with a lot of growing to do. Talking about growing! Melinda is really a big girl now. She still talks about you.

I have been growing too. Not just physically. I like school and I'm anxious to get back to Oakland. Jesse, a whole new world has opened up to me. I've gotten interested in poetry and I have written some poems. I'll show them to you someday.

Jesse, I know that during all the time we've been apart - you must have had other girl friends. I don't want that to stand between us. There may be other things that will keep us on different paths, but that shouldn't be one of them. Of course, if you've come to love someone else more than me, that would be different. They say that separation makes the heart grow fonder. I know now that that has been true for me!

Are you real Jesse? Or are you only an idea in my mind, a dream, or a spirit that haunts me.

Love, Ramona."

Jesse sat for a while, trying to get his emotions under control. Then he remembered the picture and ran the entire way to the house. Mrs. Brown had forgotten about it, but in a few minutes she located it and gave the envelope containing it to Jesse. He trotted back to the ramada and settled down to have a look.

Ramona was not just a country high school girl anymore. The colored snapshot revealed her as a young woman of nineteen or twenty, a rather tall well-shaped beautiful young woman. Melinda had grown remarkably, it seemed to Jesse, but she was three or four years old now. She looked a lot like her mother, especially the big, round eyes.

Jesse looked at Ramona carefully. He noticed that her breasts were fuller, more developed. Her figure seemed different somehow, too, maybe her hips had broadened some, he thought. She looked exquisitely beautiful, with a sweet smile and her long, wavy black hair hanging down on one side. She had a red flower in her hair, a rose probably, which set off her deep brown color to good effect.

Ramona's face revealed something of the liveliness and vitality of her character. Jesse thought about a lot of the little things that had made him love her, both as a sister-like friend and as a woman.

But he also thought briefly of Loretta, and Mary. He even thought back to other girls he had liked. How did one sort it all out?

Anyway, he had to get to his grandparent's house as soon as possible, so he reminisced a little longer while eating a cold meal. Then he took off for Delaware country.

Jesse's parents and kin were all glad to see him. If they wondered what he had been doing they didn't say anything or ask any questions. Jesse was glad to find that his grandfather was doing a little better. The leg was healing well thanks to the help of a Delaware lady who specialized in herbs.

One of the first things that Jesse did was to try to call Ramona on the phone. Failing in that, he wrote a long letter, promising to come to Oakland as soon as he could save up some money and safely leave. He also sent her a couple of his recent paintings, ones that he hadn't sold because they meant a lot to him, and a snapshot of himself squatting next to El Sabio. Jesse wanted her to see if she liked his hair long and if he had changed otherwise.

Jesse's grandfather, as he got stronger, wanted to spend a lot of time with Jesse. He wanted to talk about what was happening to the Delawares.

"It makes me sad to look around and see what is going on. The younger people don't want to talk Indian any more. All they think about is money. You know, we have what is called a claims case for money the government owes us for lands in Kansas and other places. They won't give us our tribe back or our reservation. They claim we're just Cherokees now, which isn't true. We signed a treaty with them that guaranteed that if we moved here from Kansas we would get a reservation of our own. We agreed to that treaty and came here, paying for all of this land with our own money. The Cherokees gave us nothing. We paid for it. Anyhow, they won't give us our reservation. It's all gone, allotted, they say, so that's that. But to talk about the claims case. Since we might get some money Delawares are popping up all over like toadstools! They say there are probably thousands eligible for a share! Where are they? I never seen them. They never help us. They don't come to meetings. Anyway, they're going to put in a claim. I reckon it's not wrong to accept money that's rightfully yours but Jesse, I'm not going to take any. I ain't going to let the government get off the hook that easy! When they pay us off, watch out! That will be the day they'll say none of us are Indians anymore. I won't hold anything against someone taking money who really needs it, but I'm not going to take it anyhow."

On other occasions grandfather talked about keeping the Lenápe language alive. He wanted Jesse to learn it better and to learn also about the old ceremonies and the songs. Jesse got out a tape recorder and spent much of his time recording what he heard. He was anxious to do what his grandfather wanted but he knew he would not be able to learn everything right then.

Jesse also did some painting. For the first time, he painted scenes of Delaware life, of ceremonies, and everyday things. He copied old photographs in some cases or got his ideas from the drawings of a Shawnee artist, Spybuck, who had painted the Big House around 1930. But Jesse also sketched from his grandfather's description, putting down the old man's memories, as it were, in a visual form.

To make some money he sold posters. He couldn't sell any of his Lenápe paintings, but he sent a couple to Ladell so that they could be copied.

A letter came from Ramona. She was very happy that he had found her note and that he was painting. She said she liked the ones he had sent and had put them up in her bedroom and in the living room. "I liked the snapshot too," she said. "Your dog looks very wise, indeed. I'm glad he is helping to take care of you. Oh yes, I like your hair and, of course, you too. You seem more handsome than before." She was looking forward to his coming, whenever he could get away.

New Year's came and passed and Jesse became increasingly anxious. Finally, Ladell sent him a check to cover money she felt was due to Jesse from the poster business. So Jesse prepared to leave, since his grandfather was better. He had to wait through a January blizzard but as soon as the roads were clear he started out, driving west between storms.

From Arizona Jesse angled as directly as possible towards Oakland, having to put on chains only over Tehachapi Pass. The long trip gave him many hours to think about Ramona and his future. He realized that Ramona had first introduced him to the mystery of a woman's love. Why, then, had he lived with Loretta and loved Mary as well?

It occurred to him that each was certainly unique and individual. But they were all women of great inner strength and solidness. They all had the depth of character to go on living and growing through crises and hardships. All of them had known hard work and poverty. For none of them was Jesse the first lover, at least in a physical sense.

Jesse felt that he might have been happy to have lived for a lifetime with Loretta. He wasn't sure about Mary, having known her for such a short time. But his love for Ramona was deeper, more enduring it seemed. "I guess I'm the kind of guy who can love more than one woman, but still, and at the same time, love one more deeply than the others. Or maybe it's that I love them differently. Some I can allow just to become a beautiful memory, but Ramona is too much, too powerful just to be remembered."

As Jesse neared Oakland he became increasingly nervous and agitated, as well as happy and elated. "I feel like I'm going on my first date." Then, "I feel like I'm coming directly home to Ramona from the army, and I don't know whether to shake her hand or kiss her. Wow!"

Ramona, for her part, was also nervous. Jesse had sent a telegram from Oklahoma so she knew he was coming at last. She knew, from her intense joy and the upheaval in her stomach, that her old feelings for Jesse were still very much alive. Would he have changed? She didn't know what to do. Should they sleep together in her bedroom? She desperately wanted to be in his arms but...well that would all depend on him.

Jesse stopped at a gas station outside of Oakland to feed El Sabio and to study a city map. He located Ramona's new place on the map and soon arrived there, legs rubbery, nearly exhausted, but supremely happy.

Little Melinda, refusing to sleep, watching out the window, was the first to see the truck pull up. She opened the door and ran outside to put her arms around Jesse's legs, crying "Jesse's here, Jesse's here, remember me, I'm Melinda." Jesse picked her up in his arms and she put hers around his neck. As he walked with her towards the door Ramona appeared. Her mouth was formed into a smile that told Jesse much more than words. The only word she uttered, was "Jesse," before he had her in his arms, still holding Melinda but finding a place for her as well. Jesse kissed both of them and then set Melinda down, telling her to go let El Sabio out. Then he took Ramona to his breast again, squeezing her as if to crush her, kissing her hard on the lips, and just letting the tears flow. Where their faces were pressed together two sets of tears met and mingled, forming little streams, but neither noticed.

In the touch of her body against his, so tightly pressed together that they seemed as one, in that physical and emotional contact he felt a surge of sheer elemental love, a kind of overwhelming power such as he had never known before, even with this very same Ramona. But she wasn't the same, and he wasn't the same, and their coming together could not be just a repetition of what had been before.

Red Blood

Chapter Seventeen: Sacred Oceans and Mountains

Jesse looked at Ramona for a long time, letting his mind absorb every part of her. She was sitting on a beachtowel, with her back against a large, water smoothed rock. They had just finished playing in the ocean surf and her exceptionally smooth brown skin was still flecked with droplets of water. Her eyes were closed and her breasts were gently rising up and down.

Jesse looked at her feet. Ramona had nice feet, not small but well made, very athletic although still feminine and, to him, strangely exciting. He liked the transition of colors, from pinkish underneath, to light tan, to deep, dark brown on top. Jesse imagined his hands holding her feet tight, as he had the night before. He almost got up and crawled over by her side in order to feel them again.

But as he looked at her body, Jesse realized that as fine as it was, as exciting to him as it seemed, it was Ramona, the person, who moved it, guided it, and, more than that, made it worth being with.

The world is full of beautiful women, thought Jesse, millions upon millions of them, all types, all colors, all shapes and sizes. But although they might be beautiful to look at, and although their smiles might attract you for a time, ultimately the inner nature of the person dominated all. Jesse had learned that. It was Ramona's inner self that made her outer garments of skin and hair worth being with for the rest of his life.

They had a lot of time to talk and as Ramona told Jesse of her life in Oakland, of her classes, of Melinda's adventures, of her artistic and intellectual discoveries, and as she read him her poems, he was fascinated not by the outer Ramona but by the inner one.

He understood now why he had been in awe of Ramona back on the Big Deer's farm. Her lithe, teenage beauty had, of course, seized hold of him. But more than that something vital, strong, elemental in her nature had forced him to treat her as an extraordinary person It was hard to pin down. Jesse tried to sort out Ramona's strengths but they blended together. But from her spiritually centered grandparents she had absorbed the heart of Native religion, the deep compassion for all living things, the absolute honesty, and a finely tuned sensitivity to the vibrations sent out by other people, creatures, and even trees and plants.

Ramona had also known a great deal of prejudice, a lot of poverty, and, for a time, had suffered from loneliness and confusion. But finally, thanks to the quiet examples of the elders, and their certain love, she had used those experiences of pain and disappointment to become part of her storehouse of wisdom and feelings.

Above all, Ramona was a nurturing woman. In this she was not unique, of course. But the magic of womanhood which she possessed was immensely strengthened by her other qualities and by the harmony of her thoughts and actions.

Jesse recognized that in many respects her intelligence, her mind, was superior to his. Above all, she had an intuitive understanding which often exceeded his. He was sure that she had always understood his nature, his needs, better than he had.

The sound of sea gulls flying overhead reminded Jesse of the mystery that the sea coast had always had for him. He looked again at Ramona, naked there beside the ocean, and felt that his life had come full circle. He was happy that Ramona loved to look at his naked body as much as he liked hers. She was a naturally sexual person, not one who had to be artificially stimulated or released from inhibitions by suggestive dancing or pornography. Like most Indians, at least the older ones, sex had always been part of life, just as it was part of theirs.

Jesse got up, stretched, washed himself in the cold ocean water and walked over to sit beside Ramona. She had opened her eyes to watch him and reached out her hands to massage his wet body. He closed his eyes and whispered, "Ramona." Very shortly, together, they set forth once again on that magic search for merging which the Creator has imprinted within the souls of most men and women.

After a time, deeply satisfied and in an especially receptive state, the two lovers lay next to each other on the sand and allowed the ocean, the shiny smooth ever-changing spots on the water surface, the rock ribs of former cliffs now surrounded by water, the shorebirds digging in the wet sand, and ever-crying gulls, and the smells of sea breezes, all of these things, and more, to seep into them directly, not through eyes alone but through all the senses, and not just the physical senses but others as well, intuitive and mystical.

It was warm on the sand, a thing very unusual for that time of year. But the normal rains had given way to a few warm, sunny days and it was the best kind of weather for the coast, clear as a bell, with no fog. Jesse and Ramona had decided to go off together, where they could be totally absorbed in each other, totally alone. So they had driven up the coast until locating a supremely private cove, reached only by a steep trail. Packing a picnic lunch, they had come early, hoping to spend the full day.

In the late afternoon it began to cool down and Jesse gathered firewood. They put on their clothes and made a pot of coffee on the fire. Then, refreshed, they walked up and down the beach examining the little stones and broken sea shells. Jesse saw many that could be polished and used in necklaces or earrings.

As evening came on the two bundled up together, sat by the fire and ate leftovers from lunch and drank hot coffee. Together, holding hands, they watched Gishux, the Day Sun, descend and then they both offered prayers of thanks for all the gifts of the Creator. Both Jesse and Ramona felt intensely happy, incredibly fulfilled, indefinably stimulated. For that moment, they were all alone in the world.

They hadn't talked a great deal since arriving on the beach but now Jesse felt the need to give voice to things he had been thinking about.

"Ramona, I may not be ready to settle down in one place. It seems like I still have some wandering, or we'll say, exploring to do. But I know now that I don't want to do it alone anymore. I want us to be together. I want to share my life with you, and to share yours."

"Jesse, I feel the same way. I want to share everything with you from now on. And I also want to travel, go places. For example, I've long wanted to go down to Mexico to see where the Seminoles went under old Wildcat. And I've always wanted to see the old Shawnee homeland in Ohio, the Great Serpent Mound and all of that. But, of course, I also want to finish my studies and provide some stability for Melinda."

"I feel like we're married already, but I want us to get married in the eyes of others too," said Jesse.

"I guess you know how I feel," Ramona responded. "At least you should! I feel like we are married too. If you want to get married officially, that would make me happy... Can we be married by a medicine woman or a Peyote man? Would we have to go back to Oklahoma to do that?"

"Maybe not. We'll have to ask around to see what we can do. Anyway, Ramona Rainwater! I now pronounce you my wife by virtue of the power vested in me by... love." They were both very happy.

On their way back to Oakland they talked about housing. It was very convenient to live with Aunt Elsie but the house was a little crowded since other relatives were also there now. The ideal solution was to try to get an apartment nearby or to find a larger house where everybody could move.

"You know what?" confided Ramona. "I would really like to have a place to sell paintings and posters, and maybe books – kind of an Indian art gallery and bookstore. Maybe we could talk Aunt Elsie into going 50/50 and we could rent, or maybe buy, a large older house with commercial potential."

Jesse was enthusiastic. "I could maybe borrow some money from Dewey."

Ramona liked the idea the more she mulled it over: "Well, we can talk with Aunt Elsie. She might like to have a permanent place to live, with plenty of room, and everybody could work in the store."

Aunt Elsie was enthusiastic at the idea of buying a house, so they looked around and pooled their resources. They located a large house with a big, dry basement on a busy street near the Oakland-Berkeley line. A variance was obtained, allowing for partial commercial use, and the basement was converted. The front two-thirds was turned into a gallery and store while the back part became a storeroom and studio. It took some time, but one of Ramona's cousins helped Jesse with the carpentry.

The house had several apartments so Jesse, Ramona and Melinda were able to live together, with their own indoor kitchenette, for the first time. However, they usually still shared dinners with the rest of the household.

Eventually the gallery did pretty well. It had no competition in the immediate area and they were able to get some Indian artists to place their work on consignment. Books, records, tapes, posters, bumper stickers, and some jewelry also helped to cover costs. Financially, the entire operation was only modestly successful but the 'profit' plus the rent they all would have been paying anyway was together enough to cover the monthly mortgage payment as well as to repay Dewey.

The Many Tribes Native American Gallery was successful in another sense. Family members worked there, including Aunt Elsie and Melinda, so Ramona and Jesse weren't tied down. They had time for classes, individual projects, and short trips to the beach or redwood forests. Poetry readings at the gallery also added to the enrichment of their lives.

That year, 1968, was a very exciting one in the Bay Area. The anti-war groups, leftist organizations, Black and Chicano groups, and the "Hippies" all were extremely active. Native Americans were also being quite active and such Indian groups as the California Indian Education Association, the Oakland American Indian Association, the American Indian Historical Society, and a small committee of NIYC were all operating in the region.

Jesse and Ramona went to several meetings, especially enjoying the education association because it enabled them to meet native California Indians from several tribes. The ceremonies and dances of the California tribes were unique, quite different from what they were familiar with.

Jesse and Ramona talked at some length about their future plans. Jesse said, "I'm a pretty good painter I guess, but I'm still a novice when it comes to really getting across the human face or the body, for that matter. I need to study more than just so-called Indian art. I'm getting some good instruction now but Rufus suggested that I go down to Mexico City also. Your interest in Mexico brought it to my mind again. What do you think? How about next year in Mexico? You could go to school down there if you wanted to."

Ramona was excited. She wanted to visit Coahuila of course and also the great Indian ruins and see the Aztec floating gardens at Xochimilco. It would give her a chance to study Mexican literature, a new interest after taking a Chicano course which included translations of Aztec and Maya poems and songs.

"I guess that means that Melinda's little brother will have to be born in Mexico," she said, with a half-suppressed smile. "I think I'm carrying a child, and I want it to be a boy. Oh Jesse, I wasn't going to tell you until I was absolutely sure, but, well, I just blurted it out!"

Jesse was excited. "That's wonderful!" He kissed her tenderly, and hugged her rather gently. She laughed and squeezed him hard. "I don't care, boy or girl, it's all right with me. I want lots of little Indians around. But maybe we should postpone the trip until after you have the baby, so you have Aunt Elsie and your cousins around."

"Don't worry," she said. "Women have had babies without others to help before. Besides I can stay at home and you'll be there to help."

Jesse was elated at the idea of being a father but it was excitement more at the idea of pregnancy and birth rather than fatherhood since he had already grown to regard Melinda as his daughter. In fact little Melinda had already started calling him 'Daddy' instead of Jesse. That had pleased him greatly and he wanted to legally adopt her later on.

Jesse was also excited about the idea of going to Mexico because he dreamed of introducing Ramona and Melinda to Antonio Chavis, either at his place in the desert or in Mexico, if he could be located.

During the spring break the whole family, in two cars, drove to Nevada so that Jesse and Ramona could be married by a Peyote road chief. A wedding license was obtained and the Peyote man signed the document after completing the ceremony. Then Ramona, Jesse and Melinda honeymooned in Nevada.

On the trip Jesse voiced another dream to Ramona. "You know, I have been thinking that one day I'd like to study filmmaking. I've got some ideas for films. Do you think that's crazy?"

"Here, Jesse, this is crazier still. I might want to take up the guitar! I've always liked music and the idea came to me. And why don't you and I write some songs? The Indian movement needs songs and films. What do you think? Or am I a perpetual girl always looking for something new? And while I'm on it, I want to study playwriting some day. We need our own plays too!"

"That's one reason I love you. You're so much like a young girl - enthusiastic and always exploring, experimenting, creating. I like that. So don't worry about being crazy. The only thing is, it takes a lot of time and dedication to become really good at anything, as I'm discovering with my painting. Lots of Indian artists just kind of quit learning at a certain stage. I don't want to do that. But I've got time to learn some other things, since I quit drinking and don't watch TV. I can't make love to you all the time, though some times I try. And I can't paint all the time."

"Well, I'm going to get a guitar when we're in Mexico."

"You know honey, there's an instrument that interests me."

"What is it, Jesse?"

"The marimba. It's like the...what do they call it? Oh yes, the xylophone. But the Maya Indians of Central America play it. You've heard it, haven't you?"

"Yes. Hey, it would go well with the guitar. We could have a family band. 'Big Deer Rainwater Rock'!"

So they dreamed about a lot of things that they could do. And none of them were impossible, because once you eliminate going to bars or sitting around watching television you find that there is a lot of time for doing the things you really want to do, provided that you're not exhausted from some miserable job.

Later in the spring Jesse got back to Nevada to meet some of the traditional Shoshones and Paiutes who were trying to fight the claims case issue. What it amounted to was that the U.S. government had neglected to sign any treaties of cession with the Nevada tribes, as well as with those of California and southern Arizona. So under U.S. constitutional law the Indian tribes still possessed their Aboriginal titles intact. But in 1946 the Congress had established the Indian Claims Commission to provide token money payments for all Native claims. Some tribes, like the Delaware, were just being paid compensation for having been cheated but the western tribes had never ceded their lands in the first place.

The traditional Indians were convinced that they still were the bonafide owners of most of Nevada and that it would be a betrayal of their religion to accept money for Mother Earth. One old man said, "The lawyers appointed for us by the BIA tell us that we have to agree to accept whatever the government wants to give us. They say we already lost this land but how did we lose it? We never sold it. We never gave it away. We never agreed to anything. So how could we lose it?"

Jesse was deeply impressed by the character of the traditional people. Most were very poor and without formal education, but they were wise and deeply spiritual. They seemed to be willing to fight to the bitter end.

Jesse started a series of paintings to help the Nevada struggle. One was an outline of the State of Nevada with a sign on it saying: "Indian Country: Not For Sale!" Standing beside the sign was an Indian man and an Indian woman, with children at their feet and a baby in the woman's arm. This painting was reprinted as a poster.

Jesse also painted a picture of Sarah Winnemucca, a Paiute leader of the 1860s - 1880s, chasing crooked BIA agents who were trying to cheat her people. Another picture in the series showed old Shoshone Chief Temoke refusing to agree to sell Mother Earth to an avaricious-looking Uncle Sam. Still another showed traditional Indians heaping scorn on BIA Indians in dress suits whose pockets were stuffed with money.

Jesse and Ramona also went to a lot of Native gatherings in the

Bay Area. Ramona had made, with her aunt's help, a beautiful fringed dress and a ribbon shirt for Jesse, in the old Delaware style. Melinda also had a little outfit of her very own.

Jesse loved to watch Ramona dance. She moved along gracefully with a shawl on her arm, or over her shoulders, and her hair was usually braided for such occasions. He never tired of watching her. There was something so feminine yet so strong and steady about her as she moved. Sometimes, at home, she did the male war dance steps just for fun (as a lot of younger girls were doing in public) but at the dances she always used the more traditional women's steps.

It seemed to Jesse as if she was growing in radiant beauty all the time. Perhaps the child she was carrying made her more lovely, or maybe it was Jesse's love reflected back.

Ramona also thought Jesse more handsome than ever, his hair growing longer and his face and body maturing. But then, he was more of a man and his growth in character was being reflected in his stronger facial lines.

It was a happy period for Ramona and Jesse. Hard creative work, worthwhile struggle, and lots of love proved to be a combination conducive to a great deal of inner satisfaction.

On several occasions they went back to Nevada and heard new evidence of the resolve and strength of the traditional people. At one meeting a young Shoshone woman said, "If we go along with this claims case we won't just be getting some money we will be selling our homeland.

No, I can't believe that 35 cents or less per acre can ever compensate the taking of a homeland away from our Native Indians. You cannot measure a country in dollars and cents."

Another Indian, a religious leader, said, "The land was made for people to live on, not to sell. The Creator would get angry at the Indian if he wanted to sell Mother Earth. Mother Earth provides for the Indian and keeps people alive today.

There still are mountains that wait for Indians who really believe in the Great Spirit's ways to get power. Are we going to sell those mountains for pieces of green paper? I ask you, let us think on it seriously."

RED BLOOD

CHAPTER EIGHTEEN: VIEWS FROM PYRAMIDS AND MESAS

Jesse looked to the north. There stood the Pyramid of the Moon and a series of broad avenues flanked by numerous small temples or pyramids. To the west he saw the temple of Quetzalcoatl and a complex collection of structures. To the east he gazed upon a broad valley and then the peaks of the Sierra. Popocatépetl and Ixtacíhuatl, the sacred mountains, stood before him as he swung towards the southeast and south.

Jesse felt a little dizzy. Perhaps it was the elevation or the climb up to the top of the Pyramid of the Sun. Ramona had sat down with Melinda on the broad surface of the pyramid's top and Jesse joined them.

He thought about this vast sacred city of Teotihuácan, the greatest religious ceremonial center in the history of the world. It was incredible that this fantastic place, built almost 2,000 years before, and enduring for five times as long as the United States, should be completely ignored in North America.

Jesse thought about the many hundreds of thousands of Indians who must have devoutly labored to build the pyramids, and then to make them even higher. He thought about the Cahokia Mound in Illinois and how the same impulse must have motivated these ancient Mexicans. They must have been a mountain people who, after moving into the valley, felt the need to erect artificial peaks for seeking visions and praying.

City of the Spirits. Was it still a sacred place? Did Mexicans still really worship there? Or had it been 'dead' for so long that it now only served as a symbol of past national greatness? Jesse wished that all Indians could come there so that they could see for themselves what the Native People were capable of doing. But later

Jesse remarked to Ramona, "You know, I'm really impressed by all of this, and yet, as I think about it, these huge monuments are not nearly as important as the most enduring monument of all, the Indian personality."

"What do you mean, Jesse?"

"I mean, the Indians that we've met so far down here, in Coahuila, in San Luis Potosí, and everywhere, are very much alike. They are so courteous, so honest, so respectful of others, so non-aggressive. And I would guess from what we've seen and read, so democratic and spiritual, just like the old Indians at home. What I mean is that the basic Indian character seems to be the same everywhere. Sure, some tribes may be more extroverted, full of jokes and so on, but basically they're still courteous, democratic, and non-aggressive, except, of course, when alcohol interferes."

"Jesse, there seems to be a basic Native American style of behavior which is based on deep humility and a respect for all forms of life. That's what makes Indian villages free and democratic, because democracy has to come out of that kind of respect. Of course, the so-called Mestizos are often different, especially the more Spanish-looking ones. But you remember how, in that one place, the elders were conducting a meeting? It was just like up at home," noted Ramona.

"I'll bet Indians are the same all the way through South America."

"But what about the big empires around here?" asked Ramona. "The books say that they were ruled by powerful kings who were authoritarian."

"That really puzzles me," replied Jesse. "All these Indians seem democratic today. They are jealous of their autonomy and have councils that decide matters, in consultation with the community. Now, the puzzle is how could they have become democratic? The Spaniards certainly didn't teach them. The Mexican government didn't teach them."

"But this contradicts what the anthropologists tell us about ancient Mexico, doesn't it?" asked Ramona.

"Yes, my guess is that the Spaniards exaggerated the authority of the Aztec rulers in the same way that the English used to call every chief a king in Virginia and New England. Later, the descendants of the leading Indians tried also to exaggerate their ancestor's authority in order to prove that they were entitled to be treated as nobility or royalty by the Spaniards."

"And since many Spaniards married girls from such families

175

they would have had an interest along the same lines," interjected Ramona.

"In any case, it's a puzzle. But you can't dispute the fact that the Indians, as they are today, would never think of conquering anyone or obeying a dictator if they could help it."

Evening was approaching, so Jesse, Ramona, and Melinda carefully descended the narrow steps and ate a picnic dinner at the truck.

On the whole, they were really enjoying their stay in Mexico. At first they had stayed at Casa de los Amigos, a residencia operated by the Society of Friends. Then they located a residencia in Tacubaya, not too far from the university, where a very pleasant Mexican family lived with a small number of guests. Ramona did not have to cook there and she was free to take a course in Mexican Indian literature at an English language school while Jesse studied art. She also could do a lot of reading and writing and practice Spanish with the Mexican lady, Señora Ugarte, and her children. As soon as she improved her Spanish she planned other courses of study.

They found the other guests very cordial. One was a Maya scholar who taught at the university. Another was a student specializing in archaeology. Still another was a struggling filmmaker, trying to produce innovative films. Since they often ate dinner together it was a chance for Jesse to learn a great deal. Ramona also participated in the conversations, and her Spanish improved rapidly.

Unfortunately, their arrival in the fall corresponded with a great deal of student unrest. The students were asking for reforms in Mexican politics to allow for greater democratic participation. Jesse was an interested observer but he and Ramona were warned to be careful. It was suggested that the police and right wing gangs might attack them because of Jesse's long hair and student status. When army troops briefly occupied the colleges, Jesse stayed away, and then on October 2, the troops attacked a peaceful student meeting at the plaza of Tlatelolco. At least 325 students were brutally gunned down and thousands more were injured or arrested.

Jesse and Ramona had almost gone to the gathering but her advanced stage of pregnancy caused them to stay at home. It was a terrible event, deeply shocking to everyone in the residencia. They wondered if the students and minorities in the U.S. weren't to be in for the same thing in the future.

In any case, the massacre of Tlatelolco taught them and many others about the real nature of the Mexican government and made them rather cautious for a time. They traveled to school with friends and that only after the arrests had stopped.

The horrible details of the slaughter stuck in Jesse's mind, as if he had seen it all personally. He heard the story so many times from eyewitnesses that he actually had nightmares about being trapped, with Ramona and Melinda, in the hysterical throng, trying to escape the soldier's guns.

Finally, Jesse worked on a painting, one reflecting a fact which had become apparent to him after observing the Mexican army and newsreels of Che Guevara's death in Bolivia. The soldiers were virtually all Indians in both Bolivia and Mexico while the officers were mostly Whites or light Mestizos.

Jesse's painting was a double feature, with a diagonal break dividing the two halves. On one side Andean Indian troops and White officers were executing Che Guevara. On the other half, Mexican Indian soldiers, ordered by White officers, were shooting into the Tlatelolco crowd. On the diagonal divider Jesse painted these words: "Indians can shoot to kill: It's too bad that Whitemen tell them where to aim." Jesse didn't show that painting to very many people for quite some time.

As conditions improved, Jesse, Ramona, and Melinda visited most of the museums and archaeological sites in the region. They also managed longer bus trips to Mitla and Monte Alban in Oaxaca and to Pazcuaro in Michoacán. Everywhere, they made it plain that they were Indians and proud of it. Many people reacted strangely at first, since they were neither poor nor in sandals. But they were able to meet a lot of Mexicans who were proud of their Indian identity and they shattered some stereotypes, at least for a few.

In addition to studying painting, Jesse produced a series of posters for sale to Mexican Indians. The latter featured heroes such as Cuautémoc, the last Aztec leader, and great culture figures such as Quetzalcóatl. With the help of friends, the text was written in Spanish, Mexicano, Maya, Tarasco, and Otomí.

Ramona slowed down a bit as the child inside her became larger. Finally, in October, a fine healthy baby boy was born. He was named Chitto Hadjo Antonio Rainwater after Antonio Chavis and Chitto Hadjo. They had thought of naming him Andrew but Dewey had already named a son after their father so Ramona and Jesse decided on a different one.

Ramona recovered very rapidly and the baby, breastfed and happy, proved to be a pleasant child. Melinda was delighted and served as a loving older sister. The girls in the residencia as well as

Señora Ugarte also took a constant interest in little Chitto. Jesse was very proud and was happy to spend a lot of time with his son. Soon they were able to travel again, although on shorter trips.

Ramona found a guitar teacher who also lived in Tacubaya. He was an Otomí musician who played in a mariachi group but also taught guitar on the side. She made good progress, practicing regularly. Melinda became very interested and Ramona bought a small guitar similar to a ukelele for her to learn on. She took to it like a duck takes to water and received much support from Jesse. Ramona also studied Náhuatl, the language of the Aztecs, so that she could better understand the ancient poetry, while Jesse listened in and looked at her lessons.

Jesse felt that he was making progress as a painter. The great Mexican muralists were his inspiration but he also concentrated on the mastery of portraiture and background scenery. He aspired to enough versatility so that he wouldn't be limited by his own lack of skill. Still, his paintings were not copies of any Mexican artists. He almost always incorporated North American themes and his works were much admired for their originality by his fellow students and teachers.

The political situation in Mexico was bad, what with the massacre of Tlatelolco. In slaughtering hundreds of students, the Mexican government had openly revealed its ruthlessness, a ruthlessness often visited upon groups of Indians protesting land problems in remote areas, or so Jesse was told.

It seemed clear to Jesse and Ramona that the middle-class, at least in Mexico City, was doing very well for itself and had no serious interest in anything but conspicuous consumption and the imitation of U.S. and European cultures. The TV was terrible, with heavy U.S. programming along with Mexican-style love stories and 'westerns,' most with little social content and almost all featuring peroxided blonde heroines or Caucasian-looking actors.

Many of the students and 'intellectuals' Jesse and Ramona talked with had no conception of the Native culture having any value. They saw the non-aggressiveness and conservativism of the villages as detrimental to Mexico's 'modernization.' They had little concept of decentralized democracy or of self-determination for minority ethnic groups. It was clear that if the 'left' ever came to power they would try to speed up the process of 'Mexicanizing' all the Native groups and that centralized state planning would be the order of the day.

Jesse had many lively discussions with some of the students and professors he lived with or met at various places. The Maya instructor was very pro-Indian and a firm advocate of the idea of there being one Native culture in the Americas as a whole. His studies of the Maya language had convinced him that many words had been exchanged between the Inca region and Mexico and he enthusiastically traced the Maya origin of many Mexicano or Náhuatl terms.

There were many others with whom Jesse disagreed. One prominent scholar, supposedly an authority on ancient Meso-America, remarked, "I cannot see why you, as a North American Indian, should be at all concerned with the high civilizations of Mexico. The truth is that the Teotihuacanos, the Toltecas, Mayas, and so on, had nothing in common with the wild tribes. The Aztecas were, of course, originally Chichimecos, that is to say, barbarians from the north, but they intermarried and absorbed the high culture of the Toltecas. The Toltecas and Mayas, from whom we are descended, were as different from the Comanches and Apaches as the ancient Romans were from the Vikings. Totally different. Tenochtítlan or the City of Mexico, you see, was a metropolis of over 100,000 people. It was extremely modern, you could say, with a fantastically engineered water supply system, public sanitation, broad boulevards, and a highly developed governmental system. You simply cannot compare that with North America."

Jesse responded politely, "I am sure that the people of Tenochtítlan were highly advanced in material things, as well as in poetry and the arts. But it seems to me that the vast majority of villages and nations in Mexico were not quite like Tenochtítlan or Teotihuácan. The majority of the masehuales, the ordinary Indians, lived just as they did farther north, without great monuments. Still further, they resisted the conquests of the Aztecas, sometimes effectively, and then resisted the Spaniards long after Tenochtítlan was in ruins."

"That is true," replied the scholar. "But we cannot judge ancient Rome by what was going on in the simple Italian peasant villages. We must look to the accomplishments of the elites, or the ruling classes, of the large cities and ceremonial centers. It is always the same. Today, por ejemplo, we must judge Mexico by the accomplishments of the educated classes here in la ciudad, not by the campesinos out in the pueblitos. All true progress comes from the educated center. That is why we here in Mexico City, the Mestizos, are the true grandchildren of the Toltecas y Aztecas. The Indios out in el campo are grandchildren of the maseguales y mayeques, the masses and landless classes. But we, the scholars of today, are the heirs of Quetzalcóatl and Tlacaélel."

Jesse almost choked but he tried to hide his feelings. "That must be the reason that the beautiful exhibits in the museo antropológico are all treated as art objects and not as part of living cultures. Por ejemplo, the Tarasco material is not in any way made relevant to the modern Tarasco people, nor is the Tarasco language used to explain the materials. One would never know that los Tarascos continued to exist."

"You are quite correct," the scholar responded, not realizing that Jesse was playing a game with him. "The great cultures of the past do not belong to the Tarascos of today, or the Mixtecos, or los Otomíes, but to us, los Mestizos. We are the Mexican nationality of today and the logic of history indicates that all of the Indios must be absorbed into the cultura nacional."

"But won't they always remain peripheral, just as the rural Mestizos are peripheral even though they speak Castellano and, in effect, despise their indigenous roots? What I mean is, becoming part of the cultura nacional does not solve a single problem for oppressed people. It does not give them political power or wealth. True, they might be able to protect themselves slightly better from being cheated, but on the other hand, there will be more people around to cheat them since the more Mestizos there are the more aggressive entrepreneurs and adventurers there are."

The scholar was taken aback a little. "What do you mean? I do not understand. The Mestizos represent the progressive sector of the Mexican nation."

"Yes, I understand what you believe. All that I am saying is that every study I have seen of Mexican history and anthropology indicates that when villages of Indios become Mestizos the quality of life does not uniformly improve. The culture of many Mestizos is typified by a loss of the virtues of honesty, spirituality, sharing, and respect for nature and is replaced by a more exploitative, materialistic, and individualistic style of existence. From these Mestizos then come the brutal soldiers and dictators, such as Díaz and Huerta, as well as the local tyrants who are always trying to destroy the ejido system and cheat the campesinos out of their farms, as well as the corrupt police, the corrupt labor leaders, and the party of the Institutionalized Revolution officials, always looking for a bribe. Is that not so?"

The scholar paused. He was not pleased to admit that the process of destroying the Indians did not produce scholars like himself but, more often produced equally poor peasants or sharp-eyed promoters, thieves, and social hangers-on.

"Well, I must admit that the Mestizo masses are not always as well-mannered or as patient and honest as are los Indios. On the other hand, the Spaniards, whose conquest led to the present status of Mexico, were neither patient nor respectful of others. They were rough, aggressive, and overbearing, and it is those qualities that always distinguish the rulers from the ruled. Díaz, after all, did become our ruler. He could never have done that had he remained an Indian. But as a restless, rootless Mestizo, despising his own roots in fact, he was able to brutally seize and hold power. Juárez, although an Indian by birth, had to turn against his origin also in order to lead the nation. Zapata never made it, because he couldn't stop being an Indio at heart. So it is. So the Mestizo masses, restless and turbulent as they are, represent a step forward."

"You are saying, then, that people must become brutal and aggressive to become rulers and part of the elite. Does that mean that folk democracy, la democracia de los pueblos, has no place in a progressive scheme of evolution? Does it also mean that ultimately all human diversity must disappear in great national cultures and then, ultimately, in a 'world culture' of some kind?" asked Jesse.

"I have great sympathy, in theory, for folk democracy but for Mexico such is impossible. Mexico, as a weak nation, cannot tolerate internal diversity. The Mayas of the south would perhaps like to have their own republic and certainly the Yaquis, Tarahumaras, and other groups would desert the state if they could. We cannot allow that. Mexico has too much localism, regionalism, and ethnic diversity. Perhaps 10% of our people do not even speak Castellano, maybe more. That cannot be tolerated. We need the natural resources of these areas. What if the oil of the Tampico region had been left in the hands of the Huasteca? No, it would be absurd. Even today, the oil of Campeche must belong to the entire nation, not to the Mayas."

"But," responded Jesse, "does not that same argument justify the oppression of Mexicanos in the United States? Still further, does it not justify the seizure, by the U.S. of Mexico and her resources if they are needed for all North America? Where does one stop?"

"The United States of the North is fully justified in forcing all of its subjects to speak English, even though part of its territory was wrongfully taken from us. The North Americans have a right to enforce uniformity. As to the other, you cannot compare our using the oil of the Huastecas with the U.S. coming in and taking the same oil. Mexico is a state, recognized internationally, a historical entity. The Huastecas are just a peasant group with no independence since being defeated by the Aztecas, our ancestors. They have no rights, except as subjects, I should say, citizens, of the Republica Mexicana."

"I take it, then," said Jesse, "that you have a view of human social evolution which ranks highest those societies which produce centralized states, large material monuments, empires, and which, in essence, are materialistic and have an educated ruling elite. By the same token, democracies, societies without ruling elites, decentralized social systems, and those who have no interest in pyramids or skyscrapers must be viewed as lower on the evolutionary ladder, as primitive shall we say. Is that so?"

"Aha, you are trying to trap me into appearing to be anti-democratic and in being a materialist. But it won't work because I walk freely into your trap. Yes, democracy cannot work. All progress in Mexico comes when we have a highly centralized government and one which regulates all elections so that there can be no sudden changes. Furthermore, an educated elite, transmitting its superiority from generation to generation, is absolutely essential. Our Indians do not write books nor do they produce original paintings, don't forget that, my young friend."

Jesse found such discussions provocative but slightly frustrating. He had heard that the scholar was a purely political appointee to a high position who seldom did any original research himself. Most of his papers and books were actually prepared by anonymous clerks and students who worked for him and whose only hope for upward mobility depended upon the favors of such a man.

Afterwards, Ramona told Jesse what she would have liked to have said: "I wonder if you could publish so many things if you had to teach or if you had to feed your family by hard work instead of living off of a government salary. Perhaps an Indian could write books too if he had such a subsidy and all of the advantages you have had. Besides, most of your books, my friend, are crap. They add nothing new. They are biased. They are boring. They are a waste of wood pulp. So much for the educated elite in Mexico!"

But Ramona was basically very polite, so she never said such things except to Jesse or close friends.

Afterwards, Jesse often told Ramona things such as, "These damn s.o.b.'s. They are even trying to deny the Native People their own heritage! They claim it for the White ruling class. What a laugh! Señor so-and-so is practically a Spaniard, yet he claims he is the heir of Cuautémoc. And los Indios, they're just dirty dogs. It's hopeless. Mexico is hopeless. The rulers have only contempt for the masses, but they are very shrewd. They know how to make people feel inferior and how to accumulate and control wealth".

Ramona added, "Anyway, the common ordinary Mexicans, whether they talk Indian or not, are a helluva lot better people to be around than señor so-and-so. At least, one can be honest with them and expect honesty in return. But the elite is all fantasy and falseness. You notice how they all grovel over each other and coo, but then afterwards cut each other to pieces in private? They're nothing but kiss-asses trying to get a political appointment or a fake diploma. After a while they don't know who they are, all falseness and flattery."

On another occasion, Ramona had an argument with an upper-class student who believed in the evolutionary superiority of European-style materialistic societies. She exalted ancient Egypt and Rome, of course, and regarded all progress as consisting of bigger and better machines. Ramona responded, "I guess you don't respect Moses then?"

"Why do you say that?"

"Because Moses was a poor Jew, enslaved by the superior Egyptians. Obviously, the Jews were nothing but desert nomads, living in tents, a primitive tribal people."

"Yes, but they learned from the Egyptians and seized Palestine. After the conquest they set up their own small empire and built big cities like Jerusalem. So Moses, although a primitive, set the stage for their becoming civilized."

"Well, then certainly you must despise Jesus," said Ramona. "He wanted people to turn their backs on wealth and material things, and he himself was only a humble carpenter who worshipped on the top of mountains or out in the desert. Clearly, Jesus was a primitive, a throwback."

"I cannot accept that. I am a devout Catholic."

"But Jesus was very much like these Indians you despise so. He certainly was more like Zapata than he was like Díaz or any of the PRI leaders of today. Don't you agree?"

The student couldn't agree, but she really did not believe in Jesus. Her models were people who loved to drive luxury cars at high speeds, honking horns at pedestrians and literally forcing their way ahead, or avaricious middle-class men who left finely dressed pampered but dominated wives at home while they chased after mistresses, or women who spent their hours in salons or shopping, or lazy wealthy-class men who dined for hours in expensive restaurants ogling the elegantly groomed young ladies prepared for a career of serving as sex objects for los machos. So Jesus was a word, a name, a relic having absolutely no reality at all, just as in the U.S. A talisman, but one with all of its power gone!

Another student, a closer friend said, "Jesse and Ramona, you are such idealists. No one except you and maybe some Indios out in the pueblitos ranks societies any differently. Your North American anthropologists and historians all rank cultures on the basis of their material accomplishments. They don't give any attention to the quality of life in spiritual or ethical terms. And we don't know what our Indians think. You know, it's very interesting but so true. I, although of Indian blood, do not have the least idea of what goes on in the minds of Indígenas right here in el estado de Mexico, not to mention Yucatán or Chiapas. 'They' are a complete enigma and do you know why? Because we don't allow them to have a voice. It is true. We do not allow them to have a voice. We forbid it! We deny it's existence by refusing to listen and we refuse to listen because we say that there is nothing there to hear. Claro, that we bourgeois Mexicans are extremely arrogant people! Yes, I can see that. Arrogant, presumptuous, and, at heart, ignorant and malicious. Yes malicious! You see, we know full well that our exalted positions, our claims to being needed by the society, are based on a malicious denigration of the indigenous masses, los Inditos. We say they are dumb and silent, that we can speak for them, guide them, and, of course, rule them. Their suffering, in turn, makes our exalted lives possible. We are parasites feeding on the masses. But the worst crime is that we parasites have consumed their tongues and they can only speak through us, their enemies. So they are forever cursed to silence. My friends, you make me uneasy, you make all of us uneasy, because you are Indians and yet you you not silent. Your existence raises the terrible possibility that our own Indians are not dumb, only forcibly silenced, not passive, but only conquered, not unobservant, but merely ignored. Personally, I thank you, Ramona and Jesse, for what you two are teaching me."

Jesse often liked to go up the stairs in the building they lived in, to a rooftop farmyard where Señora Ugarte kept a rooster and hens along with plants. He liked to hear the rooster crow and to listen to roosters crowing all over Mexico City in the early morning. It was nice to be in a city where one could still keep a rooster.

What was progress? Was progress moving into a fancy highrise complex where even hens were not allowed? Was 'progress' the life of the rich, whatever they did, whatever they created, whatever they valued? Was progress the accumulation of material wealth and wealth displayed in the form of huge cathedrals or office buildings or monumental arches?

Jesse thought to himself that the theories of evolution expounded by White anthropologists and historians, and even by Karl Marx, were neither scholarly nor innocent. They were not scholarly because they were, in fact, simply projections of the cultural and political biases of the European mind. As cultural projections, one could not logically argue with them since they were not based upon logic but upon cultural myth or sheer emotional conviction.

But also, as Jesse saw, they were not innocent. Such theories of social evolution were used, every day, to categorize all folk and peasant societies as being backward, as being 'primitive,' that is to say, 'early' or primal. The European also saw 'early man' as being stupid, beastly, crude, and savage, so calling someone 'primitive' was not a neutral denotation. In Mexico all of this became exceptionally clear. Here there were no 'noble savages' but 'dumb Indians' who, as backward, 'early' people, had no rights of self-definition, of self-conception, or self-determination.

No, the ruling elites, macho and corrupt, believed themselves to be the supreme product of evolution with the obligation to provide the honest but simple Indians with definitions, conceptions, and determinations.

Looking out over the skyline of Tacubaya, towards the rising sun, Jesse told himself, "I see now that education is warfare. What the blancos call education is ideological aggression. It isn't just racist, or bad, or lousy, or misguided. It is conscious unadulterated cultural and class warfare. And art and literature are all part of that."

On the rooftop, watching the city come to life, Jesse had an idea. It was that Mexicans should identify with those of their ancestors who loved democracy and freedom so much that they had struggled on for hundreds of years against both Aztecs and Spaniards, peoples such as the Tarascos, Chichimecos, Huicholes, Yaquis, Mayas, and innumerable others.

To himself he said, "Mexicanos de hoy, is it better to be a free Indian with your own land and life, or a pimp, selling women on the streets of some city...or a pimp, selling oneself to the highest bidder? The evolutionists say it is 'high civilization' to live in the shadow of huge government buildings, but, Mexicanos, does it bring you happiness? Or does it bring murder as at Tlatelolco. Have the anthropologists ever ranked societies on the criteria of human suffering?"

On another day, when Jesse, Ramona, Melinda and little Chitto were resting in Chapultepec Park, not far from the museo antropológico, Ramona said, "I like being here in Mexico. I know the government is corrupt and oligarchical, and I know it's hard for the poor, but Jesse, isn't it wonderful to not be a minority? Here we are, brown people, Indians, and almost everyone else is brown too. Look at that family over there, pure Indians, and all around us are other Indians or mixed people. No one would look at us twice except for your long hair. Oh, I just feel so good here! I miss our friends and relatives, and I miss the bays and mountains of home – but I don't miss the other people."

"I know how you feel. It is good to be part of the majority for a change. You know, the Yankee tourists make me cringe. I pretend I'm Mexicano when they're around, and they always think I don't understand English. They say the weirdest things. It makes me realize how alienated I am from them. I really do feel like a Native here and that they are foreigners but not me."

"In a way it's too bad that we have to leave soon. Can we come back someday? Melinda is learning Spanish so well. Now she and Chitto will have to learn Indian. Which language will we teach them?" asked Ramona.

"That's a hard one. Probably all of them, depending on whichever grandparent is around – but mostly Shawnee or Seminole, I guess since you and Aunt Elsie speak them."

"Ah, we'll be leaving so soon. It's going to be a shock for little Chitto to hear people speaking English all around him."

Chitto was crawling around on the grass, happily chasing Melinda. He was a chubby little boy, about the color of Ramona, with dark hair already growing luxuriantly on his head. His cheeks were fat and his eyes were big and round, almost always humorous. Chitto was a well loved, good natured baby with a great many people to hold and hug him.

Melinda was happy with her baby brother. She was about Jesse's color, a little on the chubby side, but very pretty with her long black slightly wavy hair and very Indian facial features. She enjoyed attending a kindergarten with mostly Mexican children and playing with the niños in the residencia. Melinda already was showing the responsibility and helpfulness so characteristic of older children, but Jesse and Ramona made sure she got lots of attention and love. She already was able to read some in both inglés y Castellano. And her budding musical career continued to blossom!

As summer came, the Rainwaters said goodbye to their friends of almost a year and set out for Oklahoma, going by way of

Guanajuato, Durango, Chihuahua, and New Mexico. Jesse wanted to show Santa Fe and Taos to Ramona. He also left off some paintings in various galleries and visited some old artist friends. They were impressed with his progress but most of them felt that his themes were too 'political' for the art climate of the U.S., especially as regards Indians.

They then drove to Oklahoma to visit the Delawares. Little Chitto and Melinda were both given a special welcome, as befits grandchildren, but Ramona was also made to feel very much at home. Jesse's grandparents were still hearty and Chitto and Melinda had a chance to hear the old people tell stories, just as Jesse had when he was young.

Everybody, including Andrew and Elisa, drove down to Muskogee to have a Rainwater family reunion. All the cousins and aunts and uncles made a big fuss over Chitto and Melinda. Ramona, of course, they remembered from before Jesse went into the army. Jesse was pleased to see that the civil rights movement had resulted in marked improvement for the lives of Red-Black people. Even the public library and county courthouse now employed non-Whites (which was not the case in other counties) and jobs were easier to get for the young people.

Later in the summer, Jesse, Ramona, and their children drove back towards California, stopping briefly at Fred Yazzie's on the Navajo Reservation. Jesse didn't really want to run into Loretta but he did want to see if everything was okay. Fred told him that Loretta's husband was taking care of her and that she seemed to be happy. He also told Jesse about a traditional movement meeting taking place at New Oraibi so Jesse decided to go by there.

They rigged up a camp where many tents and campers were located and then went to attend the talks. Old traditional leaders, mostly Hopis, were speaking. One old man spoke in Hopi while an interpreter translated into English:

"We still have the fundamental principles of life, which were laid down for us by our Great Spirit, Masau'u and by our forefathers. What we say is from the heart. We speak truths that are based upon our own traditions and teachings. Our Hopi form of government was given to us by the Great Spirit. The sacred plan of life on this land was laid out for us by Masau'u. This plan cannot be changed. The Hopi life is set according to this sacred plan. We cannot do anything but follow this plan. There is no other way for us. This land is sacred and is the home for the Hopi and all other Indians. This area, marked on our Stone Tablets, was given to the Hopis to guard, not by force of arms, but by humble prayers, by obedience to our traditions. We want to come to our own destiny in our own way. We have no enemy. Our traditional and religious life forbid us to harm, kill or molest anyone. We can recognize no higher authority over us but the Great Spirit."

For many days Jesse and Ramona stayed among the Hopi, listening to speakers and participating in or observing ceremonies. It was deeply meaningful to be among traditional people who not only refused to accept the U.S. conquest but who also lived exactly what they professed. They learned that many Hopi had gone to prison rather than fight in wars, while others had been jailed for refusing to obey the BIA. The traditional Hopi were really very much like the Yaquis, Tarahumaras, and many other groups in Mexico, in that those peoples also refused to be absorbed into an alien society. The form of Hopi resistance was, however, somewhat unique. It was true that all used 'passive, non-violent' tactics but the Yaqui had in the past been driven to the use of arms also, as had other groups south of the border.

One night a group of people were informally talking about the future. Ramona said out loud, "I wonder if it is really possible for a traditional people, such as the Hopi, to survive. I know they have resisted for 400 or more years. But now the government wants their coal and water and ambitious Christian Hopis are perfectly willing to sell out for money. Rich Hopi cattle ranchers also are squabbling with Navajo families. What I mean is, that each year the pressures get greater."

The response of the traditionalists was that they had to keep moving ahead on their sacred path. That was all they could do. If things got too bad the world would simply be destroyed. In the meantime, they were hopeful that the good Whites could be alerted and that the society would change in time. To that end, the traditionalists were sending out emissaries to carry the message to other Indians and to White supporters.

But Ramona wasn't fully satisfied. Many traditional people were forced, by circumstance, to use attorneys, to seek legislative help, or to otherwise engage in active forms of resistance. "What I see is that some people, mostly Indians, must sacrifice their traditional status in order to help protect the core. Like, in this day and age, a lot of people have to use planes, trains, buses, or even cars. They are all wasteful and, especially planes, are bad for the air. But to defend ourselves, to get around, we have to use them. So then we have compromised. We are harming something important for a greater good perhaps."

Jesse added, "Another thing. When we deal with aggressive, arrogant people who are also deceitful we face a real danger, that is, that we will become like them. When one is resisting a powerful evil force one is tempted – perhaps one is driven – to be evil also. One learns how to lie or at least not to be honest. After all, you would be a fool to tell all White people everything you think about them. You would be foolish to reveal your plans to your enemy. So you learn how to be deceptive, which is to play his game."

One of the men said, "You are right. But we do not contaminate our holy people with such activity. They would lose their power. And those who do go out must be very well balanced and in harmony with the people. They must keep the temptations in mind."

An experienced younger organizer added, "We face tremendous difficulty. Those who try to actively resist may find themselves getting jailed or beat up. Others will be offered good jobs or money. And we know that the government is trying to infiltrate the different movements. They are trying to start splits and factions. So it is very hard. We know what they are doing to the White antiwar movement and to the Blacks and Chicanos. They are pouring money in, splitting them, or killing them off. An old medicine man told me that within a couple of years the Indian movement will also split wide open, that the government will cause money to fall down like rain and that lots of Indians will start fighting over it."

"We have to be prepared for that. Many of our Indians, people who appear to be with us today, will prove to be our worst enemies. We will find many Indians who are going to betray us like Judas betrayed Jesus. We must be strong and alert, knowing that is inevitable."

An older man concluded, "There can be no compromising with our religion, our sacred instructions. That is our firm, solid base, our foundation. If we stick with that we will get through all of the bad things that are coming."

RED BLOOD

CHAPTER NINETEEN: EL DESIERTO

Jesse steered their camper across the wonderland of northern Arizona, aiming toward Don Antonio's place. On the way, they cut over from Cameron and the Little Colorado to the Grand Canyon, camping out close to the south rim. They were all deeply affected by the massive rift in the mantle of Mother Earth but they didn't take the time to go down to the bottom because of little Chitto.

From Grand Canyon they drove to the Hualpai country and on to the Mohave's land at Needles. Then Jesse steered west across the desert turning south at Amboy to head towards Marú and Coyote Hole. They drove mostly at night, sleeping in the shade of trees along the Colorado River for a daytime rest.

As he approached Antonio's place, Jesse began to feel that this time he was not going to find it deserted. And sure enough, as he drove up the dirt road he saw a pickup truck and what was even more thrilling, many geese, chickens, and a new turkey or two. But the biggest thrill of all came when Melinda shouted out, "El Sabio, I see El Sabio!"

And there he was! Their old, faithful friend, getting up and coming eagerly to meet them in spite of his advancing years. Melinda excitedly jumped out of the truck and hugged El Sabio. Jesse, Ramona, and even Chitto soon joined her and El Sabio, in turn, licked all of them and especially Chitto whom he recognized instantly as belonging to him.

The reunion became even more joyous when Jesse shouted, "Antonio, you're home at last!"

"Jesse, muchacho, I'm so glad to see you again, compadre," and he embraced Jesse as he spoke, turning also to hug Ramona, Melinda, and Chitto, each in turn and then all at once.

"El Sabio, you are a magic dog! How did you get from Oakland to Antonio's place?" asked Jesse of his old friend. Antonio laughed, and as they walked to the shade of the ramada, told them how he had returned from Sonora, found a letter from Jesse, and decided to go get El Sabio.

"I was lonely for my old companion. So before I got any other animals, I jumped back in my truck and drove up there to your place. I visited with your Aunt Elsie, saw your galería and store and had a good time. It was a good trip, especially when El Sabio consented to return home with me to the desert. But I had to promise him that I will stay put from now on! Except for short trips, that is!"

The adults and Chitto sat down in the shade of the ramada while Melinda made friends with the chickens and ducks. The geese were a little stand-offish but when she offered them some bread they decided to make her acquaintance. Then it was her turn to back off a little as several of them were almost as big as she was!

"Well, Viejo, you are looking pretty good," said Jesse. "Mexico must have agreed with you."

"Not just Mexico! Here I was a little lonely but now I have a new girl friend. What do you think about that? Of course, I'm not the man I used to be, entiendes, but she doesn't seem to mind. Anyway, I don't get to see her too often, since she lives in Indio. But what am I doing? I want to talk with Ramona. So beautiful! You are truly as marvelous as Jesse has written. I feel like I already know you."

"I feel the same. All Jesse talks about is Antonio this, Antonio that. I've been waiting to meet you for a long time."

"What did you do in Mexico? Ahora hablas el castellano?"

"Sí, hablo. I was very busy. Besides having Chitto, I studied la guitara with a wonderful Otomí mariachi guitarist named Dionisio José. I also studied Castellano, of course, and then indigenous literature and el idioma nahautl o' Mexicano."

"Que bien! you were very, very busy!"

"Ah, but that's not all. I also managed to write a lot of poetry and a short play, my first! I don't know how good it is, but it's an experiment."

"Ramona, I can see why Jesse fell in love with you. You are not only beautiful but also creative. That is so wonderful. To be creative is to be close to the spiritual, close to the essence of things."

"Jesse has been doing great things too. You'll get to see his paintings and drawings, I'm sure! And even Melinda has been learning to play a children's guitar."

And thus it went. They had a wonderful visit sharing the expe-

191

riences of several years. Luckily, the high desert was only in the mid-90's temperature-wise, so it was bearable, especially in Antonio's cool house (with the windows all open) or under the ramada.

Eventually, Jesse was able to come around to telling about his experiences in the army and his disillusionment with the U.S. government. He was able to unload some of his stored up pain and to tell something of his problems with alcohol and depression.

Antonio listened intently. His first response was to point out that it was common for young people to be very patriotic after graduation from high school, even when they are well aware that their own ethnic group had not been accurately dealt with.

"Pues bien, young people usually believe the teachers and the books, which are all designed to give a nationalistic point of view - perhaps more a pro-government point of view. All these lousy presidents are made into heroes!"

"I know what you mean," said Ramona. "Like Andrew Jackson is made into a democratic hero by that kind of propaganda, while nothing is said of his betrayal of the Cherokees, who had helped him, and of those Creeks and Euchees who had sided with him in the Red Cap war. Jackson also played a key role in the expansion of slavery by opening up indigenous lands to the slave-owners."

"Precisamente! You know Ramona, I wish you were my granddaughter! I feel like Jesse is a grandson and that makes you like a granddaughter. You're so right on!"

They all laughed. "I would love to be your granddaughter, Antonio. My grandparents are dead, so I really need an adopted one!"

She hugged Antonio and Jesse said, "I also want to be your grandson, Antonio. I guess I've always regarded you as an uncle or grandparent."

Antonio gathered up some salsa with a dried tortilla and then continued with his thoughts.

"I have been very worried about the future of Mexico, about it's independence. I see the U.S. becoming more and more dangerous, especially since the invasion of Dominicana. Then again, the imperialism of the U.S. is an old story, which we Mexicanos are very familiar with. In 1898 the U.S. tried to destroy the new Filipino Republic you know. They were willing to fight a horrible, bloody war that lasted until 1902 just to make the Phillipines into a colony. Then the U.S. sent troops to Cuba, Haiti, the Dominican Republic, Mexico, and Nicaragua. The last Indians here in the U.S. were defeated in 1890 except for the Utes and Paiutes in 1915. So you see, there is no break. The Indian wars just became the Filipino War and the Caribbean Wars. And don't forget the Yaqui Wars from the 1880s until after 1910. Yes, when the Yaquis tried to take refuge in Arizona, why, many of them were turned over to the soldiers of the Díaz dictatorship to be killed or sold as slaves in Yucatán."

Ramona chimed in, "So it's a sad story right up to the Depression isn't it. No breaks! And then comes World War II and after that 'I like Ike.' Eisenhower! A fraud or a fool. Maybe both. Now we are finding out that he overthrew a democratic pro-Indian government in Guatemala, another in Iran, sent troops to prop up a dictator in Lebanon, and tried to 'terminate' Indians right here. To 'terminate' means to 'wipe out' or 'finish off.' Then we got the Bay of Pigs!"

"Now take Kennedy. He started the Vietnam War but maybe he might have pulled out later. Who knows? But as you have said before his army school trained Latin American dictators and he did nothing about Somoza in Nicaragua," added Jesse.

"Of course, Johnson is worse, with over 300,000 men now in Vietnam, and he has supported the dictators in Brazil, Paraguay, and everywhere else, not to mention his invasion of the Dominican Republic," continued Antonio. You were lucky to get out when you did, Jesse, before the really big build-up."

Jesse wanted to know what Antonio thought about the reason behind this continuous tendency. "I know that greed is part of it, the desire to get cheap raw materials, markets for exports, and profitable investments, but there must be something more? Any ideas?"

Antonio thought for a while and said, "Yes, it is greed. That is one of the core elements. But you are right, there is more. It is arrogance. We are talking about greedy men, and occasionally, women, who are also supremely arrogant. In fact, arrogance is the key to their personalities. The most dangerous gente in the world are the arrogant ones. Take for example, the men who are advising Johnson, the ones with the suits and ties as well as those with the brass on their uniforms. The scholars are telling them they are wrong, the events in Vietnam are telling them that they are wrong but they don't care. They press on anyway, not for greed because they're probably not going to make much personally. No, they press on, killing and maiming millions, even 10,000 or more of their own citizens, and why? Out of sheer unadulterated arrogance. They are fighting to 'save face' to uphold their 'prestige,' to prove that they were right in the first place, and to demonstrate superiority. Almost all of the great wars of modern times were fought because of arrogance. World War I, World War II. The arrogance of the Prussian military class, the arrogance of the Russian Czar and his elite, the arrogance of the Japanese, French and British elites. Those wars were not fought for economic reasons alone. They were fought also for pride, for the glory of empire, for the desire to strut about with a sword at one's side."

"It sounds to me a lot like what Mexicans call machismo. These male big shots just have so much immaturity that they have to behave like the biggest bully on the block. In other words, they think with their huevos rather than their heads," offered Ramona.

"You're probably right, Ramona."

Jesse added, "Right now, for example, the U.S. is spending 30 or 40 billion a year in Vietnam, in addition to wasting precious oil and other resources. What will that do to this country? If it goes on long it will cause a great economic crisis in the future. In any case, it is clear that there can be no economic profit for el pueblo in such a war. We will probably have a gigantic inflation, if not shortages of raw materials!"

Antonio continued, "Arrogance goes back a long ways. Imagine the Jews believing that they had a covenant with God to conquer Palestine for themselves! And later the Jewish priests had the arrogance to suppress religious dissent and to try to impose, by the use of law, conformity. There are many things I admire about the Jews but it may be said that they helped to teach the western world a form of imperialism. Didn't the White settlers justify their conquest of Native Americans by referring constantly to biblical precedents? Of course, the Catholic Church systematized arrogance very well indeed, causing the deaths and torture of millions upon millions. Then the Lutherans and Calvinists used arrogance against the Catholics and other sects. It's an endless story. But whatever we say we have to admit that the arrogant personalities, usually men, are far more dangerous than drug addicts, thieves, or greedy shopkeepers."

After a dinner of frijoles, tortillas de maíz, nopalitos, and carne de res, Jesse took Ramona and the children over to Coyote Hole Canyon. They spent several hours examining the canyon walls and exploring its nooks and crannies. Jesse told them about his experiences there, and El Sabio guided Melinda into some places too small for the adults to visit.

After the children were in bed, Ramona returned to the subject of Antonio's new lady friend, gently inquiring about her name.

"Her name is Joaquina. She is Cahuilla from near Mecca, but

also she is part Yaqui and Tarahumara. She had some children who are pretty-well grown now and her husband is dead. I met her because, as Jesse knows, I love dates. I was down in Indio looking for a good deal on dates and I went into this small store where they sell used books. Joaquina was in there and we found ourselves looking for the same kind of books. So we got to talking and I found out that she is a librarian working in the public library there. After that I found excuses to go to the library and she gave me personal assistance, you know. Eventually, I offered to buy her some dinner and we became friends. She has come up to stay with me here, but only for a few days at a time. We are both jealous of our privacy! I'm an old codger, set in my ways, you know, so I couldn't have a woman living here with me all of the time. Oh no! That would be terrible – for both of us!" He laughed. "Anyway, she loves her work and won't be retiring probably until I'll be gone."

"So, she is not your age, Antonio."

"No, she is almost half my age, but that doesn't seem to bother her, nor me for that matter."

"Do you always attract younger women? Your handsome, distinguished looks and all..."

"Well, as a matter of fact, I have a very close friend of many years, a painter, a wonderful painter who is 75, I believe. She is still very vivacious and 'sexy' if I may say so. But she lives far away in Encinitas along the seacoast, so we don't get to visit very often. She doesn't like to drive so much anymore."

"Is she a Native person also?"

"No, she is Jewish and German. She escaped from Nazi Germany just before 1939. I have learned a lot from her, her life story, her philosophy of survival and spirituality. She follows a Buddhist philosophy now. Her name is Francesca.

Anyway, I enjoy my friends. All of my friends. One has to treasure relationships because at my age one never knows what the next day will bring."

"Antonio, you will be living for a long time yet! You are a survivor!" offered Jesse.

"Gracias, amigo, but it is more important to live a life of quality, of beauty, than it is to just survive. Remember what I told you years ago. We have only our calidad, the quality of our lives, in the end. Everything else is a chimera, transient, always changing."

"I remember your words very well, viejo, very well indeed. They have helped me on many occasions. Probably even saved my life!" said Jesse.

"But now I have come also to be closer and closer to the earth, to the sand, to the ground where I'm going to place my body before too long, and also closer to the plants, to the cactus, to the trees, and animals. Closer also to the sacred water we have to have, and to the clean pure air. Now it is becoming clearer to me that we have a different kind of existence than we normally think. Now I am feeling the other bodies which I have, the other layers. I am reaching out to the multiple universes inside of me and outside of me, like the layers of an onion, and feeling already something of what it will be like to crash the sound barrier." He laughed. "Yes, the sound barrier. When my alma starts going faster than the speed of sound, faster than the speed of light, then it becomes something impossible to conceive of. I am feeling that more and more already. Breaking loose from my shell. Going inside. Going outside. Looking inside. Looking outside. Exploring deep within. Exploring deep without. It's all me! This world that the Creator has given us is really magical, no doubt of it. And I am so glad to have the time to explore it, here in the desert, with my learned companions, the animalitos, the yerbas, the piedras, all around me!"

RED BLOOD

CHAPTER TWENTY: SOMETHING MISSING

Jesse and Ramona settled back into the life of the Bay Area of northern California, becoming active in the many movements there. They visited Alcatraz a number of times in 1969 and 1970 and also supported D-Q University, the grassroots Indian-Chicano college, when it was founded. Every Wednesday night they took Chitto and Melinda to the community dinner at the Oakland Intertribal Friendship House, renewing old acquaintances there. Aunt Elsie and other relatives often went with them.

Ramona's poems and stories had begun to appear in Native periodicals and several of her plays were being performed. She regularly recorded Indian songs on cassette, playing her own guitar accompaniment. The cassettes began to be used on Native radio programs and they were for sale in the gallery. Melinda was able to play along with her on occasion.

Jesse's murals and paintings were becoming well-known in the region and he was able to have his works shown in several other galleries. He also displayed his work at pow-wows and was able to sell some of the less expensive items there. Indian people were definitely in the mood for militant, political art. But Jesse had also begun to paint pictures with spiritual motifs as well.

All in all, they were quite successful.

Something was missing, however. They both liked Berkeley and northern California. They were so active in so many things that they hardly noticed the empty spot, but occasionally it surfaced. It had something to do with Oklahoma and the old people back there, with peyote meetings, and with Green Corn dances. It had to do with a more traditional, spiritual life in the midst of Indian communities. It had to do with the exhaustion that comes when one is always too busy to get oriented, to find out what one really wants to do.

One afternoon they went to the beach, to the same beach where they had first gone after Jesse's arrival from Oklahoma some five years before. They lay back on the sand and listened to the sea gulls. The gulls and the sound of the surf made both Jesse and Ramona introspective and reflective. Jesse said, "How long has it been since we spent a lot of time out in nature? We've been around people too much. The Indian struggle is important and rewarding but something is not quite in balance in our lives."

Ramona agreed, suggesting that the spiritual side of their lives needed renewing. Ramona's remark made Jesse think back to the way that Antonio Chavis talked. He said out loud, "Antonio says that all we have is the quality of our acts; that's all we really have. Now what does that mean to me as an artist? I paint pictures which are 'hard' products. Many of them could be destroyed in a few years. Who knows, maybe some of my original paintings have already disappeared in some furnace or garbage heap. But even if they last three or four thousand years, like some of the Egyptian paintings buried in tombs, what would that mean? That's just an instant of time, really."

Then they talked about the cave paintings of Europe, maybe 25,000 years old, and the murals of the Mayas, 2,000 years old. "What do they mean? They are interesting for us to look at but surely they no longer have their original meaning. They could just as well be the work of wind and water, or chemicals, as of men or women. The artists are all anonymous, forgotten. And anyway, what is even 25,0000 years? It's just a speck in the sands of time."

"The quality of an artist's acts must have to do with the act of creation itself and with the vibrations that flow outward to others," added Ramona.

"I guess I've been trying to use art as a part of the struggle for human decency. My motives are good, or at least I think so. The quality of my acts has been okay, I would say. But maybe the struggle for justice depends on something else, on spiritual values, on a deeper understanding. Maybe I've been getting away from that path."

Ramona looked at him and said, "Our old people used to seek after visions. Men and women had different ways of getting them but they all used spiritual knowledge to keep oriented, to keep on the right path."

Jesse thought about that. The old Indians suffered on a hilltop or in a cave or in some other private place, fasting and praying, to get a better understanding. Maybe that was lacking in his own life.

"I've had lots of inspiration. I've received many gifts from the Creator. But maybe I still don't have nearly enough understanding. Perhaps I need to follow the old way, and go out to seek a vision or greater insight, in the old Lenápe way."

"Or maybe it's that you and I are just too far away from your grandparents. Maybe we just don't get to see enough Delawares and Shawnees or Seminoles."

"Yeah and maybe I'm tired of Berkeley, as good a town as it is. The spit and dog crap on the sidewalk, the trash, the traffic, the neon lights – it's always so crowded. I guess cities are by nature oppressive. One has to get away from them. But I have a deeper need also... I hope to really be able to feel, totally and directly, that the Great Spirit is the very core of my being. Not just believe it, but know it fully in action as well as thought. But I guess that doesn't come easy. That's what mystics the world over have always been seeking. Maybe if one truly finds it you no longer are an ordinary human being. What kind of impact could greater spiritual understanding have on my art? Would I still paint about oppression and liberation, about colonialism and freedom? Or would I paint more about spiritual discovery or about praying and ceremonies like other Indian artists?"

"Maybe you wouldn't change. How can one ignore the pain of other living creatures? Even if it is only a transient pain, only an illusion of sorts, it is still real to them. They are enmeshed in it. If one has compassion one still has to share their pain. Indians don't seek to suffer just for themselves alone. They don't seek salvation alone. They don't seek union with the Creator alone. They always think in terms of all creation, of the whole world, or of the whole community," said Ramona. "I like that. That's what makes the old Indians so different from a lot of these Hindu gurus or born again Christians. It is truly unselfish, not just a craving for personal salvation. Each day is holy. We don't have to seek after some holy relics or shrines or miracles. Every dawn is a miracle. Life itself is holy. All living things are sacred, not just some cathedral or giant temple. It's so simple and yet so beautiful."

Jesse closed his eyes and breathed deeply. "The greatness of the Indian mind," he said. "But it's not too surprising. The old Indians kept their lives simple so that they could see things clearly. How few people understand that today!"

Jesse's newest art showing was in Los Angeles and it was an

apparent success. People complimented him and talked endlessly about his paintings. But Jesse realized, more than ever before, that his art was something that he could not take credit for. It was a gift. It flowed out of him in mysterious ways. He didn't make it up, it came from somewhere else. True, he had mastered the skills needed to let it flow but the flowing was like a river he didn't own or control.

And he realized now that it was time to seek a renewal, a change. There was no way that he could stand still, or look back. Like a river he had to flow to the sea and then, perhaps, he would come back to the earth again as rain, to flow once more across the land.

RED BLOOD

CHAPTER TWENTY-ONE: THREADS

It was the middle of winter by the time Jesse, Ramona, Melinda, and Chitto reached Lenápe country. A storm had left a few inches of snow on the ground and it was bitterly cold outside. Inside, however, was another matter.

Woodstoves, fast heating blue steel ones, stood in almost every room, giving off heat and a sense of comfort. The children had to learn not to touch the metal, but they were used to campfires so they caught on quickly. The children enjoyed bringing in wood from the woodpile. Melinda liked to help her grandmother cook on the big wood stove in the kitchen.

Jesse's grandfather was failing in health. Jesse spent as much time as possible with him, listening to the old stories and prayers, using the Lenápe language as much as he was able.

Grandfather told Jesse of the old ceremony they called 'doupalin' or 'scouting.' He said, "The most experienced men, those considered to be warriors, would come together. They would talk to the younger men about penahokíen, exploring, and about doupalin, scouting. They told about their dreams and visions and they trained the young men about such things and about the tekene or uninhabited forest.

When they prepared to go on an expedition or when they wanted to do something demanding or even when they wanted to play football, pasahémang, they sometimes would scratch themselves to bleed. In this way they tried to show that they were capable of suffering and that they were seeking spiritual cleansing. This is like what the Euchees do in their Green Corn dance," he said.

Sometimes other old men or ladies came to visit when the weather was mild. Jesse told them about the Walam Olum, the old hieroglyphic carved sticks of the Lenápe. They had heard of them but not of the contents. So Jesse read to them from a translation made many years before:

"After the rushing waters had gone, the Lenápe of the turtle were close together, in hollow houses, living together there.

It freezes where they lived, it snows where they lived, it storms where they lived, it is cold where they lived

At this northern place they speak favorably of mild, cool lands, with many deer and buffaloes...

In that ancient country, in that northern country, in that turtle country, the best of the Lenápe were the Turtle Men...

To the Snake Land to the east they came forth, going away, greatly grieving...

Over the water, the frozen sea, they went to enjoy it. On the wonderful, slippery water, on the stone hard water all went,

On the great Tidal Water, the mussel-bearing water.

Ten thousand at night, all in one night. To the Snake Island, to the east, at night, they walk and walk, all of them..."

Then Jesse spoke of how the Lenápe migrated eastward, contacting the Snake People, probably the people of the Great Serpent Mound, then the Huron, the Tallagewi, and other peoples, and how the Shawnees went off to the south. Then they reached the Atlantic coast.

The elders were very interested. They wanted to know where the Lenápe had started out from but all Jesse could say was that it was a land of ice and snow but one with lots of turtles, probably around the northern Great Lakes, and that from there they had gradually migrated to the Atlantic coast. "Turtles only go up to 50 degrees in North America, which is just above Lake Superior," said Jesse. He also pointed out that there were some who were skeptical of the authenticity of the Walam Olum, or, at least, of its translations into English.

Then one of the old ones told Jesse about the origin of the Big House: "The Gamwing was the Lenápe's most important ceremony. But we did not always have it. There was a time when the earth quaked and everyone was frightened, even the animals. The earth opened up and big holes appeared, reaching the world below. This was a very long time ago – then it was, it is said, that a great sound came from down below and then there came up a black fluid, sticky and looking like tar. There was smoke and dust coming up from our mother's body. And then, it is told, all the creatures came together to pray and to discuss a way to please Kishelemokong, the Creator of us all. They felt that the Creator was angry. Then they rose, certain ones, and told about their dreams. From this came the first Big House, built with doors at the east and west ends. Inside they built a pimuwákan, a sweat house, and they heated rocks and poured water on them for steam. The pimuwákan was made very hot by the rocks and steam and only the strongest could stay in there for a long time. The Xengwikáo-on or Big House, symbolizes the entire Universe and the lives of humans as they follow the Wilaúsit Mutomákan (The Path of the One Who is Good), the Wiliepelexing (Good or Beautiful White Path). As the Dancers wind around the center post and the two fires inside, they are following the Great Spirit's road."

They also talked about how the Big House was made, with carvings of faces on the center post and the main support posts, with the faces painted half black and half red. These faces represented spiritual powers with the center one also standing for the Creator and a ceremonial staff that the Creator carries.

On one occasion, Jesse told the elders that he had copied down some passages from old books about the Lenapéyok. He said, "What you have been saying about the Gamwing, the Xengwikáo-on, and the Mesingholíkan (Mask-being), reminds me of something written down by a Presbyterian missionary, David Brainerd, when he visited the Delawares on the Susquehanna River in the spring of 1744. That would be almost two hundred and thirty years ago. Do you want me to read it?" They all assented, so Jesse started reading about when Brainerd met a Delaware leader, a Mask-Owner.

"He made his appearance in...a coat of bear skins, dressed with the hair on, and hanging down to his toes, a pair of bear skin stockings, and a great wooden face painted, the one half black, the other half tawny, about the color of an Indian's skin, with an extravagant mouth, cut very much awry; the face fastened to a bear skin cap, which was drawn over his head. He advanced towards me with an instrument in his hand, which he used for music. This was a dry tortoise shell with some corn in it, and the neck of it drawn on to a piece of wood, which made a very convenient handle. As he came forward, he beat his time with the rattle, and danced with all his might, but did not suffer in any part of his body, not so much as his fingers, to be seen. No one would have imagined, from his appearance or actions, that he could have been a human creature...He had a house consecrated to religious uses, with diverse images cut upon its several parts. I went in and found the ground beaten almost as hard as a rock, from frequent dancing upon it...He told me that God had taught him his religion, and that he never would turn from it, but wanted to find some others who would join heartily with him in it, for the Indians, he said, had grown very degenerate and corrupt. He had thought of leaving all his friends, and traveling abroad in order to find others who would join with him for he believed that God had some good people somewhere, who felt as he did."

Jesse continued, "Brainerd also wrote that:

"I was told by the Indians that he opposed their drinking strong liquor with all his power, and that, if at any time he could not dissuade them from it by all he could say, he would leave them and go crying into the woods....He likewise told me that departed souls went southward, and that the difference between the good and the bad was this: That the former were admitted into a beautiful town with spiritual walls, and that the latter would forever hover around these walls in vain attempts to get in."

One of the oldest men then spoke up, "This Mask-Owner you read about. He was surely one of the Kashieesu wehendjiikaneyo (Great Men Who Perform in a Single File). He reminds me of some of our now deceased ancestors, always asking us to follow the Good Path, always trying to get people to lead a good life and to support the ceremonies. And that was over two hundred years ago? My, how long we have been trying to keep our religion going."

Another one asked, "Do you know, Jesse, about the Delaware Prophet, called Neolin? Was he the same person?"

Jesse looked among his papers, answering in the meantime, "I don't know for sure. Here is what I have on Neolin. He is first mentioned by two white men in 1762, one of whom was an adopted Delaware. He is said to have been teaching then on the Tuscalaways (Tuscarawas) River in Ohio. The Prophet was preparing parchments or deerskins for every family with a map and markings on them that showed what he had learned in a meeting with the Creator. He was telling the people that they could correct their lives by using medicine to make them vomit and cleanse their insides, by abstaining from sexual relations before or outside of marriage, by stopping the use of alcohol, and by going back to old Indian ways in every respect, even to making fire only in the ancient way. They say he was almost always crying when he spoke to the people. Thus he was deeply concerned and serious.

Another whiteman wrote that the Prophet's teaching was put on a dressed skin or on paper. Do you want me to tell you about it?" They all said yes, so Jesse went ahead.

"Well, the deerskin was painted like a road map for life. At the top was heaven and that was connected with a straight line to the earth at the bottom. The line represented a path by which the ancestors used to reach happiness. But in the middle of the map was drawn a long square shape, like a barrier, and next to it were marks representing all of the evil things which the people had learned from the Europeans and which were blocking the good road.

Neolin was teaching that the Native People had to cut off their use of the bad things of the Europeans in order to be able to get a straight road to Heaven."

The elders had Jesse read the passage over several times and then one of them said: "That sounds like a vision old Chief Elkhair had which he used to tell about at every Gamwing. Do you know anything more about the Prophet's vision?"

Jesse replied: "Well, not much is known except a version of the story told by the Ottawa leader Pontiac, who had become a follower of the Delaware Prophet. Pontiac said that Neolin had decided to seek a meeting with the Master of Life. He waited for a dream to guide him and in the dream he was told to just start out. He travelled for eight days but then he came to a place where three paths divided. He tried one but was blocked by a great fire from the earth. He tried the second but it also led to a pit of fire. So then he went on the third path, I would guess on the eleventh day, until he came to the foot of a gleaming white, smooth mountain. There a beautiful woman dressed in white told him in Lenápe to undress, cleanse himself, and then climb up the mountain, using only his left hand and left leg which are nearest to the heart.

Neolin did as he was told and saw three villages on top. He went to the most beautiful and was met by a man in white who took him to see the Master of Life, who said that it was he who had created everything. He told Neolin that the Indians should not drink alcohol to excess, should not fight each other, should not have more than one wife, and should not listen to the spirit of evil. He also instructed Neolin that the Indians should not allow White people to settle in Indian country and should not be dependent upon the Europeans' goods.

The Master of Life then gave Neolin a prayer to say. After that the Indians combined together in Pontiac's rebellion to drive the British troops out of the Ohio country. Neolin was called a 'Wolf' which is what the Great Lakes Indians and the French called the Lenápe in those times, according to what I've read."

"Ah, that is something," said one of the elders. "Now let me tell you about Elkhair's vision, which was not so long ago. In it he saw a huge bird resting on a mountain. He was led there by a spirit who undertook to take him as far as the soul of a living being could go.

The path he traveled on was a crooked, hard road, always uphill at first, leading toward the mountain. This road is called the beautiful White Path or the One Who is Good Path.

He then reached a crossroad, just as you say that Neolin did. This place, Endashowageexing, where roads cross, was as far as one could go unless you had led a good life. The bad people are turned aside here and wander off on a branch path to an unhappy existence. A cross symbolizes this crossroad and that same mark is carved on the drumsticks used in the Gamwing until the ninth night.

So you see what this means. The Prophet way back in, what did you say, 1762? The Prophet took eight days to get to the same place. We do the same in the Gamwing, because on the ninth night we switch to different sticks and we feel we are going beyond the crossroad towards Heaven after that. Anyway, Elkhair in his vision was led past the crossroad to that mountain with the huge bird. This is called 'Bird Where He Lives' and the bird is called 'Storm-Maker.' He causes storms and winds to come down to the earth below. Some Indians might call him the Thunderbird.

After passing by the mountain is the home of the Thunder, Pedhákhon. It was a terrifying place.

Beyond this mountain of storms the soul of Elkhair couldn't pass but he could see a distant ridge of mountains called Peemaxting. He could also hear the voices of departed souls enjoying their heavenly existence. Here the souls were resting until the end of the world when they would be able to cross over the next gap to where the Great Spirit lives.

There are different levels of Heaven and the Great Spirit is in the Twelfth. So that is the mountain that the Prophet Neolin was allowed to climb in his dream, it seems to me.

He must have been a special person to have been allowed to go that final distance."

Jesse's grandfather was deeply interested in the discussion and remarked on how the Prophet's map was really accurate in showing how it had become harder for Indians to follow the Good Road past the crossroad. "We have learned so many bad things from the Shewanuk. Our people have learned how to lie and deceive, how to be frivolous, how to live irresponsible lives. Even I, and I have tried, with the help of Father Peyote, to follow the Good Path all of my life, but even I am a little worried." He laughed a little and the others all laughed too.

"No, my friend, you should not be worried. If you can't make it past the crossroad none of us can," commented another elder.

"But I am thinking about the Gamwing. We let it go some forty years ago now. We were all younger men when it stopped. We are the ones who should have kept it up, but we were pitiful, ignorant.

That is true, but maybe Jesse here and some of our other grandchildren will dream it again and bring it back. It all started with a dream. It can happen again, maybe when the world is in trouble, opening up again, then everybody will see that they have to bring it back."

Another elder said: "Remember how all of the older ones used to recite their visions every year? They used to start out with the same kind of prayers. I remember how they used to say that they were sad to look back and see how much of our cultural life has been lost, about how many people used to be together inside the Big House.

Yes, and how they used to ask the spirit forces to hear them, to pity them, and to bring blessings."

Often Jesse's grandmother, mother and father also sat in. On those occasions the talk often took a lighter form, with humorous anecdotes predominating. But the older Lenápe tended to be devoutly religious and the subject usually returned to the Gamwing, other ceremonies, or Peyote meetings. Jesse encouraged the older ones to tell about some of the visions people had talked about in the Big House. Some of the elders also remembered songs people had sung while dancing on the last day. One went:

"This is how I do,
When I travel over this earth,
The Lenápe praying way!
This is how I do when I travel,
When traveling over the universe.
Their tribal relationship!"

And so it was that they spent many hours talking about the history of the Lenapéyok and about their long struggle for survival. It strengthened them to think that in the 1740s their ancestors were already facing a deep spiritual crisis and that teachers, wise ones, had appeared to help them return to the Path of the One Who is

207

Good. They thought also of the dangerous gifts of the Europeans, such as alcohol and drugs, and how they had to fight against them for so many centuries. Still, the Lenápe had survived, the language still lived, and the prayers were not forgotten.

Towards spring, when a short warm spell came, Jesse's grandfather attended a special Peyote service arranged for him. There he prayed:

"I am not asking to be made well. The Great Spirit has come to me and told me that my time is coming soon.

I am waiting to leave this world and to go on the White Path. I have good thoughts all day long and all night also. I pray every morning, noon, and evening. I thank the Creator and ask for good thoughts. I pray for everybody and especially for my companion and my grandchildren and their children.

It is said that if one lives a good life one will go on the Good White Path to be with the Creator. I am pitiful, as you can see, being a poor boy. I am imperfect. I have many faults. But I pray to the Creator and ask for his help. No man can do anything good alone. We always need to ask for help. I have come to feel pity for everyone. I ask now for help for every creature who is suffering.

I am waiting to pass from this world. My relations are all around me and I feel good spiritually. My body is old and very tired. It needs to rest. But my spirit is like a young child, ready to move on to something new. I ask you all my brothers and sisters not to grieve too hard for me. We all go on the same journey. I will see you all again. Death is not the end.

Again I wish to thank Father Peyote. Again I thank the Creator, whose servant Peyote is. Wanishi!"

In the early spring, just when the leaves were beginning to break loose from the buds, Jesse's grandfather died. The preparation for the burial was as traditional as possible, with four men playing the moccasin game all night long after he passed away. Then just before dawn those who dressed him in his clothes went out and shot guns three times towards the east. Afterwards, everybody was awakened, although most were already up. Then two men and two women began to prepare food for people to eat.

The grave had to be dug and the body placed in a wooden box. Then everyone went to the cemetery and a sermon was given.

"Here all of the belongings of the deceased are, to be divided among the pall bearers. My relatives, now, two days after this life has departed, we are gathered together...

You must also be prepared some day to join with the departed one in the place where the lenápe-ókan, the humanness, goes. As you know, we will all have this experience of leaving our earthly home. That is why we teach how to prepare and to purify the lenápe-ókan so that it can go directly to the Creator. Now wanishi, thanks. Tepilahapa, it is enough."

The speaker then turned to address all of the people present. Not only was Andrew and Elisa, Elisa's mother, Jesse and his family, and other friends and relations there, but Cary, Ladell, Andy, Dewey and their families had all driven or flown back for the service. So it was a big group standing near the grave, united in tears and sorrow.

"Since the beginning it has been known how hard it is to travel the road of our Father Pilsit Manito, the Pure Power. Nonetheless, a person who lives a good life will find it easy to be following the path...

In ten and one days everybody must bring cooked food because it is then that we shall all eat together. At that time at midday we will eat together for the last time with the departed one. And we will all know that we are with him and it will give us gladness...."

All of those who had been living with grandfather were prepared, in their minds, for his death. But emotionally it was still hard. Grandmother took it hardest, when the reality of it, the finality of it, hit her with full force. But she had her children and grandchildren around her and little by little she reconciled herself to her companion's departure. Many stayed with her for a long time late into the Spring.

Jesse felt the need for Ramona's love, and her presence, more than he had in a long time. The relationship of his grandmother and grandfather, their loyal, loving companionship through all the years, brought home to him with new force the magical beauty of the union of a man and a woman. He knew that Ramona was not just any woman but his companion and lover for a lifetime.

Perhaps it was strange, but making love with Ramona later that Sikwin (spring) gave Jesse tremendous satisfaction and helped to heal the pain of separation from his grandfather. Of course, having his dear sisters and brothers there, for a time, also helped greatly, but it was Ramona's love and her warm, strong, responsive body and ever present tenderness that strengthened him, healed him. Making love with Ramona was like a renewal, like the Spring itself, a regeneration of life after death.

Jesse for a long time had known that there was a deep mystical connection for him, between woman and the spiritual life. There was something deeply powerful about womanhood, womanness, and what it could mean to a man. He could understand why most human beings loved the Earth Mother, the Female Power, in her many forms including even the Virgin Mary.

Woman as created was so beautiful, so powerful, so ever sustaining, so enduring, so nurturing, such a never ending fountain of free flowing love and compassion. And Ramona symbolized that to Jesse, along with grandmother, Elisa, Ladell, and Cary, and yes, even all the other girls he had loved and never abused and never forgotten. But it was Ramona who was to be his special companion, knowing him as no other person was ever to know him, through the whole of his life to come.

Of course, they didn't get to make love as easily or spontaneously as in times' past. Having so many relatives around, as well as the children, made for crowded quarters. For that reason Ramona and Jesse drove off in the camper several times, staying at campgrounds along lakes or in the hills along streams. They were able to leave Chitto and Melinda to play with their cousins.

Not many other campers were around yet and they were able to find private spots where they could play at love and have a kind of a second honeymoon. The water was still cold but they jumped in anyway, bathed quickly, and dried themselves, each helping the other.

Back in the camper Jesse started kissing Ramona, as he often did, on her breasts, under her arms where he loved to rub his lips in her hair, around her neck, behind her ears, and back to her breasts again, biting her nipples tenderly. Ramona, in turn, kissed her lover everywhere she could reach, biting his nipples in a way which she knew created intense desire in Jesse.

Jesse was glad that Ramona had given up shaving under her arms. Her hair there was extremely sexy and he loved to touch it lightly with lips and fingers. Perhaps it reminded him of the soft hair around her sex.

Sometimes Ramona took the lead. She loved to kiss Jesse all over and to feel his penis growing and hardening inside her hand. The smell of his sex was stimulating to her, just as Jesse exalted in her woman-smell.

The union which the lovers achieved was sometimes quiet, sometimes like an earthquake tremor, sometimes like a roller coaster ride, sometimes like a mountain exploding, but always it felt, to both of them, as if their connection was so natural, so meant to be, so right.

Ramona was sometimes in a hurry, the thrust of her strong desire carrying them both forward without much delay. Jesse was always attentive to her body, to her spirit, and to exactly what it was she needed. He took his time because he knew that it was always better when Ramona had her orgasm. But always it was thinking of the other one which made their love so deeply enriching and spiritually uplifting.

Sex is, after all, never a physical event only. The way it is done tells a great deal about the spiritual level of development of the lovers. Is not sharing beauty an aspect of spiritual-giving, beauty of feeling, beauty of pleasure for the universal body?

The old Indians never disdained sex! They respected its power, abstained when undertaking certain dangerous tasks, but never turned away from the Creator's gift of love-making.

Jesse and Ramona cleansed themselves in love, renewed themselves, renewed their connectedness in the joy of nature. They were in nature, with nature, and of nature.

The important things in one's life are still the essentials, thought Jesse. The Kikayoyemenaninga, our departed ancestors, they believed that life was a cycle, each one repeating the steps and the stages of everyone that has gone before, just as the spring follows the winter each year.

They did not value the accumulation of goods or the searching after fame or secular power because they saw clearly that it is inevitable that aween (every creature) moves from youth to old age and to death. In essence, the outline of every life is the same.

The modern White people and many Indians try to fool themselves into believing that each generation is different, that their lives are distinct from that of their ancestors. But the Kikayoyemenaninga were more insightful.

The basic things of our lives are no different, in essence, from what our grandparents experienced. Some people are unprepared for growing old because they don't know that. Nothing has prepared them for being an elder and then an ancestor. When they are young they live selfishly, not caring about the old age that awaits around the corner. And when they are finally caught they become frantic or are cast aside by a modern society which loves only the young.

But the Indians, thought Jesse, lived a steady life, one predicated on the reality of sex, of birth, of death, of the inevitable cycle. Their old age was a rich, satisfying period, perhaps the best part of their life, because they had prepared for its coming and because their younger relatives honored and respected them, and yes, because they usually remained alive, sexual, to the end.

They did not just fall into old age, as into a trap. No, they prepared for it all their lives. Thus, as elders, they had wisdom. They were esteemed for what they had taken the time to learn, to study about.

Jesse thought deeply on these matters, and he thought about 'threads.' Threads in the tapestry of tribal life. The kikayoyeme-naninga had woven threads, strong ones to pass on to those who were to follow.

The Lenápe still had a few strong threads. Who was to carry them forward? Who was to weave new threads?

Ramona and Jesse, while camping in the country, had found several places where one could still seek greater understanding in the tekene. And so, later that Spring, with the help of an elder man who still knew the way, Jesse went out alone to seek another understanding, another message, another vision.

The time had come. A woman had given birth to him. Now it was the time to return to another mother-woman, the Earth, for the lessons that she and the other spirit-powers might bring, away from the people.

RED BLOOD

AUTHOR'S AFTERWORD

I began writing Red Blood in Spring, 1979 and finished a first draft that same year. Since then I have gradually refined that draft, cutting and adding, but about eighty percent of the final text stems from the original version.

This is a work of fiction, but that needs to be qualified somewhat. Several well-known historical personages are mentioned by their real names, although they are incidental to the story as a whole. More importantly, I have attempted to tell a story which is essentially true. On the other hand, the characters are all completely fictional, with the exception mentioned above.

I have especially endeavored to portray the Lenápe-Delaware culture of the Twentieth Century accurately and to that end have become indebted to many persons, living and dead, including Witapanoxwe and Frank G. Speck. The speeches and prayers attributed to Lenápe elders are, I hope, all faithful to the spirit of Delaware thinking and several are taken, with some modification, from traditional texts.

I wish to acknowledge specifically my debt to Vincenzo Petrullo for the insight provided in his *The Diabolic Root: A Study of Peyotism, The New Indian Religion, Among the Delawares* (Philadelphia: University of Pennsylvania Press, 1934, reprinted by Octagon Books in 1975); Frank G. Speck for the Native texts in his *Oklahoma Delaware Ceremonies* (Philadelphia: American Philosophical Society, 1937) and for the same in his *A Study of the Delaware Indian Big House Ceremony* (Publications of the Pennsylvania Historical Commission, Vol. 2); Daniel G. Brinton for his texts in *The Lenápe and Their Legends* (1885, and now reissued by AMS Press, 1969); and my old friend, the late M. R. Harrington, for his *Study of The Lenápe Religion.*

I wish to acknowledge also the assistance of those who have reviewed the manuscript, chapter by chapter, and whose criticism has been essential. This includes especially Carolyn L. Forbes. I also wish to thank Huell Hutchison, Kelly Crabtree, and Cheryl Payne for their assistance.

I must also thank Jesse and Ramona Rainwater, Antonio Chavis, Mitchell Crow, Ladell, Cary, Loretta, El Sabio, and all the other characters in this book. They are friends who have enriched my life and deepened my understanding. I hope they will do the same for others.

Glossary of Lenápe Terms

Aween (awen) : all creatures
Dálamoos : my pet
Doupalin (topalin) : scouting
Elemahákamik : all the earth, universe
Enda Sokalanheng : rain ceremony
Endashowageexing : where (when) roads cross
Gamwing : the annual Big House ceremony
Gishux : Sun
Gishte amalsi : I'm hot
Haki : earth
Kashieesu wehendjiikameyo : Great men who perform in a
single file, honored elders in the Big House ceremony
Ketemaksíhena : Have pity on us
Kikayoyemenaninga : the departed ancestors
Kishelemókong (Gishelemùkon) : the Creator of Us All
Kshilánte : it's a hot day
Lákwik (Lawkwik) : evening
Lenápe, Lenápeyok : Human Being(s), Delaware(s)
Lenápe-ókan : Human spirit or soul; Delawareness
Manito : That Which Exceeds, Creative Power
Mesingholíkan (Msink) : the Mask Being, guardian of animals
Moékanih, Moékanuk : dog, dogs
Moxúmsa : Grandfather (Creator)
Mutomákan (now tomakan) : Someone's road, a road or way
Opank (Wapank) : dawn
Pasahémang : la crosse or football
Pedhákhon : thunder
Peemáxting : mountains near Heaven

Penahokíen : exploring
Pilsit Manito: Pure Spirit, Pure Power, the Creator
Pimuwákan : the sweatlodge ceremony, sweating
Piske : it is dark
Shewanuk : white people, Europeans
Síkon, Síkwin : Spring
Taktáni : I don't really know, maybe
Tallagewi : A people mentioned in the Walam Olum
Tékene, te-ekene : the forest, an uninhabited place
Tepilahapa : it is enough
Tulape, tulapin : turtle, little turtle
Wanishi : Thank You
Wilausit (weelaúsit) mutomákan : the one who is good path, road
Wiliepelexing (weeliepelexing) : Good or beautiful white path
Wichemanen koxwísuk : help us your grandchildren
Wíchemi, wichemínen : Help me, help all of us
Xengwikáon or Xengwikao-own : the Big House
Yukwe (yookway) gatati weemi awen whichemanen moxumséna :
Now help all of us creatures Grandfather
Yukwe ki-íshkwik : this day, today

Note: "x" is always pronounced like a very guttural "ch" sound, as in some Swiss and Dutch dialects.